The Parry Garden

The Honey Strait Series Book 2

Paige Lynn Hill

TRS BOOKS

The Parry Garden

First published by TRS Books 2019

This novel is entirely a work of fiction. The names, characters, and incidents portrayed in it are the work of the author's imagination. Any resemblance to actual persons, living or dead, events or localities is entirely coincidental.

All lyrics and song titles contained within belong to their prospective songwriters.

First edition

Cover art by Dark Water Covers

This book was professionally typeset on Atticus.io

Also By TRS Books

PARANORMAL ROMANCE

<u>A Bite Lurkers Novel</u> series is a heartfelt vampiric romance about love, loss, and a hard look at that poignant phrase, *I'll love you forever*.

Dark Flames

Dark Modern

Dark Trade

<u>DARK ROMANCE</u>

The University Alley series is a dark erotic romance about a teacher who falls in love with her student who is battling a Heroin addiction.

Another Vice

Another Virtue

<u>STANDALONES</u>

A Songwriter's Death

A contemporary rockstar romance, where Tina and Michael both have been bitten by the fame bug. But when one reaches the promise land first it calls into question their whole relationship and their life.

AND MORE BOOKS TO COME!

Contents

Society should never dictate whose right for your heart.

Prologue

I broke up with my boyfriend Manny, upside down in a Camaro. It was a brief moment of calm before the shit storm hit. But who could pick the perfect moment to do these things? I unbuckled myself from the passenger side seat and fell to the floor. That was formerly the roof.

"Good, now you can unbuckle me."

"I can't get it. The steering wheel is pressing into your stomach." I utilized all the strength I could muster to get him free. Just thanking my lucky stars that we had gone unharmed. But at that moment, I really disliked Manny. "We are so over. If I so much as see your caller ID after this. I'm getting a restraining order."

"You can't be serious," he said, dropping to the floor like a log. His weight was so heavy that it seemed to rock the car back and forth. I didn't find his surprise at my statement amusing. His bad-boy ways were good enough to be its own Hans Memling painting, and I was over it today. This was the last night that I would go home with bumps and bruises that I didn't get from a fight. A person who wasn't two sheets to the wind was not supposed to be having these types of misadventures.

"Over, the end, complete, never to begin again."

Manny met my gaze, this time with a glare that would make me laugh under different circumstances. His side of the window was completely crushed. There was no way to get out on that side. My window was busted out and I most definitely smelled oil, but it was open. With some degree of nausea, I made the painstaking climb through the window. My clothes drenched in alcohol from the bottle that had burst on impact. Helping Manny secure his release after a jagged edge from the split cup holder snagged at his jacket. Scratching his hands on the glass to the point where he was drawing blood.

"Are you okay?" I asked once he was completely free.

"Never better."

It wasn't lost on me that this accident had immediately sobered him up. His red eyes the only evidence that he had been drinking enough alcohol to induce a coma. Or that he had left the party with his keys leaving behind a four-body pile up after he started a fight. Forcing me into the car under the fear, that if we walked then he was pretty sure I'd end up going home with someone else. For all the sense that makes. The sirens getting louder

"I'm testifying against you," I admitted. "You put my life in danger. I'm your hostage."

He smacked his lips, running his hands over the scruff o his jaw. "You had two drinks and you smell like how I feel. No one's going to believe that Shatterproof coming off her epic win, is innocent."

His words took all the wind out of my sails. Whilst I marveled at his capability to summon tears for my brand new car. Running his hands through his blond highlighted hair so much that it was positively sticking up. I wanted to yell that it wasn't his car to cry over, but mine. Right, it was mine. Would the cops even believe that I wasn't the one driving? Thanks to Manny's antics, I had developed a reputation that wasn't wholly true.

Shatterproof was known as a wild child with the need for speed and adventure.

Maybe when I first got with him that was what I wanted. Squinting my eyes at him as he kicked the tires with his low top Christian Louboutin's, as if that were enough to right my car. How drunk was he still? We went together to get this car, but it became clear that Manny had his own ideas. He acted like it was his purchase. Taking over the conversation with the salesman. But that truth wasn't going to get me out of this either. I had nothing to do with knocking over that stop sign. Narrowly missing a woman in the crosswalk and skipping like five red lights. But I smelled like the brewery at Bud Light and I had two heavy drinks that were still sitting on my stomach even now. And my reputation was going to kill me.

Red and blue lights finally made it to our block. We were in a small quiet neighborhood that we were uprooting at three a.m. in the morning. Heads peeked out of closed curtains. Where even were we? How much was this lawyer going to cost me?

"Run," Manny suddenly blurted. The lights and sounds bringing him out of his daze.

"What?"

"Fucking, run?" He repeated heading towards a house across the street and the backyard of a gate that was left open.

I looked around, clearly not ready for the criminal life. Before sprinting down the street. But I told myself I was only running, not because I was guilty, but because there was no way out of this. Jail time was not good for my complexion. Even if it wouldn't necessarily hurt my reputation. I didn't need more water on a problem that was already drowning me.

Three blocks down, I stuck to the shadows and saw a man pulling into his driveway. The cops just on my heel. I ran to the car and pulled open the door to the backseat. Diving inside like it was a pool and closing the door behind me. "Don't move!"

"Are you about to hurt me? I don't have any money on me?"

"No one's going to hurt you," I said anxiously, realizing that this was not was I wanted to do. Scare the pants off some poor unsuspecting man. "Just do as I say and will both go our separate ways. The cops are looking for me. Stay quiet. Cut your lights off and will both wait until they pass. I'll leave once there gone."

"Do you have a gun?"

Even from my vantage point on the ground, I could tell that his hands were at 10 and 2. His voice was robotic and stiff. "No, so you're not going to get hurt. Just stay quiet."

"If you don't have a gun why should I help you?" He inquired, as if he were a teller at the DMV.

My brows furrowed. "Would you prefer I be threatening you right now? Because I think I could muster it."

"I'm just saying, I'm not a criminal and I don't have any criminal intentions to be your accessory."

I smacked my lips. "I don't need an accessory. We're not robbing banks here. You just stay quiet long enough for me to run."

"I don't think I want to help. What did you do?"

I stomped my feet on the felt bottom of the car growing increasingly annoyed at our negotiations. "I'm not asking. Just sit still and be quiet."

"But you don't have a gun?"

"My fists are weapons of mass destruction." Hitting my forehead at how lame that sounded even to my ears. Even if it was true.

Not once did he bother to look behind the passenger side seat at me. I couldn't tell if that meant he was extremely brave or just extremely scared. So I tried a different tactic. "I don't have a gun, and I wont hurt you, but I need you to shut off those headlights. Please."

"You're always supposed to obey the law," he said turning his head towards me.

I inhaled sharply at the blue color of his eyes. "I know."

"Good," he said before leaning on the horn.

A cops flashlight beamed through the backside window.

"Fucking A."

1

Chapter One

Amber

6 Months Later. . .

Picking a boyfriend was as crucial as picking a career. I'd had time to think about this while staring up at a jailhouse ceiling that was a suspect color of yellow.

The right relationship could propel me to untold success. And I'd still get to keep the visceral reactions of having butterflies in my tummy. My heart would still beat fast at the sight of my beloved, and not because we're careening down the Dan Ryan at Nascar speeds. I wouldn't eat because I'd be too busy thinking about him, and not because I couldn't remember the last time I ate after going through some binger. Every day I'd be on the brink of falling in love instead of falling in trouble. Everything in my life would be under my control. His choices wouldn't be my downfall.

So picking a boyfriend was as crucial as picking a career. Why? It's the difference between jail time and cuddle time.

At least I got things halfway correct. I followed my career first instead of love, and I kind of wish that I would've stuck with that now.

Unfortunately, I thought love had fallen at my doorstep when Manny walked into my gym. Instead, every day with him was another tally mark on my crumbling reputation.

A reputation that now needed to be buffed out by attending Driver's Education classes at the community center. Trapped behind a desk for the next 18 weeks. It's early Monday evening and I could think of a hundred things I'd rather do. Each was more exciting than the last like waxing my pussy hairs. I wasn't even allowed to attend Driver's Ed until after I finished my court-appointed volunteerism picking up garbage. In the eyes of the law, I was a trashy human who needed to be in familiar dwellings. Being a boxer certainly had its pros and cons.

Once upon a time, Boxing was just a way for me to work out while learning to protect myself. The reality is that it became much more than that when I won my first championship and then had to defend it. I had to overcome some impossible odds being the new girl on the block, proving that I'm shatterproof. My first time defending the championship was not supposed to be that easy, but it was.

At the last minute, Michelle 'Second to Nones' team forfeited the game. I won on a technicality, and admittedly, it didn't sit right with my spirit.

Stubbornly, I wanted to fight for my win and earn it. Now my rivals had ammunition against me during the upcoming petition for replacement. They all wanted a shot at the title against a woman they thought held onto it fraudulently. Never mind that I wasn't happy about it either. The women in my division viewed that fight through a lens of right and wrong.

They couldn't believe that Michelle would walk away. My worse critics believed that my team and I somehow had a hand in it. Through money exchanging hands and back door dealings. Those people didn't care that Michelle's father had killed her manager that same day. Or that her alibi clocked her at some dance thing cuddled up with her new boo. None of that mattered. I was a fighter. Defending my championship was my game. I didn't do either. I kept the belt. It was all fraudulent.

I parked my car three blocks away from the center and exhaled loudly. Closest to the house with the biggest bushes for cover. How did they expect me to get around without a license? The bus. I resented the notion of ever going back to the level of peasant after everything I've achieved. I've earned my place. Despite everything, Michelle did unseat me. Stuffing my headphones in my ear as The River by KT Tunstall played trying to help me forget that I was running late.

This wasn't my first time at the community center anyway. I've done community service here in the past when Manny's antics have gone awry with the law. But outside of that, it also happens to be one of my favorite places. There is a beautiful plot of land outside for gardeners. They even give out awards for best potter and herbalist. The air outback was perfumed with lavender, parsley, and tea. A famous gardener by the name of Lancelot "Capability" Brown was their inspiration. They kept his photo in one of the classrooms where they meet.

If memory served me correct, my first encounter with this building was a little underwhelming. It looked underfunded and forgotten - a straight line between boring and unuseful. However, whatever anyone sees on the outside looking at the plain white staccato and bland décor, missed the spirit of the place. It's filled with so many voices and budding dreams. They kept it cool in the summer and warm in the winter. But the outside garden was its pride and joy. Mostly thanks to all the work that the gardening class had put in.

My first tour of the place made me feel like I was somehow back in elementary school. With rooms cordoned off for faculty and staff, and others designated as classrooms for a variety of activities. A swimming pool was located closer to the back door.

The hallways could also use a retrograde new paint job. Its walls were dingy and worn from too many little fingers. A visual step into the past with its cream and maroon décor. It looked like an exploration into an 80s high school drama. I can half expect my old gym teacher to appear at the door and scream, we're playing dodgeball, and he doesn't care how much we cry about it. Not surprised at all when there was no one to greet me, not even a security guard. I looked down at my paperwork and read off the information. "Mr. Beard, classroom 107."

I was a little late because I had to make the appearance of having walked. However, I was expecting this short stint to run smoothly. I exhaled loudly outside a big red construction papered door decorated like Clifford, The Big Red Dog. Shaking off all the jitters before entering the classroom. Pulling the headphones from my ear. "Your last student is here."

"No."

"Fucking A," I said, turning and realizing that, Andrew Kent, the vain of my existence, the reason this was all happening sat in the third row.

"We can't be here together," we said simultaneously.

I rolled my eyes, "Oh great, we finally agree on something."

Being in this classroom with him would be like sticking hot pokers in my eyes.

Mr. Beard raised both of his hands up to calm the situation down. My face was perfectly still. I had already won this battle. My presence here was court-appointed, and Mr. Kent would be the one to have to leave. Folding my hands in front of me like the triumphant student I was. The thrill of finally winning something over him could not play on my face. I remained as wooden as a puppet. The same way that I had come to expect him to be during my court appearances.

During those things, my only audience was other inmates and the police officers who arrested us. But sitting in the gallery opposite me was always Mr. Andrew Kent. My kidnappee. The only thing anyone needs to know about me is that I did not kidnap this man. Okay, two things, I also happen to hate Andrew Kent.

Of course, he immediately recalled our sorted meeting to everyone who will listen. It's the I was traumatized speech. To the casual listener, it might not be evident that this epic event happened without a weapon or any bloodshed of any kind. His dramatic acting was as subtle as a barking pit bull. The man had to be around the same age as me, and I was only twenty-seven. You would have thought he had flashbacks of his last days during our brief two-minute encounter. This class was my actual punishment because I'd rather be smelling garbage now.

"Enough with the theatrics. I was not charged with kidnapping because what happened to you was not kidnapping. Look it up."

My eyes widened at the sight of him visibly looking it up on his phone. Only for him to read the definition aloud to the class. I smirked.

"The action of abducting someone and holding them captive," he said before placing his phone neatly back on his desk, next to his pencils. "I suppose it doesn't."

I squinted at him in disbelief. Like the trial he sat in wasn't enough proof. Of course, he did stop attending them once he realized that court attendance wasn't work-friendly. Nothing in that place happened in a timely fashion. He should imagine how I felt being on lockdown until I could post bail.

"I'm court-appointed to be here, so." I tried to contain my glee, but I could feel it tugging on the corners of my lips.

"Everyone is appointed to be here," he stated matter of factly. It felt like a complete shutdown.

"What can be done then? Surely, this is a miscarriage of justice."

I leveled a hard gaze in Mr. Kent's direction. "This is justice at its finest because I'm being punished."

"Okay you two, at the moment I can't do anything about it. You'll both have to leave until I can fit you into another class. However, I'm the only one who runs these classes. So you both will have to wait longer to get your license."

If I agree, I'll be driving on a suspended license for longer. I'm a daredevil, but I'm not crazy. This whole ordeal needed to be over.

"Can't you just allow one of us to stay and reschedule the other?" My throat was drying up.

"On what basis? After all, Mr. Kent was first."

"I had to walk here."

"So did I."

It was childish, but I turned my head and poked my tongue out at him. "I need the most help, sir. What did you forget to help a little old lady cross the street?"

"No," he answered matter-of-factly.

I shrugged, already done with him. "I need this class. Now! Not another 18 weeks from now."

It's Mr. Kent's turn to eye me wryly.

"You both can stay in this class. If you agree to behave yourselves and not make trouble. Otherwise, you both will be asked to leave."

After a few minutes, I glance over at Mr. Kent to see him watching me. It felt like I was watching the fourth of July fireworks, in complete awe. Amazed to be in the presence of such beauty that I contemplate my place in the universe. Only to look down and see someone being murdered out on a boat. I look around madly hoping I'm not the only one seeing this. But of course, I am. So I panic because I was unqualified for whatever was about to come next. While trying not to pee myself because I already imagine the killer swimming to get me next, like the shark in Jaws, that was how intensely he looked at me.

He's so nerdy it's off-putting. He was dressed like someone's granddad in a crisp white button-down and old brown corduroy pants. A navy blue sweater was thrown over the whole get-up. I wanted to ask him where was his wife, Edith? He looked like every college professor I'd ever had. I was actually squelching the urge to check his bag for dusty old books and an old smoking pipe. Surprised, that he paired that monstrosity of style with a pair of bright orange gym shoes. Although his appearance gave me plenty to laugh at. He was kind of handsome. Which only made me mad. It was like he was hiding his sexy behind this grandfather vibe. Not that I would be interested either way. "We can do this."

"Agreed."

I walked over to the only seat left in the class - a desk in the fourth row right behind his. I took the long way around the desks so that I wouldn't touch the big baby. A kiddie mat with shapes was rolled up and propped against the back wall of the bookshelf. The low shelving was filled with kindergarten books. I noticed everything in the room except for the many eyes following me.

As it would be highly improper for them to crane their necks to look at us both. Everyone reluctantly turned back to the front of the class and the teacher.

"Now that everything's settled," Mr. Beard said, tapping the top of his desk. "I was trying to be transparent on how reporting works here."

There was no chance of this class being a simple breeze now. I was already disengaging from Mr. Beard's little speech. Be on time. . . yadda, yadda, yadda. Every time I looked at Mr. Kent, it just reminded me of how out of control my life had gotten. And that I did the right thing in breaking up with Manny. Guys like Mr. Kent have no business looking down on me. In fact, in college, it was the opposite.

But he didn't deserve any more of my attention. I looked around the classroom. It looked as if at any given moment it could be hosting a variety of activities. A chart of the human body on the back of the wall. Two teacher desks one that Mr. Beard was utilizing and another off to the right. Math books were piled on top so thick that they could be used as weapons. Seamstress-type rulers were in a small container on top of the bookshelf. It ran the entire length of the left side underneath the windows. I'm sure I would have a good laugh if I looked at the date of publishing on the stack of encyclopedias on the shelves. The dust in the corner of the shelves was its own added decoration.

I turned back to Andrew Kent's perfectly coiffed hair. The teacher was in the front of the class writing something on the whiteboard. None of which I could read.

"Excuse me, Mr. Kent."

His ears don't even twitch in my direction. The quick scratching across his yellow legal pad the only hint that he even heard me. "Yes?"

"I can't see the board. Would you mind lowering your head a little bit?"

My question was only met with silence before he said, "The less we talk to each other, the better."

I lean over in my seat to get a better look at the contact info Mr. Beard was leaving for his students. Mumbling under my breath, "I hate you too."

Chapter Two

Andrew

I was the type of person to build something up, and Miss. Spence was the person to tear it down. Everywhere I went, I had a clear direction on how to get there. Miss. Spence probably figured it out as she went along only to end up late to every appointment she ever made. Including her fights. I only knew she was a fighter because the prosecutor only mentioned it 15 times during her trial.

Not that I would have guessed that either. Today, she showed up in class wearing some white jean studded pants, and a grey t-shirt that said never settle. Her medium blond hair was pulled back into a ponytail with a simple rubber band.

For the life of me, I couldn't understand why I didn't just take the teacher's offer to reschedule. People's actions don't always follow a linear line. So predicting my own emotions wasn't as simple as putting code into a computer. Although, sometimes I wished that my brain worked a little more like a machine does. A computer can learn to do and read anything if you merely send it the correct sequence of letters and numbers. My brain couldn't accurately compute that way. Certain things just hit a brick wall and fall to the cement to be swept away by the wind. Sometimes I ask my grandmother, Dama, why I act the way I do when social norms require otherwise. She merely shrugged and likened it to my Autism. I tried to break down my words and actions in my head like a math problem. There was no logical reason why I couldn't have just waited.

Public transportation was hard to deal with sometimes, but not impossible. There were ways of predicting heavy traffic times so that I could avoid the overstimulating crowds. My work schedule would not have been affected either. But now I've agreed for both of us to remain in the same classroom.

Unfortunately, I had reached max capacity on my data of this woman. So figuring her out was going to be a feat. I was unable to compute the emotions in her voice when she was sitting behind me. Social norms would indicate that no one would be happy in a class with the person that tried to have them arrested. Although, I was only doing what was required of me by the boundaries set by the state of Illinois. Not to mention that if I had been kidnapped, it would have sent my granny to an early grave. It certainly taxed the boundaries of my knowledge on appropriate behavior. Weirdly, she seemed happier when we were hurling insults at each other.

The prosecutor had taught me how to scowl before Miss. Spence's trial. He thought my cause would be more sympathetic if I looked angry over it. Miss. Spence was merely found in my car. I was just concerned with not being charged as an accessory. It was kind of dramatic to be dragged into the police station. I look over my shoulder at her to see her glowering at me. Yup, that's anger.

The makeup around her eyes was dark. The sparkle in her green eyes was like the glint of a rare jade in the light. Eyes that were youthful and inviting. But what were they inviting me to do?

I pushed the thoughts from my head and focused on my class. Sharpening my pencils with the electric sharpener that I had brought from home. A few gazes turned to look at me.

"You're more than welcome to use it," I said as friendly as I could manage.

They simply turned back around without another word, and I wondered if I had missed another social norm. It was a cool September evening. The clock ground slowly to nine p.m. Fresh air drifted in from the open window signally the beginning of the end of summer. Hopefully, I can still get in a few more hikes before the weather made it unbearable. Already, imagining myself in my hiking boots among the silence and the birds. The class was only two hours long, and the first one was mostly introductory. So it ended quickly.

Most of the students looked like they still had plans for the rest of the night. Meanwhile, all I had to do was go home, feed the dog, and still cook dinner. I was already on the phone checking my calendar for tonight's dinner menu when I kicked open the classroom door.

It swung back and accidentally hit Miss Spence in the nose by the sound of her squeal. Her nose was all red like a cute little reindeer. "Pretty adorable Daylily."

She grabbed my arm just as I was about to walk away. "Oh, so I suppose that's payback for your non-kidnapping?"

"No, just an accident," I replied, observing her quietly. The look she gave me appeared to be both stunned and annoyed.

"I'm leaving first. To avoid any more of your accidents," Amber replied with finger air quotes.

I looked back at Mr. Beard, who was observing us with a frown. Who ironically sported a beard. "Honestly, it was an accident. You got to believe me."

"It's okay Mr. Kent, but perhaps you should wait 10 minutes to be sure."

I sighed and looked down at my watch? Making a mental note in my head to leave 10 minutes late every day. Punctuality gets you where you need to be. But its bedfellow was predictability. And my movements were down to a science.

Once I was released from duty. The world outside the community center was quiet. A foggy cold chill in the air hinted at the coming rain that was desperately needed. I walked back to my place, which was only a few short blocks away from the center. That's partly why I chose this place, to take classes, because of the convenience. I frowned, as the sound of a blaring alarm system announced itself to the world. Why don't people ever turn those things off in a timely fashion?

Because they don't know how my mind seemed to answer for me at the sight of Miss Spence bent over an open hood. Her amazing ass was backlit by the bright headlights.

"Do you need some help?" I forced out.

She looked up, almost hitting her head on the hood. "Yes, please. I was beginning to think there was no one else left in the world."

Our eyes connected as I approached, and she frowned.

"But not if you were the last person on Earth."

"Okay, but I do think I can help."

She looked me up and down and laughed. "Not on your life are you touching my big beautiful car."

"I am just trying to help. You don't have to scold me for it." I left her to stew and walked off.

"Wait," she said, holding up her hand. Her face dipped in shadow. "What kind of car is this?"

I looked at the back of the car and frowned, before coming around to the front. She looked less than impressed. "Okay scientist, and it is?"

"A midnight blue 2019 Chevy Camaro."

She let out a big chunk of air. "Please tell me how to turn off the noise."

"Can I take a look?" I said, pointing to the engine.

"Please," she begged, looking a bit desperate. That was an expression that I wasn't used to. She only ever showed me an angry face.

I started thinking about her a lot. Especially after I stopped attending her trial dates because it was interfering with my work. Women as a whole had always served as a puzzle to me. My granny assured me that wasn't my Autism that was just most men. Still, it appeared to me as if most women treated me like a kid once they found out about my Autism. If I were lucky enough, I'd become a toilet to cry on for all their shitty relationships. Even though Amber was only one note, angry, talking to her was the only time I ever really felt like a man. Not someone's friend or helper. There were no kid gloves. She gave me the full barrel, and she expected me to handle it, and I did. Now she was asking me to do it again.

I didn't even remember the last time I felt this free with someone. My only other relationship was with my high school love. And we simply grew apart after she ended up pregnant with someone else's baby. Although, I'd been set up on many dates since then.

The tubes and nuts on the car were hot to the touch. Making it a little hard to make sure the fittings were in working order. Out of the corner of my eye, I caught sight of her chewing on her already short fingernails. I slammed the trunk shut and went to check her doors. The blaring alarm stirred up some uncomfortable feelings within me.

"Do you know what's the matter or what? I fully expect the cops to catch me breaking my probation if I can't get my baby to stop screaming."

"You've got a faulty door switch simulating a break-in. You'll need to take it in to get it fixed."

"Fuck," she said, taking her hair down from the ponytail and massaging her head. As if she were stimulating her thinking process.

I wasn't even offended. Just impressed. Other girls I've met would already be apologizing to me as if I were from the planet Krypton and cursing doesn't exist.

"In the meantime, what will help tonight. Don't try to remote lock with the key fob. Just lock and unlock your door with the key."

She went over to the passenger side door and did as instructed. Biting her bottom lip as the alarm went off. She spread her hands in the air and wiggled her fingers. "Glorious silence."

I smiled.

She looked back at me with appreciation. "How did you even know?"

I simply shrug. "How do you know if the mechanics are overcharging you if you don't first understand what they're fixing? Cars these days or no different from pulling apart a computer and putting it back together."

She laughed. "I guess. You are so weird."

Offended that she called me weird, I pointed out what was starting to be glaringly obvious. "Is this your car?"

She rubbed the hood of the car lovingly. "Yes, this is Christine 2. Christine 1 died in a tragic accident. She was led astray by my ex-boyfriend, Manny."

"You're not supposed to be driving!"

"Right," she said with a chuckle. "How else was I supposed to get here?"

"The bus, like the other participants, or walk as I did."

She leaned on the top of her car and raised an eyebrow at me. "The three blocks to the building was all the walk I needed. Why don't you just forget you saw anything."

"I can't do that."

She opened the door with her key, preparing to get in, but she froze. "What do you mean you can't?" her voice dipping a little lower. "Just mind your business. If I get caught breaking my probation, I have to spend a year in jail."

I swallowed the lump in my throat. "Well, you shouldn't be driving then."

She slammed the door shut and approached me. So close that she could smack me and I almost feared she would. The smell of sea salt, vanilla, and sandalwood wafting off her skin. Like a summer beach day with friends. "Do you hate me that much?"

"No-No," I said stuttering, which always happened when I get too nervous. "But I'm not going to lie for you if someone asks."

She broke out into a smile. "No one's going to ask. We're not speaking to each other, remember?"

"Yes."

She looked back towards her car. "So what do you have planned for the rest of tonight?"

"I have to go home and feed my dog, Hubert, cook, and then get ready for work tomorrow." I glance at the time on my watch. "By now, I'm sure my granny has fallen asleep on the couch."

Her eyes widened, but she didn't make any other outward facial expressions. "You live with your granny?"

"NO, she lives with me. I pay the majority of the bills."

She laughed before leaning over. I stood still as if she were a dream that might evaporate as soon as I touched her. Her sweet perfume tickled my nostrils. Startled when she did nothing more than kiss the collar of my shirt. Like a woman who had told me all her secrets, she stepped back. Her lips grazed my cheek as light as a feather. "There, that's all the explanation you need when she asks you why you're late."

I pulled my collar away from my neck to see a pink print of Amber's lipstick. "You messed up my shirt. It will have to be dry cleaned."

"I like the one on third street. They're miraculous when it comes to getting blood out. Nothing to worry about, wonder boy."

Miss Spence didn't reenter my head until I made it home. I lived in a beautiful house with my grandmother. A two-bedroom colonial that I rehabbed on a plot of land left to me by my deceased grandfather. I had just enough land to add on too if I so chose. But right now, the backyard is being used as a garden oasis for my grandmother. She doesn't tend to it as much as she said she would. But I completely understood. She was getting older.

I walked in to find the small woman asleep on the couch. A small fan was blowing in her face, barely keeping the heat at bay. We had forced air, yet she insisted on *controlling her weather*. Strands of her grey hair flew across her face as if it had a mind of its own. A swimming competition watched her from the TV screen. I touched her shoulder gently to rouse her. "Grandma, you should go to your room."

She groaned softly as she began to stir. Looking at the TV with bewilderment as she reoriented herself. "Oh, Andrew, you're home from your class?"

"I am, but not that long. Just long enough to see that you are tired."

She grabbed my hand and forced me to sit beside her. Not even in her pajamas yet. She wore a plain flowery tee and blue capris. Her pink slippers were on the floor beside the couch. I leaned over to put them within her reach. Brown age spots were across her feet like freckles.

"Tell me how it went first?" she asked, slipping her shoes on without another thought. "Will you be able to make any friends?"

My granny had single-handedly been the mastermind behind any social life I had managed to have. It was kind of sad. But I didn't mind having a fan even if it was just my granny.

"I don't think that is likely to happen here. Miss. Spence is also in the class," I replied smoothly without thinking about how she felt about the woman.

"Miss. Spence?" she inquired, patting my cheek as she tried to remember. "I know it's important."

I got up and turned off the television. Moving to cut on the living room light to see Hubert, my Dauchsand, lift his head from the chair. He wasn't acting like he was hungry. I glanced over at his food bowl next to the kitchen island. It was half full of kibble.

"I guess granny must've fed you," I said, leaning down to scratch his ears. His rough tongue scraped across my chin. He was lucky I was about to get into the shower.

"She was the girl that hopped in the back of my car after you had fallen asleep," I said to my dog without looking at her.

"The woman that almost kidnapped you and held your life in the balance." She stood up and began to pace.

"It's okay because we've both decided to attend the class together. We just wont speak to each other, and I'll leave 10 minutes later than Miss. Spence will."

She made her way over to the coat closet. "We've got to call the police."

The corners of my mouth turned down in a frown. I came up behind grandmother and took the sweater from her hand. "Grandma, no. It bothers her more than it bothers me. I can get through 18 weeks without incident. I don't need help."

She patted my cheek again, this time lovingly. "You can handle this, can't you? Sometimes even granny underestimates you."

I remove her hands from my face and place them between mine. "Yes. But only cause she worries."

She laughed a hearty laugh that I hadn't heard in a while. Allowing me to escort her back to her room. "You're only saying that because I told you too."

"You know I can't do that."

"If I ever lay eyes on that ruffian. You just point her out, and I'll teach her a lesson not to mess with my grandson." She sat on the bed and cocked her head to the side. "What's that on your collar?"

"A girl in class put it there."

She laughed and got up under the covers. "See Drew you can make a joke. You're getting better every day. You just have to practice more."

I cooked myself dinner. Preferring to maintain my autonomy so that my grandmother didn't have to take care of me. Hubert was also my dog to care for. Changing out his water bowl before settling down at the dinner table to eat dinner for one, appreciating the quiet. I had yet to change out of my clothes that still held hints of Miss Spence fragrance and lipstick. I had to see that woman every day. How was I going to get through it?

Chapter Three

Amber

Now that I wasn't defending my belt. It felt like my hands had been tied behind my back. The next person to fill Michelle Nunn's shoes wasn't going to be easy to find. There was too much sports politics at play. My manager had to talk to their manager with lots of posturing and boasting going on. Then there were the questions. What fighter had the biggest TV draw? Who had the most money? What fight would increase my ranking in the boxing world? My opinion didn't matter in this process.

And the one person who would make me feel better in times like these wasn't here anymore. My longtime trainer, Don, died seven months ago. My fight with Michelle Nun was dedicated to him. And I never got the chance to make him proud. He'd probably find this whole, find shatterproof someone to fight, business funny. He'd make it okay. It would be less overwhelming.

Now I was alone at Boxpad with a delivered letter from my old trainer, Donald Blanchard, as my only company. His former lawyer had dropped off the letter after my workout. Sticking out like a sore thumb as he made his way through the women's locker room. Shielding his eyes with a newspaper, despite there being nothing for him to sneak a peek of. It was almost comical. But I knew his appearance was serious. He was the one man in the whole world that I never wanted to meet because it would mean that my Don was not here anymore. And I wanted him more than I wanted anything that was in that letter.

When I first started here, he was literally my only friend. We would be the only ones at the gym working late, and we would often get dinner together. The others saw my fresh-faced college dew, and no one wanted to take me seriously. It was hard finding a personal trainer once the boxing defense classes were over. They just gave me the runaway and a list of fancy hot yoga gyms to join instead. Don looked at me and saw my potential. He promised that he could turn Barbie into G.I. Jane.

I met Layla, my best friend, because of him. Apparently, I was the first woman that Don had agreed to train in years. Layla was furious and frequently wanted to take me on. Don taught me never to turn down a challenge. However, Layla and everyone else was never my real competition. It was just me. Convincing myself that I was noth-ing outside of the box that people were putting me in. That somehow, Layla was right, and she was more deserving.

Don gave me confidence. Something that couldn't be taught. It could only be felt. I won my match against Layla and eventually, I won her over. But it started with one man giving me the chance to prove myself. He named me, Shatterproof when I refused to let everyone's mean-spirited bullying sway me.

Now no one would dare tell me that I didn't belong here at The Boxpad. This was Shatterproof country. When others ask me my opinion on their form, I speak with his voice, and I see their mistakes with his eyes. The respect that he commands was something to aspire to. I knew I'd never get there. But that didn't mean that I didn't rule this place like the Queen I was. I keep one eye on this place at all times, even as the vultures start circling. Everyone wanted to get their hands on the deed. Don owned The Boxpad. Well, he used to.

But no one had the real cheddar to buy it. No one, but me, anyway. I just wasn't sure I was ready to make this my permanent kingdom. It just felt empty without him. I turned the envelope over and over in my hand, and I wished it was a cell phone instead so that I could call him. Maybe I would just turn the phone over to Manny for an intervention. A connection could be drawn between Don's death and Manny's antics kicking up a notch. The man was lost without him. I knew how he felt. But he was going to hurt himself, and I don't think I'm wired to handle that. I couldn't just stand by and be a witness to his decline. He'd certainly never stop for me.

I got up and rubbed my only photo of Don affectionately. A small photo of us was poorly taped to the inside of my locker. It was a selfie that I had stolen after one of our training sessions. He hated taking photos. He used to say that there was nothing about him worth memorializing in a picture. So I took this one in secret when he was standing behind me. His attention was directed to something off-camera. It was just the side of his face, but I could already picture that familiar scowl. Neither one of us was feeling particularly smiley that day. I was probably cursing his name under my breath after being pushed too far in one of my training's. He always did know more than me. No one ever reached their limit.

Layla appeared in front of me and pushed the door close. "Who you grieving girl? Your man or your trainer. You've got to snap out of this."

My nostrils flared. "Watch what you're saying. Of course, you wouldn't understand."

Every winter, Layla pops up with a new trainer. She likened it to finding her spirit animal. Justifying her right to be picky. I think she's just holding out for her own Don. However, she's setting the bar far too high. I felt sorry for her because she obviously loved him. Yet, she never got to be close to him in the same way that I did. But I could tell that he cared for her. She wasn't ready to hear that, though. Layla would only think that it was lip service. I closed my locker and put the combination lock back on. Ready to blow this stand in favor of my driver's ed classes.

Layla looked at me expectantly, "So you not going to tell me what the suit wanted? I saw him come out of here."

I blinked back my tears, holding them at bay as I remembered Don's legacy. But a mere mention of the stiff suit had me going into a panic attack. I sat back on the wooden bench and fanned my face with the letter. Looking up at the ceiling as if gravity would be enough to hold the tears back. "I haven't opened it yet."

I feel her hand on my knee. "Honey, do you want me to open it?"

I exhaled slowly and looked back at her. "How did you even know that the suit was for me?"

She laughed. "Come on. Unless Viva's baby daddy was serving her papers. What else could it be?"

I nodded, unable to even joke about it. "You open it."

She looked on pensively as I gave it to her. As if she half-expected it to blow up. She ripped it open with all the fervor of someone who had just won the lottery. But when her hands stilled. My heart stopped.

"To Shatterproof." The slight tremor in her voice was enough to bowl me over. Did she hear his words in that scratchy smoker's voice that we had all come to know and love? "I was trying to figure out what to give everyone who made an impact on me. You were the easiest. Truthfully, the day you walked into The Boxpad, you breathed life into this sport once again. I began to feel like I had done and did everything. Like I had accomplished my purpose. Then I met you, and I knew that by 40+ years of experience wasn't for all the championships in the world. Or the great guys that I've come to consider like my sons. It was for you. My last greatest achievement. So what can I give you? But the very place that changed your life. Ownership of The Boxpad."

My hands flew to my mouth. I knew Don didn't have any biological descendants. But he trained some greats in the boxing world and maintained a relationship with all of them. Surely, they would be the ones to carry on his legacy effectively. I was still just a stiletto masquerading as a gym shoe.

Imagine what the others would think once they got wind of it. Would there be a mutiny afoot? Would they band against me to take it from me? This decision would ruin any goodwill I had with everyone. I looked back at Layla surprised when there was more.

"You don't need a bunch of instructions to make this happen either. Just follow that big beautiful heart of yours. I've already given special instructions to the people that I expect to help you on this journey. P.S. Tell Layla, I'll miss my funny girl. In another life, she would've been my wife."

I snatched the letter from her hand. A copy of the deed was attached. The yellow sticky note on top listed the contact info of the lawyer for more details. I stuffed it all back into the envelope and hid it in my bag. He should've talked about this with me first. What if I don't want to be a gym owner? Maintaining the status quo doesn't seem so bad. I know where I stand. My future was open, not shackled to a gym located next to a strip club. The only friends I had were likely to reject me because of this coup.

"At least you don't have to buy it now."

I was never planning on buying it. It was simply passed around that I was the only one at the gym currently with the means. However, it was never my cross to bear. I was still trying to figure out what to do with my life. Don passing away might be my chance to course correct. Finally, make my parents proud. Maybe go back to my dream of being a landscaper. Get away from Manny's daredevil ways that have recently turned toxic.

"You can't tell anyone that I received this until after I figure things out."

I practically stare her down until she relents. "Okay, your secret is safe with me. What are you going to do?"

"Talk to that lawyer?"

I stood up, ready to leave.

She waved her hand at me. "It's almost 6 o'clock. You can't now."

I shook my head. "Oh no, I have Driver's Ed tonight. That's where I'm headed. If you're finished, can you take me?"

"I thought you bought a new car?" she asked, with uncertainty in her voice.

"I did, but I can't drive it."

"Since when?" Her lips quirked up on the end.

"You know I lost my license," I impatiently reminded her. Switching from one foot to the other.

"See my previous statement. Since when has that stopped you?"

I grabbed Layla's arm and pulled her up from the wooden bench, halfway dragging her to the door. "Since the guy that had me arrested showed up in my class. He saw me with it last night and threatened to call my P.O."

"That asshole," she declared, grabbing her purse from behind the reception desk. "The same guy that said you were kidnapping him, right?"

Now that Layla had read the letter, her special privileges around this place made sense. Like her never having to use a locker. I wondered if she was even paying for her membership when I was paying for mine. "Yeah, the one and only."

She scrunched up her nose and looked at me pityingly before lacing her arm through mine. "Well, if he's going to be petty then you know what to do right? Be petty back."

I looked at her curiously. "What do you mean?"

"Prank him."

I opened my mouth to protest but then thought better of it. Layla can be so silly, but maybe she was right. A laugh at his expense might just do my body good.

Once we arrived at the community center, I made a show of getting out of Layla's car in front of the center. If Mr, Kent had seen the siren call from my car. There was no telling who else did, and I didn't need any more blackmailers.

Layla just laughed. "Hey, you want a ride home after?"

"Yeah, could you."

"Sure. Be back at 9 pm," Layla said before freewheeling out of the small parking lot. It was mostly staff cars and a single drop-off lane. I thought about how funny it would be if she were caught by a cop just now. She'd be attending this class with me.

I walked inside to see that Mr. Kent only arrived five minutes ago. A fast-food bag crinkling in his hand. What a nightmare he must be at a restaurant? I only want two slices of tomato without the seeds and crisp lettuce on the side. I'll add it myself. No skimping on the fries, I will be counting. Just crazy.

He looked over to see me walking towards the classroom as well. I remember him hitting me with the door last night, and it took everything not to gut punch him. Mr. Kent simply stepped back and allowed me to go first. It was the first time that I noticed how much taller than me he was. He had to be 6'0 to my 5'7. Naturally fit, although he certainly didn't work out. I appreciated the gesture because if I didn't clear the door this time, I really would punch him.

He wasn't dressed any better today than he was yesterday. No sweater this time, but he was still dressed like a man prepared to do my taxes. A pair of bright green gym shoes on. I wondered what the story was there? It was such a stark contrast to his bland everything else. He looked like the physical embodiment of white bread. Handsome white bread. Such wasted packaging. He was overdue for a mall trip. So that some witty fashionista in a boutique could upgrade his style. He would be pretty hot then. Not that he wasn't hot now. Stopping my thoughts in their tracks, I turned my attention to the teacher.

Everyone said hello to him as they filed in.

"Okay everyone, there is no need to be so formal. You can call me Joseph. We're all adults here."

"Okay, Joseph," I sang. I don't think he liked the way I said his first name. So he might be regretting his little concession.

I don't even think I realized until now how tall Joseph was - too wrapped in my problems with Mr. Kent. He had to be at least two feet taller. And he looked kind of cute in his jean jacket. His warm smile was inviting. He wasn't bad looking either - an average guy. I wouldn't sleep with him though. He looked like just the sort of man to drink tea at sunset while questioning the meaning of life. Yet down to Earth enough to be considered the cool teacher. Just not my type.

My type made you question if they were all-natural or on steroids. But of course, it was all-natural brawn because I just don't roll with cheaters. Manny wasn't a boxer, but he worked out aggressively. The sidekick of one of the brawlers that Don used to train. He was a funny guy, but I wouldn't call him a weasel. He could bench press 240 and eat men like Joseph and Mr. Kent for breakfast. I just could never picture myself with a guy who wasn't serious about working out.

At least Joseph was close. Mr. Kent was the complete opposite. He wore nerdy black glasses. His hair kind of falls into his eyes in the front. In a way that makes you want to brush it back in place. A square masculine jawline that beckons you to map its lines right up to those kissable lips. Okay, so he's not ugly, just dorky. His eyes are a coffee-colored shade of brown that could see to the bottom of the ocean if they wanted. Or maybe just the color of my soul.

He looked soft and adorable. Yet he was calculating and stoic. A mean-spirited, by the book, sort of guy who needed to get laid. Whose favorite gift to give would probably be a reading list.

No, I like big guys. They're just more fun. They live by the seat of their pants and know how to make you scream. Of course, in my case, that was part of the problem. But Manny had lost his way without Don to reel him in. I just wasn't interested in being his sponsor. That spark in his eyes was gone now. And I didn't want to wait around to see what he was going to replace it with.

I reluctantly get up to play Joseph's pet after being called on to pass out some diagram of a four-lane highway with cars moving in different directions. Passing Mr. Kent's desk on the right side, it was easy to pick up on the notes of Lavender, Cedar, and Cardamom in his cologne. He smelled like the edges of the woods. It wasn't a strong scent by any means, but it had a spicy flare. Something I would never pick out for the stiff Mr. Kent. The smell was reminiscent of young blossoming love in the fall.

As I handed him his paper, I tried not to drop my gaze to his neck. I was avoiding the searing heat of his gaze altogether. There was no way that I wanted to see another look of disapproval. He had told me all I needed to know last night. Even his kindness was wrapped up in burnt cigarette paper.

I went back up to the teacher's desk and handed him the extra worksheets. Catching a glimpse of some pretty stickers of men's and women's accessories in a small red tray.

"Those are so cool," I squealed, picking them up to view them closer. I must have been loud because I drew a stare from Andrew who was looking at me with cynical interest. The others looked too bored to pick up on much of anything outside of their phones and fingernails.

"You like stickers?" The teacher inquired clearly surprised.

"Yeah, why not?" I would typically come back with a hot retort about people judging others on looks alone. But I actually wanted to keep these. I already knew what page in my bullet journal I would use. The men's stickers were a vibrant shade of brown, and the girls were red. I love picking up cool stuff like this at hobby shops when I get a chance. Not that I've had time. Unable to stray too far from The Boxpad these last six months. "Can I keep these?"

"Since your so excited about them. I don't see why not. There's more where that came from."

I smiled and turned back towards Andrew, whose sudden cough sounded suspiciously like a laugh. "They are pretty, Daylily."

Since when did this Daylily stuff start and how do I stop it. Was Andrew trying to insult me on the low? I'm not Daylily. I'm Shatterproof. And if he thought he was going to get to me by resorting to childish name-calling, he had another thing coming. I had developed a thick skin thanks to Don.

Still pouting, I *accidentally* kicked his bottled water that he sat on the floor, on the way to my desk. I was picking it up before it rolled too far, when an idea came to me, and I placed it behind the left leg of my chair. Game on.

It isn't long before Mr. Kent gets a little parched. Rummaging through his backpack and looking on the floor for the elusive bottle. There are vending machines just down the hall before you reach the swimming pool. Since Joseph allowed us to leave, I imagine that's where he's headed when he leaves his bag. A sick sense of victory at the thought that he would think he lost it. I stared at the notebooks sticking out of his backpack. Did people really need all that just for Driver's Ed? I looked around at the other student's bags for confirmation. Curiosity got the best of me. I waited until Joseph's back was turned and pulled out the smallest notebook. A red spiral pocketbook that I quickly dropped in my gym bag. Zipping it before folding my hands on top of my desk. Joseph turned back around to address the students and all he saw was me smiling like an A student. Pretending to listen to him rattle on about the changing rules on the highways of Illinois.

I managed to take Andrew's bottled water five more times before I become bored with the whole thing. Catching the eye of a newbie who wasn't here the first day. I leveled a stony glare at him, daring him to say something. He merely smirked and said, "you wildin'," under his breath. I took that as his stamp of approval.

Joseph eventually paused the class for a 15-minute break. I stepped out into the hall to stretch my legs. My stash of water bottles was safely tucked away behind my bookbag. Unable to stop laughing at the sight of Mr. Kent drinking water out of the fountain.

"What's the story between you and that guy?" Andrew's desk neighbor asked.

I propped one leg up against the wall and crossed my hand in front of my chest. "Too long to tell."

"Well, I ain't never been no snitch."

"Then you don't have anything in common with Mr. Kent then," I said sarcastically. "Thank your lucky stars."

He leaned against the wall next to me as we both watched Mr. Kent take off his glasses and clean them. "I'm Jamal by the way."

"Amber," I said, shaking his hand.

"Hey, neighbor," Jamal called out to him.

I groaned inwardly. What was this guy up to? I didn't need a co-conspirator. This wasn't Mean Girls. This was my beef alone.

"Yes. It's Andrew by the way or Mr. Kent."

"Kent," Jamal huffed. "That's fitting." He nodded in my direction, rubbing his finger along the back of my hand. "How you sitting next to this pretty girl and maintaining? I'd be faced in the opposite direction flunking like a mother fucker just to stare into her eyes."

I pulled my hand away, unable to even smile at his flattery. So it comes out a little more like a sneer.

"It's a struggle," Mr. Kent answered. "But I need my license more."

Was I crazy, or did that sound like a real answer?

"I could take it or leave it," Jamal said, licking his lips.

I tore my eyes away from Kent to smirk at this man. It felt like a Velioceraptor had caught me in its grasp with how hard he was staring. I pushed myself off the wall and followed Kent inside. Choosing the lesser of two evils at that moment. Commenting over my shoulder, "Thank you for the compliment, but not interested."

"We've got some time. You might change your mind."

"I'm going to have to get out the pepper spray, aren't I?" I asked with a chuckle.

"Only if I get to lick it off your body," Jamal warned, giving me a wink.

Kent just sat at his desk and put his head down as if he were studying his notes. Meanwhile, I didn't completely hate the pepper imagery. But I wasn't going to entertain it.

"Alright guys, thanks for coming back on time. Let's knock this last hour out of the park."

Everyone buckled down at that point. Even I refused to take any notes because there is absolutely nothing wrong with my driving. My presence here was purely Manny's fault. A cruel justice in the world, when that man was allowed to walk away, and instead I took the fall.

Blessed with the one Prosecutor in the world who wouldn't listen to reason. Just glad that they had gotten their hands on some C-list celebrity.

My stomach began to rumble. I've got to start grabbing more than some apple pie cups before I come here. But I hadn't had much of an appetite lately. So focused on everything behind the scenes at The Boxpad. I slunk down in my chair once I realized that Kent heard it too. Whispering, sorry I'm hungry, would probably only draw his contempt as he wondered if I even knew how to take care of myself. I wasn't a sucker for his punishment.

"Okay, pop quiz before we go. On average, the human body can dispose of the alcohol in 12 ounces of beer in how much time?"

"Hours." Kent wasted no time in responding. I think the class unofficially voted for him to answer every question.

"Yes and since you're the only one that answered. Here's a sandwich," he said, handing Kent his untouched sandwich. Which was a little weird. "But I'm looking for an answer a little more specific than that."

"One hour." I chimed in.

"Yes, thank you, Amber."

"A lush after my own heart," Jamal leaned over and whispered with a smile.

I rolled my eyes. Jamal was definitely off-limits now. I didn't care if I never set foot in another bar. This time around, I needed to do things differently. I just didn't know what that was. At least I knew what it wasn't.

"Okay, everyone—-"

I threw up my hands in fake horror. My stomach growled in agreement. "Where's my reward?"

He stared at me blankly, before turning around and handing me his coffee. I don't remember him drinking from it. But I'm still disgusted. Staring at it like it would grow legs and walk right back to him.

Kent turned around and gave me his sandwich. "Here, we can switch."

I eyed him warily as we slowly made the exchange. What did he put in this sandwich? Hissing Hot Peppers from Madagascar. Why would he be kind to me? I bit into the sandwich, and my stomach quieted. It tasted pretty good too.

"Thanks," I replied genuinely, kind of wishing that we could be friends.

Joseph dismissed everyone 10 minutes later. It wasn't until Kent got up and gathered his things that this movement brought me out of my Kent-imposed stupor. I reached back down for my gym bag, tossing it over my head to the opposite shoulder. Before lifting six bottles of water in my hand and placing them back on Kent's desk. "Here, I only drink sparkling water."

Jamal burst out laughing. "I guess that's your lunch money for the week, huh Ken?"

Chapter Four

Andrew

September was holding on to the last days of summer by its finger-nails. I usually welcomed the fall. Enjoying the smell of pumpkin spice and hot chocolate on a cold night. But when part of me saw, Amber, I knew I was open to changing that opinion. She had on some Nike red and white shorts, that stopped just below her butt to show off her long-toned legs. A black ball cap on that matched her black jacket with a red hood. Some cute low-top sneakers on that showed off a gold, rose-shaped ankle bracelet.

She hadn't even noticed me come in, not that I could be mad about it. Instead, I was grateful, she was an unpredictable firecracker. Her laughter was like Christmas bells as Jamal sat in the desk next to her whispering in her ears. He was a lucky guy because my proficiency at flirting needed work. Standing next to him, I looked like a Windows computer next to a Mac. I'd never draw the eyes of a woman like Miss. Spence except in anger. Her skin was glowing like warm ivory. I realized I'd been staring for too long when she looked up and scowled. I've got to try to remember that you shouldn't stare at someone just because they're pretty.

I quickly sat down at my desk and the teacher opened the class, causing Jamal to return to his seat. I slowly unpacked my bag to appear as normal as possible. Placing my whiteboard and black marker on my desk to the left of me. My pencil and pen for my notes were carefully stacked above my notebook in front of me. A portable electric pencil sharpener that I grabbed from work in the upper right-hand corner. Perfectly organized as usual.

But I couldn't seal the deal without the winner for tonight. Pulling out a small coke bottle and placing it on the floor in the same position as my waters from weeks ago, I carefully zipped up my bag afterward. I know she doesn't drink regular water, but I was hoping that Coke was still fair game. My prank for her tonight wouldn't work if she didn't.

For the past three weeks, she had been pranking me every day in class. One time she put clear glue in Purell and swapped it out with the real thing I sometimes keep on my desk. But not before I ended up sharing with the teacher and Jamal. The worse was probably when I walked in to see a turd on my chair. Only to find out after I had gotten out my plastic gloves and wipes that it wasn't anything more than an old toilet paper roll that she had manipulated into looking like shit. Which still didn't keep the woman on my left from thinking that I had shit myself in class. Much to my chagrin. The only one that left me with questions was when she papered my desk and chair with pictures of my face. They were all in black and white so that it looked like a prison photo. Joseph looked equally as surprised as I at how she managed it. But clearly, she had to get into the classroom before everyone else and then leave and circle back. I definitely understood the dedication needed for that one.

As the whole pranking phenomenon was fairly new to me as I only ever went to specialty schools growing up. And Dartmouth College is not exactly known for its rowdy pranks. I briefly considered asking my granny about this, but I didn't want to worry her. She would only insist on coming up to the school and speaking with the teacher. I'm not a little kid anymore; I had to troubleshoot problems on my own.

My disability made it hard for me to find most of Miss. Spence's jokes, funny. I was also out of the loop on what the socially expected norm was as well. So instead, I was frustrated and angry with her. Yet, that only seemed to make things worse. So yesterday, I asked a coworker what I should do. A boisterous man who talked unusually loud to the point of making me uncomfortable.

Some people can't help it though, and my coworker Feng Longwei was one of the worse. A Tier I Programmer at Bridgewater Health Planning. I'm Tier II. He used to report to me until I had to switch him to another supervisor. It felt like someone was blowing into those dog whistles that are too quiet for human ears, but usually, send the dog screaming. Some human's natural octave speaking voice was like a siren call that made me want to run home and never come out. But I'd developed a system of counting to get me through it, which I utilized as we were speaking. When I usually would just avoid him. But if anyone would know he would. He said they sounded like pranks and there was nothing to do but prank her back. She might be playing a game, or she might not like you.

Considering our run-ins together, it was most likely the latter. However, if I reciprocate in good humor than perhaps I could turn it into a game. Games, I understood. There were set rules, and there were winners and losers. So I left work early to give me time to stop at the library and check out a book on pranks. I found one prank that I could prepare on short notice.

It wasn't until the teacher had given us our 15-minute break and I went out into the hall to get some water from the fountain that she made her move. I returned to find the bottle gone, so this was what making a joke felt like. I sat at my desk and smiled. Folding my hands on my notebook as I waited for class to restart. Amber stepped out into the hall with Jamal, her gym bag over her shoulder. I knew it was in there.

Her disgusted squeal from out in the hall drew my laughter.

"Yo, teach, clean up aisle seven. Amber dropped something," Jamal said, coming into the classroom and waving for him to come quick.

Joseph just looked disgusted as he grabbed some paper towels that he had set on the bookshelf closest to his desk. He said early on that if he was going to allow everyone to eat in class, then he might as well be prepared. The only reason that I couldn't feel bad for getting him involved. Miss. Spence stuck her head in the door and leveled a disbelieving look at me. Sprite and soy sauce dripping down her white shirt.

"Gotcha."

She disappeared, and the teacher called the class back to order. A few of the students patted me on the back after they got wind of what was happening. Everyone except Jamal. But I began to feel bad when she didn't immediately return. I wasn't trying to send her home. Just play a game. This time, she reappeared wearing a black t-shirt.

She plopped the coke bottle that was half empty back on my desk without another word - not even looking at me as she took her seat. I grabbed my whiteboard and wrote down Miss. Spence and Mr. Kent's names at the top. A line down between our names. Before putting 0 under hers and the number 1 undermine. Casually I lifted it on my desk next to my left elbow, and away from Jamal's prying eyes.

I heard a loud cackle behind me reminiscent of a cartoon villain and knew that I had won this round. Putting my whiteboard down as soon as Joseph looked up to locate the source of the noise. To avoid suspicion, I wiped off my board with a cloth as soon as I could. I didn't need to keep a record on the board anyway. There was no way I was going to forget the joyous feeling of my first victory. However, I could keep a running tally in my social book.

I had lost it a little over two weeks ago and just assumed that I had left it at work. But since it had yet to turn up, that meant I would have to replace it. My first installment would be winning the game against Miss. Spence.

However, getting back to normal after Amber's spilled coke incident was easier said than done. At every turn, it appeared as if she were trying to one-up me. Everyone knows that I answer the questions in class. Yet it was becoming a race of who could get their hands up first. Sometimes she wasn't even giving Joseph real answers. Her participatory efforts were also paltry. She threw out idiotic questions like how do you drive effectively during a zombie outbreak? And should you drive if you have the flu? Are there exceptions for driving with the flu if you're going to the hospital and you're pregnant?

Having had enough, I threw up my hand to interrupt the teacher's lecture on driving in bad weather. It was unlike me to do so, but this was a desperate measure. "Could you please instruct Miss Spence that you're only entertaining serious driving questions? Your previous policy of no question being stupid was admirable until we met Amber."

That elicited a few chuckles from the students that caused me to look around in confusion. I wasn't trying to make a funny. This would have to be noted in my book later.

"That's not—-"

"Come off it wonder boy!" Amber spoke up instead, interrupting the teacher.

I turned and looked at her with apprehension. "Excuse me?"

"It's questions like mine that make this fucking class bearable. Everyone here already knows how to drive, but I'm starting to wonder about you."

"Word." Jamal nodded

"This class isn't just about learning to drive. It's about driving effectively. My questions are an attempt to parse out the scenarios that the book doesn't necessarily address when you are out on the road."

She merely sneered, shaking her head. "So do mine?"

"A possible Godzilla sighting in the middle of an expressway during rush hour is not a question," I said as if I were talking to a mental patient. Did she genuinely believe she was helping?

"Maybe not, but something has to be done to break up the boredom."

"Okay, guys let's calm down and bring the class back to order," Joseph replied, rubbing the frown lines forming on his forehead.

"Class is not supposed to be stimulating, Daylily. That is a fallacy. Its importance should be measured in how much information you pick up. And you do so by asking questions and taking notes. Your behavior only interrupts the class's ability to do so," I stated quickly.

Her brows furrowed as she leaned back and put one foot up on her bare desk. "Let's ask the class then?"

"Can you two, please, focus?" Joseph replied.

I was about to comply when Amber continued her appeal to the masses.

"No, really guys? Would you rather hear more of his boring questions in class? Or my more exciting and realistic ones?" Pointing at herself as if she were running for Class President.

They all clapped for her.

I merely grimaced. "As it stands to reason that everyone is here and not at home on their couches. There are at least two people, one being a judge and the other being a cop, who think that you can't drive. So everyone needs the questions I ask even if they don't want it. After all, children don't want to eat their vegetables, do they? But they should."

A pretty smile tugged at her lips as she tried to suppress it. "Are you calling us children?"

"No, you're adults," I said, turning in my seat to face the teacher indignantly. "You're acting like children."

A few of those students hauled off and hit me with balled-up pieces of notebook paper. I sighed; at least I was right. The teacher used the segway to bring everyone back to order and resume his teaching.

I cast uneasy glances over my shoulder at Daylily. She touched her soft pink lips with her finger looking almost appreciative. Perhaps I didn't lose this argument after all. I made another mental note, 2-0. Turning around to face the teacher, when I really wanted to trace the lines of her every expression.

She's got this young innocence about her, with just enough edge to let me know that she was surely out of my league and planted firmly on the other side of the world. As my granny has often reminded me many times, my future wife will probably be some sweet girl that I meet in church. It wouldn't be this girl sitting behind me. A badass rockstar among swine, who could kick even the coolest man's butt, cursed like a sailor and was quick-witted in a way that I'd probably never be. A femme fatale in only gym shoes and sweats. Maybe if she were the opposite of all those things, she would give me a chance. She has me shaking every time she's around and it's not from anger. Yet she's off-limits. It's like I was given an exclusive preview of some hot new technological laptop that wont come out for another year. Meanwhile, everything I come into contact with dulls in comparison. I don't think I want my type anymore. I want her.

"Okay, with those last few rules drummed into your head, and trust me if you live through a Chicago winter you will need them. Today's class is dismissed. See you all tomorrow," Joseph said, stuffing his things in his bag to pack up. "Oh, Mr. Kent and Miss. Spence, can you please stay behind."

She leaned over and whispered, "Ohhh, we're in trouble."

However, when we stepped up to his desk after everyone had left, she wasn't wrong.

"The behavior demonstrated by both of you tonight was deplorable. I've put up with a lot from you both these past couple of weeks. Mostly Miss. Spence. However, I'm putting my foot down tonight. "If you two don't learn to get things under control. Then I will kick you both out of class. Report it to your probationary officer and testify at your next court appearance. And you will be starting this process all over again. Am I understood?"

"Yes, sir," we both said quietly.

"This is all your fault," she said when we stepped out into the hall. Matching my steps tip for tap.

"I remember him replying that it was, mostly Miss. Spence."

"Oh, but why am I even here?" she asked.

"Because Daylily was running from the law."

She threw up her hands and stormed off. "Grrr."

Chapter Five

Amber

Boxing is the only thing that relaxes me, but by the time I'm finished with this punching bag, my nerves are at their wit's end. I was supposed to be meeting with Don's old lawyer, Taddeo Fuschi, any minute now. I'd since let my receptionist, El, in on the secrecy. But I threatened to fire her if she said anything to anyone else. Harsh tactics for sure, but I didn't need this getting out and making my life any worse. After the admonishment by my Driver's Ed Teacher, I went to my happy place to think. There it just came to me what to do.

I showed the lawyer into Don's old office. It still smelled like him. I could still picture him smoking a cigarette after eating an Italian Beef sub. This place was not mine. "I want to put The Boxpad up for sell."

He shook his head. "Don wouldn't like this."

"Sure, but Don also should have talked to me about this first," I sighed. "I'm not going to change my mind. So how can I keep my recent inheritance of this place a secret?"

Mr. Foschi unlocked his brown and faded briefcase that looked like it had survived two world wars. I held my breath. He frowned and handed me a folder. I took it and went around the desk to sit down.

Leaning back in the chair to read what he gave me before realizing what I was doing and sitting up.

"Don may be surprised, but I'm certainly not." Somehow I'm not shocked that he couldn't simply walk away without getting a dig in first. "I told him not to trust you with his legacy."

"What?"

I knew that he probably had a long history with Don. The man never threw away, people, just garbage. But how much he knows about me is a mystery. It's certainly not enough for him to be spouting this hate.

"I don't plan on ruining Don's legacy. This job may not fit my description. However, I fully intend to find someone with the right heart and spirit for this place. It's not going to turn into some fucking hot yoga studio if that's what you're thinking and fuck you for saying so."

"Just sign the paperwork in your hand and give it back to me by the end of the week. I'll put the gym on the market as soon as possible."

"Okay," I said.

"As for that other stuff. Time will tell."

I pursed my lips.

"I'll put my own feelers out as well. I know of a few other people who are more deserving of this place."

He shut the door behind him, and I flipped him the bird. I threw the documents back on the desk. A sudden headache was coming on as I rubbed my temples. I sat up and fumbled with the calendar on the desk as the door opened. Unsure of how I would explain my presence here. I let off a sigh of ease when it's only Layla.

"Hey, I saw the lawyer left. So unless Don's ghost has come back from the dead, it could only be one person. Need to talk?" She came and leaned over the front of the desk.

"I'm selling the place," I said, deep in thought. Once the words were out of my mouth, I half expected a light to part the clouds and shine down on me. I was hoping for a sign that I had made the right decision. But nothing came. I felt as knotted up inside as I did this morning.

Layla stood up, ramrod straight. "Amber, you can't do that."

I rubbed my forehead. "Not you two?"

She rolled her eyes, clearly ready to snap her neck too. "Don trusted you with this place. If he thought The Boxpad needed you, then, then I know it does. Tell me you're not about to abandon it and us."

I played with the faded pleather that with a simple nail scrape could be lifted off the fabric. "There is no plan to abandon anything. It will just be someone else running things."

"That's not what he wanted," she declared. As if all I needed was to have that one statement repeated to change my mind.

Biting my tongue in order not to scream, I know that, Layla. "This is my chance to kind of, course correct my life. I only got into this because of Don, and I've never regretted a minute of it. But maybe there is something else I'm supposed to be doing. And I'm not going to figure that out tied to a boxing gym."

"Course correct," she said, swinging her hand at me. "You make, I wish, money. Why are you trying to be selfish now like you ain't about this life?"

"Layla?" I began feeling like I was just about to sit down in a dentist's chair.

"Save all that," she said, storming off and slamming the door in her wake.

I got up to follow up behind her. Giving El the, I'm leaving gesture. Glad that I had already put my gym bag in the car. Only to be stopped at the door by Erin 'Right Hook' Palmer and her sidekicks. One of which I was sure she was sleeping with, but that was none of my business. Her new short buzz cut was fierce. But I wouldn't dare compliment this brown noser.

She looked like she could star in a play as Peter Pan. Her, I don't ever want to grow up looking ass. Just a big, my bark is longer than my reach, because I hate the truth, dumb ass. She's closer to a Chihuahua than a Pitbull, and I occasionally had to punt her across the street like a football. Just to get her annoying ass to leave me alone. Naw, this trick wasn't getting any compliments from me.

She'd get plenty of that from the catcalls. Foregoing the usual work outwear for skimpy shorts and a sports bra that looked more like a regular bra. Then again, she always did like attention; it didn't matter from who as long as they said that she was the best at everything. But I know she was missing Don, who else would be willing to pretend that she's not a problem around here.

She was one of the original members that never came around to my presence here at The Boxpad. Even caught me unaware one night and had her friends jump me after I left the Pad. I couldn't prove it was them because they were all wearing masks. We all know the truth, though, and Don knew too before he died. But to fit in, I asked him not to do anything. Her day was coming.

Her friend Lolita was a different story, but I understood. Loyalties come first, and Erin was her girl. After hearing the rumor that Erin had found love close to home I erroneously thought it was Lolita along with everyone else. However, she set us all straight that she was strictly boxing and her personal life didn't matter. She certainly earned my respect. And I liked to think the shots I got off all of them even when they had me down on the ground won me hers.

"Get out of my way," I said, trying to move past them.

It was Lolita who blocked my way looking back at Erin for confirmation. Like the perfect stop and fetch-it dog.

"Was that Layla I saw running out of here?" Erin asked, spryly. "What happened? Did she finally realize that she was the right the first time and you don't belong here?"

"Maybe she smelled that fishy pussy of yours coming and wanted to leave before it got into her clothes," I laughed.

The next thing I knew Lolita was pushing me against the wall. Her hands crushing my windpipe made it hard for me to breathe. Erin and her girl danced behind her like laughing Hyenas. I looked up at El, who looked poised to jump in and shook my head. That would just make it evident that I owned the place now. Everyone knew El had a see no evil, hear no evil, policy when it came to the dealings surrounding this place. Now it was just me and Lolita's cold dead eyes. One hundred and fifty pounds of pure muscle. "Did your daddy turn you into this robot?" I managed to squeak out.

Relieved when Erin tapped her shoulder, giving her the signal to release me. "I saw you coming out of Don's office, what's that about?"

I clutched at my neck, gasping for air. Bending over as if there was more air, the closer I got to the ground. "Just checking to see if Don left me any letters because clearly, I was his favorite."

"Fuck that! We all know it was Layla," she said, dapping Lolita. "What he leave her? The keys to the Rolls. We all need to be checking that fucking parking lot."

"Good one baby," her love chimed in, grabbing her chin to pull her into a kiss.

She looked positively anorexic, so I knew she had no plans of actually working out today. There was no way she'd survive one round in the ring with Lolita or me. Obviously, she was hanging out for the clout. And from the looks of her coordinated workout gear, the fashion wear. But it wouldn't surprise me if she actually loved Erin. She just needed to love herself more.

"You got jokes. Let me go find some of my own," I said slinking off with my tail between my legs. It was the only way I was going to get out of this without more questions.

This time she grabbed my wrist. "Don's not here to protect you anymore. You're not special. Instead, you're just the sickly runt of the litter. And if I catch you in that office again, you wont like what happens to you."

I pulled my arm out of her hand and looked behind her at her flunkies. My blood pressure rose until I could only see shades of black. Hopping into my Camaro, Layla's anger was the furthest thing from my mind. I hit the steering wheel over and over with the palm of my hand. "Fucking Bitch."

My tires screeched across the asphalt as I peeled out of there. Looking at the building through my rear view mirror. "Even now, this place was as welcoming as a pit of Vipers."

Thirty minutes later, I parked the car at home and took the bus to school. Curiosity peaked when we passed the path that Kent walked home. My thoughts on what his home might look like. Was it all beige like his wardrobe? Were the walls wholly made of books? I bet it smelled like a sterilized hospital on the inside. If I dropped a spaghetti meatball on the floor in the bathroom, I could probably lick it up with my tongue and not get sepsis.

But the short walk to the building was surely going to give me a heat stroke. Looking up at the sun, I wondered what happened to Fall. The weather in Chicago could be so unpredictable. I walked in to find Kent already sitting. He was staring at me in that intense way that he sometimes does.

"Why are you wearing that?"

"Why am I wearing what?" I asked, my thoughts positively frozen to the inside of my head.

He merely pointed up and down, and I looked down at my clothes. Almost missing that I was still in my workout clothes because I was only focused on him. I laughed. "Oh, I came straight here from the gym and didn't have time to change."

He nodded. "Where do you go to the gym?"

Were we actually going to try to have a civil conversation? This had to be the product of Joseph's little conversation yesterday. I quickly got to my seat before answering his question. "The Boxpad. It's the famous one that everyone has heard of because it's located right next to the strip club, Champagne Lux."

He shook his head. "I haven't heard of either."

I just smiled. "Awww, you're so innocent."

He frowned and sat down at his desk.

I leaned over and rubbed his shoulders. "Don't worry, wonder boy; it's not a bad thing."

He shrugged off my hand with a brush of his shoulders. I sat back down in my seat. And just like that, we're back to being enemies, and I thought he looked cute in his blue button-down shirt. His company logo was in small lettering on his shoulder sleeve. At least I wasn't the only one running late. Kent here worked at Bridgewater Health Planning. So he wasn't an accountant. I'd never peg him for a doctor either. Weren't they supposed to have a better bedside manner?

"Okay, class, thank you for being here. Let me take a quick attendance."

Ten minutes into class, I was fanning myself with the Driver's Ed pamphlet and receiving a paltry some of air for my troubles as I leaned back in my chair. I was sweating through my sports bra. Some janitor forgot about the evening crowd because they turned off the air conditioning and went home. I turned my gaze to Jamal's desk that sat beside a vent. The dusty string clinging to the vent for dear life suggested that there was air coming through. And Jamal wasn't here today. We were only allowed to miss three classes. He already missed two. But if we're going to skip out on something like this a spontaneous heatwave was the perfect time to do it. Maybe he did like me because he knew I needed the seat.

I got up and moved at the same time Kent did. He grabbed the desk, and I grabbed the chair. But it was all connected. "What are you doing?"

"I'm about to ask you that."

The teacher through down the little book he was reading.

"It's hot. I'm simply moving my desk."

"I'm doing the same," he glared.

"Okay, well, women first," I said, hoping to appeal to his chivalry. Wasn't he a man of rules?

"You're half-naked. You'll be fine. I'm still in my uniform from work." His grip on the desk as strong as ever.

"Are you slut-shaming me?" I said, defensively.

He stood up, clearly flustered. "No that's not what I meant. You look beautiful. Not that it was appropriate to say. Just take the chair."

He quickly went back to his seat, and I smiled at how red he got when he blushed. I almost wanted to reach out and kiss his cheeks. And maybe his lips too. Before jumping on his lap. Whoa, where did that come from? Taking my victory seat.

He is not your type, Shatterproof. I still remembered the conversation that I had with my dad when I was only seven. We were watching wrestling together, and as usual, I was asking too many questions about the matches. So he sent me off to fetch him a beer from the fridge to shut me up. I did as I was told. Dad ruled the roost when mom was working late at the hospital as a Nursing Assistant.

It only took him two more of those to start waxing poetic about my future. Still an impressionable child, I listened with rapt attention as he declared that men who look like wrestlers were the new Prince

Charming. Not those pansy guys at moms favorite coffee shop. If I wanted to live happily ever after like mom, I needed to get a big muscular guy who knows how to bench press and can spell protein. Admittedly, his advice was a little light on the intelligence part. However, life was about survival of the fittest, and I'd always be on the winning team.

"Man, chicks are something else," said a grumbly old man with grey bushy eyebrows who sat in the front row of the class. Still upset over my win of the air-conditioned chair no doubt.

"Feminism, eat your heart out," I replied to the back of his head. Not at all concerned with the opinions of a 70-year-old man that I would have to run from on the road. I looked over at Kent who was busy scribbling in a small notebook that resembled the one I had taken. What did I do with that notebook?

I shook my head to refocus. Did a person who was selling her trainer's gym, his pride and joy, have time to be this childish? I could lose my friend and a couple of teeth if Erin got wind of my plans. But I didn't want to be forced into some sort of manifest destiny. I wanted to choose. I chose boxing. Now it's become so much trouble that it might be time to choose something else.

I took out my phone and flipped through my video to a clip of me with Don. Turning the volume down as low as it would go before I pressed play. Hiding it underneath my desk, I smiled at the sight of him yelling into the side of my face. Trying to force me to listen to reason during one of those times when I just knew I was doing the right thing. In the middle of a fight that would cost me my first title shot. Although, what round it was had long since faded from memory. Thanks to him there had been so many.

Talking to him in my mind as if he were right in front of me.

"I'm not making this decision to upset you. I know you had your reasons for leaving me the gym, and they were probably some damn good ones." I sighed. "I kind of wish I could hear them, no lie."

Tuning out the teacher's ramblings. I paused the screen on my phone and just stared at Don's face. "Naw, don't give me that shit. I'm not giving in to Erin. You know me better than that. Boxing just ain't my happy place no more. Don't I get a right to be happy? Even if it takes me some time to figure out how to be, happy. Kent here pissed me off the other day, and the last place I wanted to run to was The Boxpad. Instead, I went to my second home. I found peace of mind there. The behind-the-scenes stuff in boxing always made me feel dirty. When you were here, you had a way of explaining things to make them better. There's nothing better about what I'm going through now."

I pressed play on my cell again, unfreezing the phone. "I'm trying not to hate the fact that you died. I know that I need to be an adult. But every day it's getting harder. It feels like my love of boxing died with you.

How could you give me a gift that you knew I couldn't keep?"

"Joseph. Joseph," Kent called out, raising his hand higher than anyone in class because no one else was asking a question. "Miss. Spence here is back on her phone, and I thought we had all discussed as a class that such behavior is a poor use of our time."

"I remember it being less of a decision and more of something you just said," Joseph said, pinching the bridge of his nose. "But yes, Miss. Spence, if you didn't want to pay attention. All you had to do was, not come."

"Fucking A," I said, leveling a hard glare at the side of Kent's face. A face that I wanted to punch in.

"But since you two have decided to interrupt, again, with your entertainment show. Then you both can stay after class and do the reading together."

"I'd rather stare at the wall," I said, turning to the side to physically stare at the wall. My cheek rested in my hand. It was good practice for talking to Kent tonight.

Chapter Six

Amber

Joseph's afterschool work had nothing to do with driving. He handed Kent a book on weather patterns, of all things. Sensing my reluctance teach added an extra five chapters to the five he had already assigned. We even had to do a book report like fifth graders. So not only was it in his job description to turn us into competent drivers. He also wanted us to become talented weathermen and women. This class is going to be harsh on my beauty routine if all I do is frown all day.

He wasn't even going to stay and watch us complete the task because he had a life. So we would be the only two nuts in the entire building.

"Do you want to read, or should I?"

I scratched my cheek with my thumb and said nothing.

He recoiled back as if he might strike me when he turned his desk around to face mine. Wonderboy never ceases. Kent even opened the book and got out his notebook and pen to take notes at the same time. He was so irritating. Only to stop and look at me expectantly.

"I don't bring a pen and pencil to driving class because it's Driver's ed Kent." He was dressed today in a dark grey shirt and blue blazer and jeans. Unlike the old man I'm used to seeing, he looked hand-some and intelligent. How?

"You can use your phone then. I don't think Joseph expects any fancy structure. Just that it's completed," he said, pointing to my phone with his pen.

I smile even though I'm shooting daggers with my eyes. Reluctant-ly, grabbing my phone that was still turned to the video of Don. I clicked off, trying to search for a writing app when an email from Fuschi came through with an appraisal for Boxpad. An angry emoji in the subject line. Does that man even know how to use emojis?

"Did you want to read?"

I tore my eyes away from my phone and said through gritted teeth. "No, go ahead."

The sale of the gym would only net me between $50,000 and $75,000, but this wasn't about the money. The money just made me feel worse. Thanks to my successful bouts, I was covered in the money department. I didn't want anything because of Don and the gym I had more freedom to find what I really loved.

But what about Layla and everyone else who already did. Was I risking their happiness by leaving it in some stranger's hands? A stranger who might not agree with the fact that Boxpad wasn't some fancy specialty gym. It didn't have crazy membership plans and offer you smoothies and protein bars when you walked in. Would the new owner be able to maintain a sense of community? Or would people slowly stop coming, under the belief that they couldn't share their fears and weakness out in that ring? At that moment, I knew why Don had chosen me to inherit the gym.

I experienced the best and the worse that place had to offer. It tore me down only to build me up. I understood that as long as someone stood in that ring, they could always defeat any opponent that tried to tear them down. That wasn't always a person either. It was loneliness and sadness and feelings of inadequacy. Everything could be battled out.

But Don was also not acknowledging something else. It also gave him extra wrinkles and put stress on his heart. Even El developed a life policy of see no evil, hear no evil. The Boxpad brought out the worse in people until they could sometimes be unrecognizable as humans, like Erin. Or make me wonder if there ever was a part of this sport that hadn't been sullied by darkness and back dealings.

And this is what Layla wanted me to take on eagerly.

A place that gave me anxiety without Don. Sending my heart racing until I almost had a panic attack. There were people here that I wouldn't dare meet in a back alley.

I stared at Kent's lips as he read about the unpredictability of nature and joyous wonder. His voice was low and appealing. A five o'clock shadow covered the rich ridges of his philtrum. He was begging me to suck his top lip into my mouth. His silvery tone dragged me out of the dull drums. I put my phone down and listened to his voice that was like the slow rat-a-tat-tat of a little drummer boy. Lifting me and setting me back down like a roller coaster.

His voice was like a soothing blanket for my cold thoughts. A reprieve from the trouble that had taken root in the pit of my stomach and sometimes made it hard to eat. It was like I finally discovered the cure to my racing, anxious thoughts. Some temporary peace, but that was all I needed. It was silly to use him for it, though. He was just a stranger with a complex. Yet, his voice as he read cut through all the bullshit. It told me to focus on him.

"Do you want to maybe do one of the questions at the end of each chapter? That may be enough to prove that we read each one. As well as get an understanding of the overall theme of the book?"

"Why are you like this?" I know this would start our feud anew, but I genuinely wanted to know.

"Like what?"

"Stiff. By the Book. The guy in the room who does the extra credit assignment even if he's passing the class. A guy who would pass out if he had to go out to a bar on Friday night because he needs to be home to do his taxes."

"What does any of this have to do with the assignment?" He said, putting down his pen in an apparent thought over this.

"You're literally reading a chapter and contemplating more ways to give us homework."

"And you avoid homework as if you're scared you might be dumb."

"Well, I'm not." I fell into that one. It was just that I was sitting in front of an anomaly trying to make it do something. I kicked off my sneakers, in nothing but my white ankle socks, and settled down to do some real work. Rubbing my favorite rose earring, that was part ear cuff, part earring stud.

He dropped his eyes back to the book but didn't begin to read again. It's hard to crush on your arch-nemesis if you hate him.

"For the record I didn't think you were, dumb, I mean."

For the first time, I think I can see myself through his eyes. I was wearing workout shorts, that fell to my knees and was much longer than the bootie shorts I normally rock in summer. My blond hair was braided into a simple side braid. I looked like wasted potential.

"And it's not my intention to make this harder, but easier for the both of us."

I turned into more of a degenerate with each passing day, and I see him Monday through Friday. I'm going to be a smoking, alcoholic mess by graduation. Rattling off about how much feeding my stray cats cost me. My age of change that started after my incident with Manny was undoubtedly off to a poor start and finish.

"I'm open to suggestions if you have any?" He had completely stopped reading the book now.

I wanted to ask him to go back to it. And forget that I even said anything. I could use that soothing voice right about now. I'm not even sure what I wanted from him.

"Or is Daylily only critiquing me because she's trying to maintain this bad girl image?"

"I'm just trying to get us out of here at a reasonable time." I'd rather be doing laundry than sitting in here. Kent should feel the same, or maybe this was just the highlight of his day.

"Joseph decided that when he gave us 10 chapters. So you can settle down now and just do the work. There is no one here to watch you perform." His eyes lit with an amused knowing like he had it all figured out.

"Perform." The word comes out of my mouth like a curse. He thought I was fake. What everyone thinks when they meet me. They make it up in their heads who I need to be, and anything else is fake. Putting on a show. Well, there was no faking how much I hated Kent. "I'm out of here. You can finish the rest on your own."

That's enough to wipe the smile off his face. He gets up to follow me, but I level a hard glare in his direction. If he so much as touched me right now, he'd get third-degree burns. I was so mad. Catching my red cheeks in a classroom window as I passed it.

If I was bent over flowers, people find it odd and disconcerting. However, if I'm punching it out in the gym, I'm fickle and hare-brained. Most white-collar suits like Kent expect me to be kissing Justin Bieber posters and working for a company that my dad started. For people like Kent, a blond girl boxing is just her way of acting out because she hates her parents.

Newsflash, I love my mom and dad. I may even call them tonight and listen to the drama concerning the neighborhood association that they both frequent. That won't change the fact that I hate reality TV and it will take me forever to find something on. Only for me to end up entertaining myself by practicing the magic tricks I learned as a child. But not before I commemorate my decision to sell The Boxpad in my bullet journal using too much glitter and red ribbon. Red because I have mixed emotions over the whole thing.

Then I'll get up in the morning and make myself a simple protein shake of Watermelon Breeze before going to the gym to box. Where it might calm my nerves. Or I wont get anywhere close because I'm dealing with so much shit there. Most likely avoiding Layla and her peer pressure to keep the place.

Before being forced to come to Driver's Ed. Instead of the one place outside of boxing that gives me some peace. And the whole time I'll be cursing and wearing shorts and a tank. But that doesn't mean I don't like to be pretty and can't do it up a little bit for class. It's the only time I have a real opportunity to wear something cute and sexy.

What about any of that is fake?

I was stuck in a class with a guy that tried to get me some serious time with a kidnapping charge. All because my ex-boyfriend made a stupid decision in my car. I tried to make the best of a karmic insult with some silly pranks and a few harmless laughs, and that's fake. A performance for the masses. I was so insecure that the opinions of 10 people matter.

I hit the locked door hard. It wasn't budging. But I was not to be deterred. Instead, I tried all three doors. "They're all locked."

Rolling my eyes as he came behind me to try them himself. I sprinted down the hall to the swimming pool, where I knew the back door was located. A huge red exit sign was above the door. It was locked too. I turned to see Kent's huge frame filling the doorway. "We're locked in here," I said somberly.

The glow of the waves played off his shirt like a reflection, and he looked as cool as the water. When I was starting to panic, swallowing the lump in my throat.

"Don't worry, will just call for help. I have Joseph's contact info," he said, turning back towards the classroom.

"Or the police. Whoever comes first," I replied quickly, going for my phone that I had stuffed in my pocket.

It was still on Don's video, and it slowly faded to black. I pressed the home button, but there was no resurrecting this dead battery. Walking back into the classroom, I found Kent holding his cell phone in the air. That can't be good. "Mine is dead, and my charger is still in my locker at the gym."

He hit his phone against his hand. "I'm not getting a signal either."

I grabbed his wrist and twisted the phone where I could see it. "Well, we have access to every part of this building. Let's go and stand there."

He laughed. "Technology, huh?"

By the time we reached the lobby, I was rubbing my head in exasperation. "What phone company are you with? If I have it, I'm switching."

He put the phone down and looked at me with frustration. "What are we going to do?"

I went back to the front doors. A dense fog had rolled in, making it impossible to even see a street light. Or even a parked car. "Looks like we wait."

"I can't do that. I should be at home. This surprise homework assignment was already making me late. I can't stay here any longer," his words came out in a rush. Tugging on the neckline of his shirt as he began to sweat.

"Let's go back and sit down," I said, trying my best to guide him back to the classroom.

"My throat is dry." He stopped at the water fountain and gulped down the warm water as if he lived in the desert. Splashing it on his face.

"Come. Sit," I said, growing increasingly worried at Andrew's disheveled look. But when I touched his arm he was trembling. Like an Earthquake had taken root in his chest. "Whatever is waiting on you will survive until you get there. It's going to be okay."

He bent down, breathing heavily as he tried to catch his breath. Squeezing his eyes shut as if they hurt from the light. "The room's spinning. I know I shouldn't be here. It's not safe."

I looked around the room for something to help. My gaze settled on the rolled-up kiddie mat. I pushed three desks to the opposite wall and cut off the classroom light. Returning to unravel the small blue rug. Before guiding him to sit with me. His head resting in my lap. "I need you to listen to every word I say. We're going to get through this together."

Chapter Seven

Andrew

When she told me the doors were locked, I instantly wanted to be Bruce Willis in the Fifth Element; *I got this*. It was my chance to be the kind of man that I knew she would like. And I didn't even know why I wanted to make her happy, but I did. Instead, she's rocking me like a baby on a Kindergarten mat. I didn't have to phone a friend to know that this was the least sexy thing to happen between us. But boy was she beautiful doing it.

"Let's repeat. Start with your hands."

I clenched my fists like we had been doing for the last five minutes. Trying to focus on my breathing. My heart was loud in my ears.

"1-2-3-4-5."

The tension in my body was all-encompassing to the point where I could crack a walnut with my bare hands.

"Now relax your fingers for 15."

I gripped her hand hard, smashing her fingers together. I stared up into her green eyes. Her blond hair cast shadows over the right side of her face. It begged me to tuck it behind her ear. But my neurons weren't firing on all cylinders. Gritting my teeth so hard, I knew that I would need a dental check-up after.

"You don't seem relaxed," she cooed, running her fingers up and down my hand.

It kind of tingled and itched at the same time. I flexed my fingers. Releasing the hold I had on Amber's right hand.

"There you go."

"Thank you," I managed to get out. The muscles in my neck wound tight.

"He speaks," she said, her smile unwavering as she ran her fingers over my brows and the designer stubble on my face. Every movement was calming and grounding. "Let's repeat the same thing with your forearm and bicep."

I did as I was told for two more reps before catching her hand in mine. She looked a bit scared as I sat up. I brushed her cheek with my thumb. "I'm sorry, I scared you."

She blinked and then shook her as if she were snapping out of some trance I put her under. "Don't be. I'm just glad you're feeling better."

"How did you even—"

She blushed and looked down at our hands. Pulling them away when we both realized that we were still holding on. "My sister used to help me through my panic attacks that way."

"Used too?"

She leaned over and straightened the neckline of my shirt. "Olivia moved away when she got married."

I smiled when I realized that our hands had somehow found their way back together. An invisible tethered chord between us. "It's hard for me even to imagine what you lost. I'm an only child."

She shook her head and pulled away again. "It's okay. I became a little too self-reliant on her anyway. I've since come up with a solution for managing my emotions."

It was hard for me to believe that this walking Goddess would ever be able to relate to me on any level. But here she was sitting in front of me telling me that she gets panic attacks too. I want to jump into the deep end of the pool and ask her so many questions. What? Why? When? But I'd been on the receiving end of those questions. And I know it's none of my business unless they volunteer the information. I would never make her feel uncomfortable or like she was a freak of nature. Instead, I took off my shoes and folded my legs just like hers.

I chose a safe question instead. "Like what? Smashing heads, Daylily."

She threw her head back and laughed. "That's part of it, sure." She lowered her gaze. "Do you want to tell me what triggered yours? Are you claustrophobic?"

"Not at all. The only thing that triggered my episode was me," I sighed.

Volunteering information on my Autism was the last thing I wanted to do. People tended to treat me differently afterward. They usually operated from a good place of misinformation. And those who wanted to know more could get a little too personal with their questions. But Amber deserved an answer.

"You don't have to tell me if you don't want to."

"No, I can," I insisted. "Sometimes it feels like my brain is a six-way highway, and at any given moment, two lanes are closed."

She smiled. "I know a lot of steroid users like that."

I kept going because I didn't need a reason to stop. "Yeah, in my case traffic is flowing lightly. But once it reaches gridlock, nothing moves."

Her eyes darted to the window at the sound of a car riding by blasting their music. We both peered out at the stalled driver. Who looked like she had only stopped to answer a call. They wouldn't hear us yelling for help. Not over the noise of Dancing With A Stranger by Sam Smith blaring from the speakers. One of my granny's favorite singers.

"Want to dance with a stranger?" she asked, twirling her hips as she made circles around me.

I did my best to follow along feeling awkward. My movements were stilted and unnatural. Two arms and neither knew what to do but churn butter. I doubt Amber noticed in her butterfly world. She was coasting above the song lyrics looking like a goddess. It only lasted seconds before her gaze kept drifting to the door. She made me look in expectancy.

"How about we pause this dance session? We can raid the vending machine for sustenance. Or is that too criminal for you?"

I looked down bashfully. "Starving is even worse for my anxiety. Let's go."

I was used to being the man with the plan, but Miss. Spence was innovative. She had me lean the vending machine forward. Then she used a ruler up the mouth of the machine to knock bags of chips out of the row. We got five before she grew exhausted. I had a couple of dollars to get us some water. Holding our bounty up in her hand. "So Kent are you a Cheetos man or ruffles?"

I took the ruffles. "You can call me Andrew."

She slid back to the door with the help of her white socks. The bottoms of which were probably black by now. Cocking her head to the side. "How about just Drew?

"That's cool too. . ."

She giggled. "I'm Amber, but you knew that boy wonder. Is there anything you don't know?"

She leaned against the door of our classroom. Her Bambi eyes and small voice did something to my manhood. Almost as if she were flirting with me. Deliciously scrumptious even in her workout wear.

"I don't know boxing."

She raised an eyebrow at me. "Which under every circumstance sucks for you. Unless you're standing in front of a judge, then you may want to be an Obstetrician."

I looked at her puzzled. Unable to follow her sugar-induced logic as she ripped into a small bag of chips.

"Come, I'll teach you boy wonder," she declared, dragging me back into the classroom, sounding like a wizard from a magical world.

I laughed and turned into a 16th century, Englishmen. "I am at your command, Daylily."

She dropped our bounty on the Kindergarten mat. I did the same. Brushing the salt from my hands as I turned to face her. It wasn't lost on me that this mat had somehow become home base for both of us. She wasn't trying to chase me out of it either. We were getting along without arguing or pranking each other.

She stepped back to challenge me, and admittedly, I was clueless. Were we supposed to wrestle or play patty cake? "What do I do?"

"You want to start with your feet a shoulder-width apart. Then bring your left shoulder forward-tilting sideways," Amber began. "Here mimic me. Your stance would only be different if you were left-handed."

"You've been paying attention to me," I said, my voice a little high. Basking in the small win where I could get it.

She playfully rolled her eyes. "I do sit behind you."

"What's next?"

"Tuck your chin and place your hands at cheekbone level to protect your face. When you're ready to hit your opponent. No here—" She stopped mid-sentence and adjusted my arms. "Now as fast as possible, extend your front arm straight out and jab."

I connected with air and still felt pretty badass.

She laughed. "Good job. It's a little more than that, but you've got the basics."

I boxed the air for another five minutes before re-joining her out on the rug. She was looking at me with such joy as she drank from her water bottle that I was almost taken aback. Where was that cold malice she displayed in court? Or that cool aloofness in class like she didn't know I even existed? I think I liked this Amber much better.

"What do you do for fun?" she asked out of the blue. Putting the water she was drinking between her legs.

"I put together model rockets."

"Wow, that's actually interesting," she said in surprise.

"As opposed too. . ."

"Sitting at home and watching Jeopardy. In between yelling at kids to get off your lawn," she said with a shrug. "I mean, how do you even get into something like rocket modeling?"

"One cool meeting during a field trip in Elementary School. I met an Astronaut, and it just sparked a lifetime love of space. Specifically, this hulking transportation apparatus that gets them there. A machine that started as nothing, but letters and numbers on the page."

She shook her head, sucking the cheese from her fingertips. That single action gave me impure thoughts; I could never say aloud. My eyes were drawn to her rosebud lips. "I bet you were so cute as a kid. Running around your bedroom in a space helmet. Is little boy you upset that you never became an Astronaut?"

I laughed. "I'm a Computer Programmer at a Health Planning Facility. This is my dream job. I wasn't in love with the Astronaut. Instead, I wanted to build the machine that he trusted with his life. My work now requires me to input data and code into the computer to get it to achieve certain actions. Hundreds of Health Professionals rely on my programming to help their patients, and accurate medical records are a part of that."

She looked up at the ceiling as if the answers to all of life's questions were there. "The only thing I've ever been that passionate about is boxing. I got into it my junior year of college. A string of robberies was happening on campus, and it had a lot of women in a panic. One of my friends recommended a self-defense boxing class. The rest is history. It turned into my primary mode of working out. Which I was already in too. Then it became my passion. Until, that little push in that direction, I was going to be a landscaper. I was studying architecture. My parents were pretty proud of me until I dropped out. No surprise there. My mom has recently come around though because of girl empowerment, and all that.

Before that class, I hadn't thought much about sports. Outside of what guy was cutest in their team uniform. I wasn't even that heavy into exercise. Being on my own brought on a few revelations. Like there really was something to this taking care of your body thing.

I started simply with spin classes. Those robberies ended up being some students taking paying for student loans to new heights. But that scare they put in the hearts of everyone traveling at night, I was able to harness it for something good. Something amazing. My parents didn't find out until I had already dropped out. It didn't go over well."

"Parents, they have your best interest at heart. They also make it hard for you to make any decisions on your own," I acknowledged, thinking of my grandmother.

"Spoken like someone who knows."

"When I could sufficiently live on my own. My parents figured that was their cue to make up for the lost time. I was a challenging child to raise. Now they live on cruise ships going to exotic beaches. So they don't police my decisions," I said, rubbing the back of my neck. "I was thinking of my grandmother."

She clapped her hands and shook her head. "I keep going back to the image of little you. Even then, your dreams were ambitious and beautiful. I think the only thing I wanted to be growing up was a garbage man. Those guys who drove past my house were my super-heroes."

I laughed. Amber simply stared, and it caused me to falter. Was I missing another social norm?

"I don't think I've ever heard that kind of music before. At least not this much."

I tilted my ear up to the window. For a minute, I thought she heard actual music. Like the car was back. Or someone was walking home late, perhaps.

"Drew, I meant you. Your laughter. You're like uber adorable when you smile."

I felt my cheeks turn hot. "Thank you."

"You're welcome. Now don't change because I said something. I much prefer you like this. I need a chance to get used to it." She got to her knees and came around my back. Kneading my shoulders with her hands. My muscles putty under her fingertips.

However, I hated being touched. When she did it in class, it caused a knee-jerk reaction. I quickly shrugged off her touch like it was a deadly spider crawling up my back. Yet this time, I wanted her to run her hands up and down my body.

She would then lean over and whisper into my ear, 'Fucking A, I want you so bad.'

My heart would be beating too fast to hear her. Running on instinct, my hands went around her like a belt. I'd pull her down on top of me. But she was no wallflower. Straddling me on either side. Her kisses would be deep and hot, like a Jacuzzi. Pulling me under, until the only air I could take was what she gave me. She massaged all my senses and awakening aching limbs that were so needy for her every touch and taste.

And the feeling would be mutual. She would give me a full impression of just how much when she grabbed my hand and stuffed it down her pants. But I wasn't used to this feeling, and I wanted to savor it. So I would only toy with the bikini strap on her panties until she whined my name for more. Begging for my expert touch. My member straining to be released from the confines of my cotton pants.

Plunging two fingers into her wetness like an unforgiving master. Her growl into the night indicated that I was definitely doing something right. Biting down on my bottom lip and giving it a small tug like a sex kitten. Her forehead rested against mine as she rocked back and forth on my fingers. We had all night, and there was no rush.

"You better not sue me for that massage, Drew," she laughed, going back to take a sip from her bottled water. Snapping me from my daydream.

The realization that I had been thinking sexy thoughts about Amber sent me into a stuttering mess. My heart raced. Her touch was jarring to me when she grabbed my hand.

"It's alright Drew; I'm just joking."

Her lighthearted tone allowed me to relax a little and get back to the task at hand. However, the evidence of my thoughts was threatening to expose me. A print outline of my member was obvious in my pants. I quickly grabbed the weather book and placed it over my lap. Already open to the page we left off. "Maybe, we should finish the reading."

She glared at me menacingly. "I'm not doing any homework now, but you can read it."

I cleared my throat and moved next to her. My back leaning against the wall. Adjusting my member a bit so that I was more comfortable. Within five minutes she was asleep, her head resting against my shoulder. I put the book down and pushed it to the side. This would be the best and worst sleep; I'd ever had, resting my head against hers.

Chapter Eight

Amber

I was jolted awake when my head hit the floor. The sound of Drew exclaiming that he had one bar orienting me to where we were. Did I fall asleep on him?

Looking up as Drew eagerly texted Joseph that we were stuck in the classroom and needed help.

I snatched the phone from Drew's hand. "Call the police if you don't get anyone. We need out of here now."

Handing the phone back, he called the police right after. Two minutes later, he received a ring from Joseph, our teacher. The man was so loud that I could hear him and he wasn't even on speaker. He wasn't happy either. Like a boss who found out that his employees at the factory are under production because of a strike. Nevertheless, he agreed to call the owner to get the janitor over as quickly as possible.

I hung up quickly. The last thing I needed to hear was a lecture. Drew just snickered.

It was five o'clock in the morning, and the police arrived first. They didn't want to break down the door after having contacted the owner. Instead, they assured us that the janitor was coming over. He had some sort of family emergency last night and didn't thoroughly clean and check the rooms. All that was left was too clean up our mess.

"Hello, you still in there. Janitor here." Someone bellowed as we rolled up the kindergarten mat. Drew placed it back where we got it. And I grabbed my shoes and my useless phone. "Hellloooo."

I ran to the front door, my socks sliding all over the floor. Managing to trip over my own feet as my sneakers fell from my hand. Instantly, I felt stupid like the first victim in a B-Slasher movie. But like a bird of prey, Drew swooped in to save me. Cradling me in his arms. I stared into those big beautiful kind eyes and said, "Let me go."

But I wasn't talking to him. I was talking to cupid.

I couldn't believe that I would ever feel anything about this man outside of loathing. Still, the beginning tingles were there. At the same time, he'd only see me as this criminalistic wild child. I carefully got back to my feet. Putting space between us as I approached the door. Why did I need to remind myself that this man was almost responsible for me getting severe time? And yet he almost stole the air from my lungs.

I got a glimpse of his humanity, and that was worth everything. We had spent all evening together, and I couldn't allow him too confuse my heart and mind. But maybe we could be associates. Hating him a little less would be good for the soul. The shock of anything else was just bad news. I needed to kill the urge to want him. It was like a seed planted on the inside. If it got to big it would kill me.

"Now we get to sleep in a real bed."

"I'm definitely blowing all my plans tomorrow. Or should I say later today." Fucking A, when were things going to go back to normal. We should be jumping down each other's throats. I definitely shouldn't be noticing how good he looked operating on little sleep. When I probably looked like a friend to the raccoon family. I wanted to de-pants him in front of everyone and run to the safety of my comfy bed. Like a childish bully.

This janitor was a co-conspirator in my pain. I watched with amazement as he took out a plethora of keys like he had one for everyone's soul. Clueless as to which one fit this door. The cops stood behind him with a look of boredom on there faces. Their lights twirled as if this was a medical emergency of epic proportions. Most likely discussing their need for more downtime through boring cases such as these.

"Are you going to be okay getting home?" he asked.

"Yeah."

"I could accompany you half-way to keep you company if you need?"

He was the ultimate gentleman, and it was getting on my nerves. He's probably waiting for me to say that we're friends now. It does my heart good, knowing that he still doesn't know me at all. "I said no. I'm fine."

"What's the matter? Not a morning person."

I looked at him evenly. "I'm going to say this one thing, and then we're going to go back to hating each other."

He looked at me as if he were afraid I might slap him. And it completely changed what I was going to say. I couldn't slap someone I wanted to kiss. "I'm sorry."

"What?" he stuttered, with a small laugh.

"I'm sorry for the prank in the bathroom. You know, when I taped pop pop fireworks to the bottom of the toilet seat. Your face, when you ran out of there, made it clear that it was a prank gone awry. You were seriously upset, and for that I'm sorry. I went too far."

We turned back to the doors as soon as the lock released with a click.

"Thank you."

Joseph showed up just as the melee was dying down. As usual, his face was redder than a Georgia Apple. Walking towards us like he weighed 350 pounds and the very ground should tremble in his wake. I was so tired I couldn't even laugh. My hair now was more of a mop than a hairstyle.

He stopped in front of us, like a parent who had to leave work to be called to the principle office. Teaming with righteous indignation and disappointment.

"This is the last straw." His voice dripped with disdain.

"Mr. Beard. Joseph, please calm down." Drew's halo must be a little crooked because he looked upset.

Joseph ignored him. "How many chances have I given you two? If I had made a bet that you ended your tomfoolery, I would have lost. This is way above my pay grade. You both are out."

Fucking A, this can't happen.

"Sir, we are completely blameless in this. And need I remind you that we had a deal," Drew chimed in.

"One you broke by turning an extra credit assignment into a scene out of mission impossible," Joseph countered. "It stops tonight."

"Surely, there are several things that we could do instead. We'll switch off and attend classes every other day. Or we could rotate week by week. I think I can speak for both of us when I say that we just want to pass. Prolonging this fight isn't going to make our lives easier."

"All reasonable reasons to stick with the program. Both of which you have treated like a trip to Disneyland," Joseph pointed out.

I couldn't argue with that. It's an ugly truth, but I wouldn't have gotten through an hour of this miserable class without the pranks and jokes at Drew's expense. It helped me alleviate the depression I had at even being here. But until the powers that be saw me as more than another delinquent, here I was.

"We're only here because of your stupid extra credit assignment. Now we're being punished because we actually made an effort." I paused for dramatic effect. "Some teacher you are."

"One with the patience of a saint," he cackled like a gremlin.

"We can report you for this," I warned.

He nodded smugly as if to say try it.

"Let's be honest. You just want us out of your hair. But do you really think this is the way to go about it?" Drew asked, trying to assuage the man's anger. "All you would be doing is ensuring that we have to take the class here again. Maybe the court system will take pity and assign us elsewhere. But when has court ever done exactly what we needed them too."

"Okay, what's your point?"

While they negotiate like two cowboys in a bar stuck in a western. My temper flared, growing as big as a balloon capable of being its own person. Once again, I'm in a full-blown shit storm, and it's blasted me in the mouth. Fecal matter everywhere. Nothing about this was fair. I'm the innocent one.

"If we agree to do some group study on our own, then maybe we can fast track this," he told me.

"In that case, we can meet for one hour before driver's ed class," Joseph said archly, and I almost kissed his hand. Like he was granting us a pardon. He wasn't going to torpedo our only legal means of freedom.

"As I said, you'll kill each other first. But at least you wont be wasting my time because now you have to finish Driver's Ed in seven weeks."

"Not a challenge at all," I said, shaking the man's hand. I waved goodbye at him like I was trapped in a black and white photo. Only turning back to Drew after I knew he was gone. "We're screwed."

He looked at me strangely. "Why is that?"

"It's obvious today was a fluke." I started to walk to the bus stop, needing to put feet in between me and Drew. It was like he was the Sun, and I was just trying to avoid his gravitational pull. Looking upon his face like I would a rose.

"It's not obvious to me." He stopped my forward trek by blocking my path, holding his hands up weirdly as if he were trying not to touch me.

"Move out of the way."

"I didn't think I could get him to agree, but I have. That means its time for a truce. One that allows us both to get what we want Amber."

"It's not that simple." I wrapped my hands around myself. The cool, windy air whipped my hair into my eyes. My exposed bare mid-riff reminded me that I was still in my workout clothes. Leaving me feeling exposed under the bright morning glare. Like I had been caught doing the walk-of-shame.

"You're right; it's not. Joseph's going to make it harder for us. Both of us will need to study. And afterward, will both qualify for Nascar and be able to predict the weather conditions before we leave the house."

"Okay, you're a man of ideas. We spent one day together, not killing each other. How are we going to do that for seven more weeks? Our issues haven't evaporated. If there is anything fun, you kill it." A bus arrived, but it wasn't the one I needed.

"And if you can do something illegal, you will." I felt a big chill at his words, but don't show it on my face. His eyes were dark and intense. For all that posturing, he looked as if he were contemplating my words.

Maybe he secretly agreed that we were more like oil and water. We would ultimately end up killing each other. The cops would walk in on our fighting and automatically think I was a threat to him. They'd ask him all the questions. Meanwhile, he would have questioned my love for my grandma because I refused to wait for a green light in favor of jaywalking. I would have had to beat his ass. Only for him to tell the cops that I put my granny's life in danger. No, this was not the guy to get lost among the poppy fields with.

"We shouldn't spend time together." I wished that I didn't sound so heartsick over it. Looking over my shoulder to see if another bus was coming.

"I understand why you would say that. But isn't your license something you want more than than a fight with me?" He leaned against the back of the bus shelter.

"Nope, not if I can't trust you."

He let out a deep breath and pushed himself off the shelter, standing in the shade cast by its shadow.

"We can try, but neither of us should be surprised when this crashes and burns. Maybe Joseph Beet is right." I took a step around him to sit on the small wooden bench inside the shelter. Trying ineffectually to cover my mid-riff with my arms. Or maybe just my sports bra. Before throwing my hands up in defeat.

He followed, leaning on the inside advertisement for toothpaste. "Let's do something to break the ice then. Get you to trust me. So that we can pass this class."

Spending more and more time together was not appealing. However, I was at a bus stop in my sports bra. I missed my car. "Only if I get to choose the activity."

"Okay, but likewise," he said, standing up straight like a general in preparation for war.

But this lady was ready to throw in the white towel. "Then we have a deal."

"Good," he said proudly. Nodding his head and walking away.

But I knew that I would get him with one word. "You don't look like you will be any good BOXING in a REAL gym. But will see."

His back stiffened up like a broom handle. But he didn't turn around. Shatterproof would have fun with this one.

Just like this bus was playing with my intelligence. Was it invisible, and that's why I had missed it? Were they always this slow? God, I missed my Camaro. By six-thirty am, my leg began to shake. I'd never needed a shower and a good rest so bad. Okay, maybe after I got out of jail.

"Fancy meeting you here."

"Fucking A." They had a tracking device embedded in my ass. My parole officer, Mrs. Herman, pulled up in a Toyota at the bus stop. The cops must have given away my position after I gave them my name.

"You had an interesting night. Want to tell me all about it?"

"Not particularly."

"Let's go back inside. It's probably the last place you want to see, but I'm afraid I have to insist." She held up a urine cup for me to see. I looked around, glad that I was the only one at the bus stop right now. A smug look on her face like she was waiting for me to fail one of these tests. It would only feel good if every wrong thought she had about me was right.

"Fine. Whatever." I couldn't even stir up enough fury to be angry. Instead, my spirit left my body and walked home with Drew. Maybe then I could remember a time when I was a good girl, and everyone knew me as such.

Now it was Shatterproof's turn. She had the wild boyfriend that let her rot in jail instead of posting bail. He missed every day of her trial because he thought it would call attention to his guilt. Then she got the punishment he deserved. So I wasn't peeing in a cup after a massive mistake out of my control. Shatterproof was.

Mrs. Herman knocked on the door and flashed the janitor her badge. "We just need to use your bathroom."

He reluctantly opened the door looking as tired of authority as I felt. Of course, she was given carte blanch use of the ladies bathroom. We moved into the first stall. She broke the white seal on the cup and handed it to me. I didn't look her in the eye as I pulled down my pants and pissed in the cup.

This wasn't me losing my dignity; it was Shatterproof.

I handed her back the cup, and she already had on plastic gloves. Putting on another yellow seal and placing it in a small cooler like container. Her earrings caught the light. They were round and large and looked like something to be worn on a Friday not out. Not work.

It tickled me to think that we might be doing the same thing on opposite ends of the world. I spent too much time with the wrong guy. But she was innocent, and I needed to be checked for drugs.

"How did you know I was here?"

"Mr. Beard called and notified me of what happened." She zipped the cooler closed. "Stay out of trouble now."

She left me alone in the bathroom to clean up. I flushed and went to wash my hand. The mirror drawing my gaze to my pale, drained face. The water was so hot that it felt like a hundred fiery pinpricks. My hands were turning red under the pressure. But all I did was throw it back in Shatterproof's face. I smeared the mirror in front of me until she was barely visible. The good ones aren't for you.

"You're always trouble."

9

Chapter Nine

Amber

It's laundry day by the time I find that notebook I took from Kent. After hauling my laundry basket three blocks down to the Laundry Mat on the corner and starting two loads. I sat by the window and flipped through what I got. My foot propped up on the seat beside me. No sense in accidentally creating an audience.

Kent had missed Friday evening's class. Our last one with the group, and weirdly it was boring without him. There was no one there to crack jokes and make fun of. A visible outlet for my hate and anger.

I was expecting it to be gibberish about work and intended to return it if that was all it was. Instead, it was like a bomb had been dropped on my chest. The first page was convicting in itself. What had I done? I was going to hell with lead paint in my panties.

Social Norms for My Autism

This was such a Manny mistake to make. Not me. I quickly flipped to the second page and the third and fourth. It appeared as if he were recording social incidences in his life that he was trying to remember.

It's not polite to tell my coworker, Shannon, that her outfits at work looked terrible. Only if she asks and even then no. Avoid her because I can't tell a lie.

I laughed out loud, drawing the gaze of one cranky old woman. We were the only two people washing our clothes on a Saturday afternoon. She should be flattered. A woman half her age was just as pitiful as she was. But there would be many more fun instances like this in his book. I didn't know that Kent was so unintentionally funny. Feeling me with warm fuzzies like jumping into a bed of teddy berries. And I couldn't remember ever feeling this good from something that didn't come at the end of a boxing glove.

The feeling didn't last as I skipped to some pages labeled trial. It was mostly notes to remember to scowl as it will help the case. I didn't know what to think about that one. Unsure of what to do about any of this. I'm tempted to beg Andrew for forgiveness for pulling all of those pranks. But then he would surely know I took the book. And he may have a disability, but that doesn't mean he wasn't a jerk. It would be more prejudice of me not to continue to prank him. Of course, I couldn't continue to like him either.

I was seeing him later today, and that wasn't enough time to figure it all out. Maybe he didn't understand that I didn't kidnap him. Leaving my actions towards him to be wholly inappropriate. "Fucking A."

The old lady crossed herself and kissed the tiny cross around her neck. I frowned. I know lady, I'm going straight to hell.

After I got home and put up my laundry, I called Drew to make sure that he was still meeting me at the gym and hadn't changed his mind. He sounded a little stressed out, but he confirmed that he was still coming in.

The words, you have Autism, and now I know, and don't know what to do about it, crossed my mind.

I put so much thought into my workout outfit that anyone would believe me certifiable if they had seen my room. Settling on a dark green stretch-knit athletic leggings the color of grass after it rained and it's been stepped on by hundreds of muddy shoes.

The top was tougher. But then I had spent all night in a sports bra. So I stopped on a pure white mesh tube top with full sleeves over a white sports bra. An angelic color for a wild child. Both the top and bottom were a perfect representation of who I was.

My every decision was reviewed through the prism of guilt and regret. How could I salvage how badly I'd been treating this guy? Maybe I should just take today seriously. This could be our unofficial restart. My cowardly soul wasn't going to bring me to apologize. Although, I had planned on sneaking the book back into his bag.

That was enough incentive for me to head to the gym early. I even told El to assign him a specific locker that I already knew the combination to. That way, I could sneak away at some point and slip the notebook back into his bag. No questions asked, and he would think he merely misplaced it.

I put all my things in my locker and headed back into the main gym to wait for Drew. It smelled like leather and sweat in here, and I would never love a scent more. I sat on one of the benches and fit my hands with sparring gloves that said fuck off across the wrist. Then in walked my worse nightmare. Manny, wearing a tank top that said, Luke, I Am Your Spotter. A physically fit perfect specimen of a man. He was just different in how he saw the world. He lit up the room as he cracked jokes with the receptionist and dapped the guys who came up to greet him. Owning the place as if he paid for it. The guy in high school who was invited to all the parties. And now as an adult, he made you feel important if he showed up to your anniversary party. Dammit, I was staring, looking away as soon as our gazes connected.

He slid in next to me, resting his elbows on his knees. Leaning over me so that I would have to look at him.

"You've been avoiding me," he chides like he's my father and I'd forgotten to call.

Suddenly, I wished that I had something to drink. My throat was dry and in bad need of some Powerade. I shuffled my feet so that no part of me accidentally touched him, worried that we'd attract the intention of the others in the gym. Not surprised that El was the only one with her eyes on us. Making a hmmm noise with my throat to low-key alert Manny to our audience. Not that his renewed selfishness would allow him to think of anyone outside of himself.

"I've been here. So, I guess I'm not that great at hide and seek," I shrugged.

"I just miss you." So much so that he even cleaned underneath his fingernails. The only pet peeve I had with him. He gave me half a shrug as he followed my gaze to his manicure.

"Sorry. I'm good without all that."

He turned his body away from me. Staring down El, who he just realized was watching.

"I have someone I'm training coming, soo…" Grabbing my hair and braiding it into one long braid. Squinting at him as I wondered how much he enjoyed this dental visit.

"It ain't got nothing to do with the accident though."

"What do you mean? Your new daredevil profession and general penchant of not giving a damn about my feelings is the whole enchilada."

"Naw, that's just all excuses. And you need them if you don't want me involved in the decision-making for The Boxpad. Now that you own it."

I had to do a double-take. My voice was soft and shaky. "What do you know about that? Our problems existed before The Boxpad." Someone started jumping rope behind us, so I lowered my voice. "I don't want any of your shit."

"The information on this place was public knowledge. Until you hid it that is."

"Then maybe it's imaginary. Like all the love in our relationship."

His mouth fell open, and I hoped something would fly into it. I wanted a random person to pop up behind us with a ready-made quip on how dumb he looked.

But someone was utilizing the ring with their sparring partner, and it was drawing attention away from us. Not even a string of curse-laced rants would draw their eye back, and that was a good thing because I was considering letting loose in Manny's direction.

"I'm going to ignore that because I know your hurting," He looked up at the fight in the ring as if he forgot that we were talking. And we were merely two friends who had come to work out together.

"Manny Dubon. I'm training a school friend today. He will be here any minute now. That's where you leave. What else do you want?"

He said nothing for several rounds. I looked around the gym, knowing that there were quite a few killer beauties here. Any of which could be Manny's type. Yet, he chose to warm the bench with me. I would be flattered except I'm not.

"Did you think I was going to make you the manager of this place or something?" Technically I could, but after the sale, I wouldn't have that choice.

"I just figured you would need some help." His friendly tone suddenly had an ominous flare on the edges. A dark cloud crossed his features.

"I don't need anything. I don't know what I'm going to do with The Boxpad. I'm not even sure I will keep it." Not pleased at all that Manny was the first person to find out. "The only thing left for you to do is keep your mouth shut on who the new owner of this place is."

"You're going to sell it?" Dragging his nails down over his scruff. "I want in."

I stood up, unable to take his presence anymore. Signaling to El that we might need security. I considered Manny to be at a code yellow right now. The memory of this man ever being my confidant, a silly notion now.

"This isn't some get-rich-quick scheme. I'm not going to be a millionaire if I get rid of this place."

He matched my height, grabbing a fist full of my braided hair. And I immediately thought he was going to pull me into a kiss. I was preparing to push him away. Instead, he pulled like he was going to yank it from my scalp causing me to squeal in pain. To an outsider, we would have looked like two lovebirds locked in a passionate embrace. Instead of a man threatening his ex-girl. "I want half."

"And why would I do that?"

I brace my hands against his chest. His eyes were unrecognizable to the man that I used to love. There was no way that Don used to call this man, son.

"Because you don't want to see what I'll do if you don't." He told me honestly. His eyes were cold and devoid of any light.

"He loved you and me." My tone was confidential. He pulled my head in close. Resting his forehead against mine with his eyes closed. His breathing was rocky and unsteady. A small bubble of fear grew inside me like an ulcer.

"I was the hype man for this place." He yanked my head back, causing me to wince.

"And I never got acknowledged for it. But now you're in power, and you can make sure that I get something out of it."

"Okay, but why half?" I know I could take him, but the cost of causing a scene wouldn't payout. Instead, I gritted my teeth and tried to calm him down.

"Because I'm owed nothing less."

"You did what a lot of people did to make sure that this place kept going when it hit a slump. You kept the family together." It was a truth that he wasn't ready to hear - laughing off my assertion.

"I did more than anyone."

"A few people could argue that with you."

"They'd be wrong. That man had always been an ungrateful bastard. But you are not. So you're going to even the score."

"I don't know if I can heal age-old beef, Manny," I stated uncertainly.

He nodded, pulling me until my face was stuffed in the crook of his arm, and he whispered into my ear. "You'll get me half of what this place is worth, or I'll break your leg and make sure that you never fight again."

He only smiled as he pulled back. Sporting the proud look of a hunter that just killed Bambi. Leaving me alone to simmer. He was gone for almost 15 minutes, and I could barely socialize with anyone at the gym. Just angry that I had to clarify to El that I was indeed not getting back together with Manny. And the signal for the code yellow was real. Hitting the punching bag repeatedly as if its contents spilled across the floor would give me my solution like tea leaves.

"Maybe you should try gardening instead," Drew commented, his face open and sincere. Like an inquisitive child, wondering about the world.

"I already do," I laughed, stepping away from the bag. "And you're late."

"I'm sorry about that. An unforeseen circumstance popped up with my granny. I didn't mean to be late. I know it looks bad because this is our reconciliation date. But I want you to know that I meant what I said and I'm taking this seriously. We both need our driver's licenses."

I stopped and made a beeline for the vending machines. Needing something else to drink. The blue-flavored drink quenched my thirst. "Did you just call this a date? Because it's not."

"Okay, but I am sorry for being late. The bus was right on time. It was just everything else. Trust me; you don't need to retaliate with my thing. It was all just unavoidable."

"It's fine Drew. It happens, and I get it."

"You look well-rested after our little harrowing event."

I raised an eyebrow at him. "Thank you. Sleeping in helped a lot. But you ready to get to work?"

Drew was wearing a striped mesh tank top and jogger pants. White wristbands in his hands. As if he were still deciding whether he would need them. Some New Balance gym shoes on. All of which indicated that exercise was not a part of his routine. On the other hand, if I do this right, maybe it would be.

"Do you remember everything I taught you about your boxing stance?"

"Yes, I think so," he said, going into position.

"Good. In boxing, you have to control your breathing. Inhale to prepare for a punch. Exhale through your mouth like a snake's hiss as you throw."

I stood behind the punching bag and held it. "Jab...Jab...Jab." I held up his hand to stop. "Let's correct you. Your front hand and your front foot should connect simultaneously. That means you should take one step forward. We don't run from fear. We meet it head-on."

"Believe it or not, I wasn't into sports as a kid either."

I snorted. "Really," I said sarcastically. Drew looked at me wryly. And I had to apologize. "Please, go ahead."

"I just meant that I was intrigued with magic shows. I always wanted to know the science behind it. The magician's secret if you will. I guess that does make me a loser by your estimation."

I looked back at the bag feeling a bit embarrassed for admitting this. "Only if I'm a loser. I learned a few magic tricks. Most of the little kids on my block were younger than me. I embraced it by learning a few things to impress them. Just so I could walk around and have them think I was a god," I laughed. "That gave me hours of entertainment, that I still enjoy every once in a while."

His encouragement gave me the strength to talk about my first trick and how long it took me to learn it. Opening up in a way that I usually never would. He even swapped stories with me on famous tricks he solved. I watched the flicker of expressions cross his face like a parade. Maybe he wasn't the robot; I had come to depict him as. We exerted more energy laughing than we did getting his technique down. He found me interesting and it wasn't for boxing.

Like the miracle he was starting to be, he took my mind off my problems. I wasn't even thinking about the notebook or his Autism. The only thing that crosses my mind was how much I loved his laugh.

He seemed to understand the mechanics of the cross move fine too. Number two in a fighter's power punch. However, having to learn the hook was turning him into a marionette. He was all legs and arms but in the worse way. Like he couldn't get them to behave the way that he wanted. Despite me having shown him how to do it three times.

"You look awesome doing that. You could bounce a french fry off that ass."

I just moaned, almost missing the compliment. "I wish I could eat french fries."

"You think if I read Men's Health Magazine, some of these fitness terms would make sense Daylily?"

I laughed. "Well, it certainly wouldn't hurt."

"See you Sunday at 9 am for some hiking among mother nature," he said, shaking my hand.

I hesitated thinking of his Autism, before returning his handshake. "I'll be there before the birds will."

Chapter Ten

Andrew

My coworker, and fellow Tier II supervisor, Rutendo Eze, texted me and interrupted my thoughts. Out of all my coworkers, he was my favorite. He was the only one who believed that the weekend was a workday when up against a deadline. But for once, his messages weren't about the horrors of double-checking someone's work. The only problem that I could never identify with. My subordinates knew that I expected perfection. Instead, it was about Feng Longwei, getting someone else to do his work as a part of some bet. This had to be a sign. Longwei was the perfect person to answer my questions. I could send Rutendo a hugging gif right now, but that would just be weird. I completely ignored Rutendo's righteous indignation and texted Longwei instead.

Andrew: Hey

I retained his number after the short period he had been working underneath me.

Feng: Hello, sir.

Andrew: I know this is a little inappropriate but I could use your help on a more personal level. Would you be open to calling and talking to me?

The phone rang two minutes later, and I almost dropped it. I was startled that Longwei would get back to me so quickly. Then again, I am indirectly his boss. I still wouldn't hold it against him if he said that he held me to a certain level of professionalism. So he wouldn't respond in that manner.

"Goodmorning, Kent. How can I help you? What sort of problem would have a genius stomped?"

I sat down in my chair in front of my home computer. His voice was like a dog whistle, I counted to myself to focus. "The girl kind. I'm going out with someone today, and I wanted to know how I get out of the friend zone?"

"Wow, this question has left many men in the dust."

Today wasn't just about a simple hike. Looking up the bus schedule for this morning's hiking activity. Maybe for one day, I could stop being Andrew Kent, the guy with Autism. And morph into a regular guy spending time with someone he was interested in. My mind flashed to Amber's laugh when I told her how I accidentally ruined this street magician's trick during our training session. She was worth every trick in my book.

"I've even had it happen to me once," Longwei surmised. But he wasn't forthcoming with the advice.

"Listen, I know this call is inappropriate, but I don't have many guy friends. If you help me out, I'll owe you one at work. This girl is really important to me. And I need more than a sound bite to get me through today."

Longwei paused before he said, "Where did you meet this girl?"

"I'd rather not say."

Maybe it wasn't a good idea to blur the lines this way with Longwei. But in the past, I'd been able to hide my questions under the social norm of guy talk. Now, I'd be billed as terminally unprofessional and stunted when it came to women. I shifted uncomfortably in a chair that I had picked out from 100 options to be my perfect fit.

"Good morning Andrew," My granny sang, as she headed into the kitchen.

I covered the bottom of my cell and the speaker. "Good morning, grandma."

Pulling out a notebook and pen just in case it occurred to her to start eavesdropping. I needed to take notes, and typing it was now out of the question.

"Okay, but barring any specific details I can only give you general advice."

"General advice," I repeated, writing that at the top of my notebook. I found my original in a gym bag that I rarely used. Rubbing my head against the headache his voice was giving me. "I'll take whatever can help."

I could hear him chewing on his pen. He always did that at work when he was thinking.

"I can tell you that she's the complete opposite of me. A free spirit. Wild. She could beat up a brick wall if it got in her way."

"Well, first you got to show her you're interested. More is more. Find reasons to be with her as often as you can. All gifts are approved." His words came in clipped like he might be brushing his teeth now.

I hurriedly scribbled down his words. Longwei was the perfect man to ask. His advice flowed off the top of his head like he was an encyclopedia on dating 101. I looked up briefly to follow my grandmother's steps as she made eggs benedict. All of it split my attention, but I needed to focus on Daylily. His voice pushed me to shut down and it took all of my effort not to. My leg shaking uncontrollably underneath the desk. "She doesn't look like the gifts type."

"All women are the gifts type," he said, spitting and gurgling.

I pulled the phone away from my ear and frowned. Needing less noise to focus, I picked up my notebook and took it into the room with me. The clothes that I had laid out this morning were already on the chair. I sat on my bed and wrote the word, gift, with a question mark. It would take a little time for me to research what she might want.

"But just in case she throws you a curveball. You can fall back on rule number two. Every time she shows interest act aloof. Like you're not interested."

I tried to untangle his words in my mind. "I'm not sure how to go about that."

"For example, if she gives you a hat. Act like you don't even give a shit. Excuse my language," Longwei supplied. "It's the most boring hat you've ever seen. You'll take it, but don't look eager about it. Women love mystery."

"A puzzle they can figure out," I concluded. This made perfect sense for the little I knew about women.

"She can't see you with other women either. You risk her thinking you're taken, and you can't walk back a misunderstanding," he pointed out.

"Yeah. That would defeat the purpose of why I'm doing all this."

"And I know you're wondering when you should make your move? Don't! She'll come to you, but only if you're following the rules exactly."

I nodded, writing down his last tip. "How did you get so knowledgeable? I'm kind of jealous. You must be like James Bond with the women."

Meanwhile, I'm living off the scent of her perfume. My vision was tormented with flashes of her smile. Her touch ignited a fire in my belly. I had experienced things with her that I would have gone an entire lifetime without. There was no forgetting that I'd ever met Amber Spence. This Driver's Ed class was turning into nothing but a challenge. At least, I had the secret keys to get past our hiking date now.

I got up and closed my bedroom door, throwing my notebook on the bed. Grinning from ear to ear. "I think you answered all my questions."

"Glad to help good buddy," he chirpily said as if God were stamping get into Heaven free cards. Get seven stamps, and you open the pearly gates.

"How do you know so much about women?" I asked stiffly. I began to wonder if I should even take his advice.

What he said next surprised me. Although it wasn't enough to discredit him. "I've only had one long-time girlfriend and we kind of joke that cab #626 brought us together. But I did pledge a fraternity. That was all we did was trade stories about girls."

It made sense. For most of my life, my friends had been girls. They would give me advice, but from a skewed bias that intended in turning me into prince charming. That may work in the movies, but not in real life. Dating was often much more nuanced.

Now thanks to Longwei, I could finally stack the deck in my favor. I could woo a woman. Possibly changing the stereotype that it was hard for an Autistic person to understand emotions. I may be very analytical, but I'd stolen the formula to Amber's heart.

"I know you're going to be great."

"Thanks." I smiled at my reflection in the bathroom mirror. Time beckoned me to get moving because if I missed my bus, I'd have to wait another hour and a half for another. The nature preserve itself was only an hour away. But it was a frequent visit stop that I enjoyed. I'd never taken a girl here before either.

Longwei cleared his throat, "Anyway, call me if you need anything else. I'm always available. If it's work, please wait until Monday."

I laughed, as that last statement wasn't surprising. And come Monday, Rutendo would have a few surprises for him.

I showered quickly and got dressed before eating a quick breakfast. Once, grandma saw me grab my walking stick; she didn't have many questions. If she were more observant then she would have had tons. In the past, I only went hiking on Saturday mornings. But being with Amber required doing things differently. Modifying my schedule slightly wasn't too much of a pain. However, a complete change might send me into a panic. Like the evening I was trapped overnight at the center.

But I enjoyed the scenic bus route over. Only a handful of people were on the bus because everyone was at church or spending time with family. No one stared at me because I had a walking stick on the bus. I was both seen and anonymous. Officially, this would be the first time she would see me out of work clothes and exercise gear into something semi-casual. My La Nuit de L'Homme cologne was complimented by every woman I passed on the bus. This had to be a great Sunday for me.

I stepped off the bus to see Amber waiting for me on a nearby bench. For a moment, my mind caved in on itself. Lusting after a woman in a grey quilted shift sweater and ripped jeans. Even fully clothed, I wanted her to be mine. Does love travel at the speed of light?

She was her usual bright and flawless self. That rare kind of person that could smile through the pain. And you wouldn't know something was the matter until she said so. The floral head wrap around her hair was adorable. It added a softness to her fall outfit. She was a goddess in her kingdom. The foliage was a witness to her beauty. And as I approached, she looked at me as if she had been waiting for me her whole life.

I wanted to hold her hand until my fingers go numb. Lift her into my arms and twirl her around. Run my fingers along the bare skin of her stomach. The way she looked at me, I just wanted to be worthy of that look.

"You brought a walking stick on the bus?" she asked, showing me the backpack of refreshments she had brought. Her small feet were ready for the worse in a pair of brown walking boots. The shoes were so thick if you burned them they would keep you warm for an entire month. It indicated at least to me that she didn't go walking much.

"No one complained." To hide my nervousness, I approached the booth at the gate and paid the entrance fee. It was sunny, but it was also cooler today. The perfect atmosphere for walking and perhaps even a hot chocolate later. Once paid up, the bar blocking the entrance raised, and I wasn't able to escape the feeling that we had entered another world.

"Let's put everything out there, okay? We are starting over after all." She took some sunglasses out and put them on. I wondered if it was because the sun was bothering her or if she just needed to hide? In elementary school, sunglasses were like my coat of armor. So I understood the latter need.

So I said nothing and waited for her to tell me what was on her mind. Guiding her down the trail path to the right. Once we got to the middle of the nine-mile trail. It would take us to the gatehouse. We could stop then and get something to eat. There was a beautiful view of a man-made pond from the cafeteria.

I pointed out a cute squirrel on the trail just ahead. Kicking up a light layer of dust, gravel crunched under our feet. "You can tell me anything. I'm an open book."

"I know you have Autism," she blurted out. Closing her eyes as if she couldn't look me in the face when she said it.

"What gave me away Daylily?" My tone was devoid of anger. I knew the truth would eventually surface. Hiding my diagnosis was just like ignoring a huge part of my life. I'd never be embarrassed by that. I was just a little upset that she was. Yet, when our gazes finally connected, it was like a lightning bolt hit us simultaneously. Something was happening between us, and I couldn't put my finger on what it was.

"Nothing, actually, it was revealed through something I read."

My hands clenched into fists. So that's where my notebook had been all this time. Amber's also why it reappeared yesterday. I certainly anticipated her questions, but not her drastic change in demeanor. Was that why yesterday went so well? She figured that I needed her pity and not her ire. I immediately turned into a child she had to appease.

"I know what you're thinking, and I did take your notebook. I didn't read it cover to cover or anything. Just enough to form a picture. I immediately knew I needed to give it back. I only took it as a prank." Grimacing, she bit her bottom lip. It sounded as if she felt guilty about the whole thing, as she should.

I wasn't quite ready to let her off the hook. The sounds of birds chirping in the trees did little to quell my anger. Anger that was curdling like spoiled milk at the thought of all my private thoughts being violated. "And what picture is that?"

"That I need to get to know you better. I can't seem to make up my mind whether I like you or not."

Before we got trapped together, I felt the same about her. But her acknowledgment that she was in the same place wasn't getting me any closer to forgiving her. All I wanted was to be her man. I wanted to take her on the floor, in a car, and on a bed. Take time to find out what grabbed her mind. I wanted to ruin her for everyone, but me.

It didn't take us long to cross a bench. So I stopped unsure if I should go any further, and I wasn't thinking about the length of the trail. "You invaded my privacy, but I can forgive you because my Autism was never a secret. But how do I trust you?"

"I wont prank you anymore. Or take any more of your stuff. I didn't even do a web search for Autism. Most people would probably find that irresponsible. But I want to learn about you, from you."

I could tell that she was telling the truth. Her eyes were solemn and nervous. I nodded and just like that we were back on an even keel. Her outing me wasn't a bomb to our relationship, but only time would tell. I hoped that today still goes as planned. We were still in nature's wonderland. The day could still end with Amber telling me that she would like us to go out on a real date one day.

"I just need you to understand something." Her voice was almost carried away by the wind. Wringing her hands behind her back as if she were trying to hide a pistol.

"I am trying here."

"I curse a lot, and my job is violent. And you irritate me sometimes, and I should be allowed to say so. Basically, if you're asking me to change because of your diagnosis, then you may want to include my name in that notebook of people you should avoid." She turned her face up to the sky - a steely resolve in her stance.

"You are so beautiful when you do that. And you should know that there is nothing about you that I'm not satisfied with."

She gave me a half-smile. "You're only saying that to make me feel better."

"Only because I want you to feel better. We've got to get past this contention between us that originated in court."

"This driver's license is really important to you, huh. It's important to me too in a symbolic kind of way." Her tone was light and cheery. So

I figured we could start walking again. We still had a long way to go. The conversation flowed much more naturally than it did yesterday.

"My grandmother needs me to drive her to her doctor's appointments."

She seemed a bit disappointed in my answer. "So you want it so that you can play chauffeur?"

I exhaled loudly. Making noise with the back of my throat. "She's slowly going blind in one eye."

"Wow, I just put my foot in it big time. You're definitely not going to want to be my friend. I have no chill." She folded her hands in front of her and looked away.

I reached out and brushed away a leaf that had fallen in her hair. "And I have no social filter, so we are a perfect match."

"We should go on the road and do holiday parties."

She switched her backpack to the front and pulled out a healthy snack. Like the Santa Claus of snacks, she offered me some of everything. I picked one out determined not to focus on the notebook. It was just us, and mother nature. There was no going back.

I told myself that up was the only plan now.

Today quickly turned into the best day ever. I had nothing to write in my notebook. All along the route, she pointed out the plants that she had just begun to learn about. Commandeering my walking stick for her use. Underneath, all that physical power that would make a grown man crash into a wall was a heart made out of a paper mache rose. My beanstalk wanted to come out and salute her.

It had only been two days, yet all I could think about was her falling asleep on my shoulder. The trail was positively quiet as if even mother nature knew that all we needed was each other.

"These are American Bittersweet," Amber chimed in, grabbing my hand and taking me to the bridge's edge. A short bridge was built over a slightly larger body of water. "We have these at the community center. They cover the gates of the Garden Love Project."

"You know about that?" I asked, pulling her away from the bridge. As we still had ground to cover.

"Yeah, I'm in it. For the last two years anyway. Everyone's great there. Almost everyone."

I wondered if she knew my grandmother. Maybe if I knew she was there, I would volunteer to help out more. Squelching a laugh as she ran five blocks just to escape a bee in love with her perfume. "I think it's gone now."

"Shut up," she laughed, out of breath.

"Hey, do you know my grandmother, Dama?"

Amber tripped over her shoelaces but managed to catch herself. I ran to her side, the warmth of her hand on my shoulder as she leaned down to retie her shoe.

"Yeah, I do know Dama. We speak almost every day. She can't wait to comment on my flowers." She righted herself once she was done and pulled away.

"That's great then. You two are friends."

She ignored my statement as she riffled through her backpack. "I think we're out of snacks now and I could use some lunch. How about you?"

I nodded. "It's just around the bend, and they have some delicious specialty hot chocolates. I'd love for you to try some."

We approached the gatehouse, which looked like the world's largest greenhouse with shock and awe. Only to be stopped outside by a middle-aged woman selling roses. This was my chance.

"Excuse me. Roses for a dollar. Or two for a dollar fifty. Buy for the lovely lady."

"We're not together. No thank you," Amber replied bashfully, try-ing to wave her off. She hid behind me slightly as if the woman was planning to carry her off.

"Maybe you could be if you bought this pretty lady flowers," she said, blocking my path.

"I'll take all of them."

"Drew you don't have to do that. I'm on the bus too. I don't even know how I'd get the roses home. Besides, I'm into watching plants grow, not watching them die."

This was a first, and I wished that I could call Longwei right now and ask a question. What do you do if she doesn't want the roses? At that moment, his words, more is more, replayed in my head. It's a symbol of my feelings, this wasn't about the roses. "I'm getting them all. They will look beautiful at your house. I'll help you carry them on the bus. No worries."

"If you insist," she said, tapping her foot. Averting her eyes as she looked out over the pond and the family of ducks. "I'm going to go use the little girl's room."

"I'll get you a hot chocolate." I ended up having to shell out another $30 for the cute little red riding hood wicker basket that the flowers came in. It would be easier for both of us to carry. I grabbed a seat for both of us inside after standing in line for a Peanut Butter Hot Chocolate.

She must've gotten lost because I was sitting there for at least ten minutes alone. I was debating whether to go seek her out when a busgirl approached me.

"Looks like you went all out?"

I looked over at the flowers that she was referring to. Touching the petal of one that was turning brown around the edges. An imperfect beauty just like my relationship with Amber.

"Don't let her get you down. You're a great guy for even thinking of all this. Anyone would be lucky to have you. And on the off-chance that it doesn't work out, then here is my number," she said, sliding a blank receipt paper over that she had written her number on.

I looked over at her for real this time. As if I had just discovered that dragons existed. My eyes were wide as my pulse quickened. Just as I was about to turn her down, Amber reappeared. Trying to look around her to read Amber's expression. "Please move, I'm not interested."

She gave me the stink eye before moving to another table.

"Hey, sorry about that," Amber said, taking the seat across from me. Her eyes never left the girl's backside, indicating that she had seen us talking. "Were you two, like flirting?"

"No. Busgirl's ugly. Not interested. She tried. She lost. Let's eat."

She laughed and got up with me as we approached the buffet table. "Okay, but she's pretty adorable. Just your type I would think."

"Her type never finds me attractive. I'm staying single for the right one. She's close, but no cigar," I replied quickly.

She tucked some of her blond hair behind her ear and simply replied, "Hmmm." Her eyebrows slightly raised. "I think I'll settle on a simple salad."

She left me alone to visit the salad bar. Her eyes drifted to the kitchen where the busgirl had disappeared. It felt like I was losing momentum. However, I wasn't sure how I was supposed to stop the plunge. Instead, I ordered a grilled egg sandwich and took it back to our table. She was already waiting for me, looking a bit jittery as I sat down.

"Okay, my bathroom break wasn't completely innocent," she smiled wickedly, twirling a tomato around with her fork.

"I'm listening," I said, taking a bite out of my sandwich.

"I stopped off at the gift shop," she hesitated. "You bought me roses so I thought I'd return the favor." She pulled out an Arboretum bag and handed it to me. Before digging into her salad, but it wasn't the food that was exciting her.

I pulled out an eight-by-ten box. Inside it was a wooden puzzle of a tree-lined landscape. Beautiful art painted on thick solid maple hardwood. It was the perfect gift, and it couldn't have come at a better time. Now I could prove to her that I was relaxed and mysterious. Just like the guys she usually dates.

"It's good," I nodded, placing it back in the bag and setting it to the side.

"They didn't have much there," she offered.

"It's cool."

She looked down at her food and finished the rest in silence. Barely touching her hot chocolate. Amber opted to call it a day instead of finishing the rest of the trail. We took the same bus home. So I waited with her at the bus stop.

"So today was a success. We can work together without killing each other."

She pursed her lips. The basket of roses hanging off her arm. "Right."

"We could even be friends," I told her honestly, blurting out my true feelings on accident. I knew I just broke a Longwei rule about making the first move. It felt good to get it out though. But there's a bus coming, and she's so distracted that for a minute I'm sure she didn't even hear me.

She let the others get on first before she turned back and said, "No, we're not going to be friends."

How am I supposed to get her to fall in love with me if she wont even be my friend? Maybe this wild child was too hot for me to handle after all.

Chapter Eleven

Amber

"You don't look happy to be here," Layla said, dropping me off behind an abandoned factory. The parking lot was so big that it could be a state. Not what I pictured for my Monday afternoon.

"I feel like we're about to do a drug deal."

Layla laughed out loud. "You know that's not what's got your skirt in a bunch."

I shot her a glare, before hopping out of her car. She was right, though. After what happened yesterday, I was dreading seeing Drew. Everything started great, just for there to be a massive crash at the end. Beginning with the roses, I didn't want. And the gift he ignored as if it were too much of an inconvenience to feign interest. It was a pretty clever gift I might add.

Maybe weirdly, the thing that bothered me most was the incident with the girl. She was a softball of cotton candy. I thought she was interested in Drew and was cute enough. Yet his reply to me when I asked him about it was that women like that don't find him attractive. Women like what? If she wasn't capable of finding him attractive, and she was arguably on the opposite end of the spectrum from me. What was I doing? Maybe my feelings for him were some sort of adjacent mental breakdown because of what happened to Don.

Him being the grandson of the gardening troll, Dama, just made perfect sense. No wonder we don't like each other it's in their blood. I'm allergic to all of the Kents.

"Hey," Layla called, leaning out of the driver's side window. "I know your non-date with nerd cutie wasn't so hot. But keep the pepper spray close. This lot is where murderers dump their bodies."

"Shouldn't the murderers be scared of us?" I huffed.

She gave me a wink and pulled off. I knew she was leaving to pick up her daughter from daycare so she couldn't stay. But she'd be back to pick me up. Layla had yet to meet Drew, and that was probably a good thing. By the time she started attending my trial dates with me for support, Drew had already stopped coming. All Layla had to go off of was everything that I had told her about him. I wondered if she saw him if she would think I was crazy or see the appeal.

I got out of my head long enough to see that I was alone in the parking lot of a building that was falling apart. Whole bricks were falling to the ground like a landslide. It looked like a bulldozer had been taken to the building, and then they changed their mind. The surrounding homes were more like ghost towns. I half expected an old woman to come out on the front porch, throwing cats and shaking chains.

Relieved, when Drew finally showed up in his 2017 Toyota. However, that was short-lived when I remember everything that happened yesterday. I sighed and moved out of the way as he parked near me.

Today, Joseph through us a curveball. Instead of five days a week, we would only be meeting with him for three. The other days, he expected us to put in driving hours. Drew even had to go to the community center to pick up our paperwork. For some reason, Joseph didn't trust me not to lose them. I figured that I would just be forging mine or getting Layla to sign off. But teach, really did think of every-thing. The only person who could sign off on our driving hours was the other person. In his mind, we hated each other too much to lie. He wasn't exactly off about that either.

Drew got out and slammed the driver's side door shut. "Hopefully, you haven't been waiting long?"

I looked back at his car, wearily. "You think he's trying to sabotage us on purpose?"

"He certainly feels like we were doing that to him."

I bit my bottom lip. Trying not to throw a pity party. "Joseph doesn't want me anywhere near that classroom, does he?"

He shook his head and went over to open the passenger side door. "No, but you don't want to be there either."

"Touche." I smiled.

After about thirty minutes each, riding around the parking lot. Our perfect driving record was getting a little boring.

"So...you drove the car here? Alone," I asked, staring out the passenger side window. Not paying attention at all to his parallel parking skills.

"Yes."

"So, isn't that like illegal and stuff?" I replied, clearly with an agenda. One he wasn't picking up on.

"Yes, but I don't live far from here. And we needed to practice," Drew explained, throwing the car in park. It was so clean inside that I would have thought it just rolled off the lot. Unlike my Camaro, there wasn't the smell of stale pizza and half-full beers in the air. It simply smelled like the strawberry car freshener hanging from the rearview mirror. A lucky rabbit's foot behind it.

I took it down and twirled it in my hand. Rubbing the scraggly fur as if it were a genie bottle. "Can we take the same route to practice driving on the street?"

"Oh no——-"

"You have to take that route going home. And neither of us can afford to take the easy way out doing figure eight's in the parking lot." I hung the chain from the rabbits foot on my finger. Making it dance with the slow movements of my hand. "I'm just suggesting that we take that route several times. Not for a joyride, but for educational purposes."

"Okay."

"Okay?" I asked nervously, having fully expected to extend my little speech for the next 15 minutes. This man was usually a hard sell.

"Yes, but I get the wheel first."

I kiss the rabbit's foot and returned it to its home, pressing the automatic button to lower the window. Adjusting myself so that the seat leaned back. "I'm ready. You go first."

"Shouldn't you be watching to see if I'm doing everything right?"

He had to be joking. "Your ability to stay exactly two inches to the right of the centerline is like fucking A1. If I had watched you parallel park, then I would have had to smack you because you're like weirdly great at everything."

Smiling, he flexed his fingers on the wheel. His hands were perfectly positioned at nine and three. An adorable red blush on his cheek that was uber kissable. However, I should have offered to take the wheel first. It didn't take me long to figure out what he had gotten his tickets for. Fifteen minutes later, this man was still on the same block. We hadn't even turned the corner. And there were no other cars on this barren side street that time forgot.

By the time we made it to the main street. We both ran into our friend, Buddy. A stray mutt with dirty blond fur, who was using the road as his runway, trotted casually beside us. Like he had not a care in the world, and we weren't stuck behind him. We watched him awhile, which is why I named him, Buddy. No one else appeared to be having these issues because they mastered the art of going around. Something that was going to take more than a day for us to master.

"What do you expect me to do I can't just run Buddy over?"

My seat was now in an upright position. I shook my head hopelessly on top of the car frame. The frame was hot against my forehead. "We could pull over and put him in the car?"

He pointed straight ahead. "You see how dirty he is."

"Yes, but at least he will be safe. Will find a place for him where he can be taken to a farm. Where he can run free."

"Are you patronizing me?" He frowned. "There is no farm for dogs. Only pigs go to farms and there eaten. It's not Heaven. It's animal Hell."

Despite myself, I laughed. Picking my head up to view our progress. "Maybe you should let me out so that I can gently shoo him to the side."

"He's still a wild animal. My license doesn't make exceptions for panicky trips to the hospital."

I smacked my lips at that one. Instead, I directed my ire at the rabbit's foot menacingly. It was just like that monkey paw that granted wishes but only with a catch. The powers that be knew exactly how to get me. I sat back and turned on the radio. "Let's scare him off."

"I'm the one scared here. Doggy brains could be splashed across my bumper. I'm pretty sure animal cruelty is a sin."

I unbuckled my seat belt and leaned across him. Aware that a healthy portion of my cleavage could be seen over the top of my tank top. He stiffened up like aboard. And it made me perversely happy that he was having this reaction to me.

"What are you doing, Amber?" he asked through gritted teeth.

"Breathe," I mouthed. His body was as sturdy as those bricks that lay on the ground crumbling. Looking no less dangerous. Swallowing the lump in my throat at the feeling of our bodies pressed together.

I lowered down his window and mine before returning to my seat. Staring at him as I tried to get my heartbeat under control. "Sing. Send him back to the sidewalk."

I turned the radio up obnoxiously loud. Just as the song, I'm So Tired by Lauv and Troye Sivan began to play. I stuck my head out the window. The wind whipped my hair out of my face. But I didn't think I looked as menacing as I was trying to go for.

So I stuck my whole body out the window, sitting my ass on the door frame. And I belted the song as if I was Ariel and I was going to lose my voice. The dog howled a few times like he wanted to join in, but made no major moves.

"Daylily, this is insane. Come inside."

"Sing Drew," I barked this time.

He joined in with me, and I knew that he had gotten into it when he started honking the horn in rhythm. All this combined was enough to spook the old boy and send him towards the sidewalk. I screamed into the air, feeling exhilarated.

"Okay Amber, come inside," Drew begged, turning the radio down.

This time it was my turn to obey. I accidentally hit my head on the top of the window frame.

"Ow," I said, rubbing my forehead.

"You're amazing, Daylily," he said, taking his eyes off the road long enough to check out my head.

It was enough time for the dog to circle back as we rounded the corner. Drew slammed on the brakes. He narrowly missed the dog by a nose. Luckily, his runway days were over. He was just trying to cross the street.

I sat back in my seat and put my seat belt on.

"That was close. Do you want to come to my house for hot chocolate and fruit roll-ups?"

I laughed, but it turned hysterical halfway through. My life flashed before my eyes. Starting with my parents and ending with my championship wins. My limbs displayed across the hood of the car like a Rorschach blob with glass sticking out of my forehead like a unicorn's horn. But once the moment passed, I took a deep breath. "I'd actually like some hot chocolate and fruit roll-ups."

"Good."

"But Dama?"

"She's not home right now. I think she's at the community center."

That put me at ease. We pulled up to Drew's house, and it wasn't like anything else on the block. It stuck out like a glittered thumb. The houses around it were nothing more than colonial-style single-family homes when his was a modern marvel. A minimalist design fit for an urban boro with sharp angles and wooden touches. My mouth was on the floor. I followed him back out to the front door.

Stepping back to get a full view of the place as he put the key in the door. The accented wood was strategically placed to make this place pleasing to the eye. When otherwise it might be a temple for robots. The kind of place that put all the others to shame. There was no fucking way his granny was paying for something like this off of a retirement check. She really was living with him.

"You have to—" He stopped when he turned and noticed me gawking at the place. "Right, I bet you can tell that I built this place. I know it's at odds with the neighborhood. They've told me at length."

My eyes nearly dropped out of my head at the mention of him building this place himself. I guess he didn't lie about being a computer programmer either. Thanks to some profitable wins, my wallet was pretty heavy, and my bank account carried some large rocks. Outside of paying off some student loans; however, I hadn't done anything to spend the dough. My Camaro #1 and now #2 had been my only major purchases. I figured now that I had stepped back from boxing, the unlimited funds could help me get my mind right.

"You're still staring. Something's awkward, isn't it? It's the clean lines. It was my only specification when I built this place. That's why I had to go for a more modern finish."

I looked back up at the two-story home and really saw it. It was almost a perfect square. Except for the wooden chimney-looking structure that extended past the second floor. Leaving enough room for a small wrap-around porch on the second level. The whole thing was enclosed by frosted glass. This old man had style after all.

"It's a beautiful home," I shakily said, failing miserably at sounding casual.

"Hey Ken Doll," yelled his neighbor, at the next house over. A guy in his mid-forties carted a pregnant beer belly and wearing a red Hawaiian shirt.

The house was so impressive; I hadn't seen him next door watering his lawn. Drew was positioned in the middle of a cull-de-sac. His house drew the eye like a laser pointer. I could see the neighbor's complaints. They were jealous.

"You finally anatomically correct. Now you can pull in a real woman."

I merely smirked. This from the guy who looked like he had to inhale Viagra just to get it up. Only to ask, where was the hole. I shuddered to think.

Drew stuck his head out around the hedges that divided their property and waved. Awkwardly laughing, he said, "Hi Joe, funny joke."

I joined in to play it off, but I knew the truth. Joe was a jerk. He must know about Drew's diagnosis. What kind of soul do you have to have to take advantage of someone like that? Just to make himself feel good because his trips to the doctor's office with the kids and guy's night out on Saturday wasn't cutting it. He had to knock his neighbor down a peg for a thrill. But it wasn't my battle to fight. So I ignored it the same way that Drew, did.

"Sorry, you'll have to take off your shoes," he said, closing the door behind me.

"Sure," I said. No qualms about showing my chipped nail polish. Or my chubby feet that looked like they belonged to a big toddler. "Does he do that often?"

"Who Joe?" he said, pointing behind him. "He's a crass joker."

I cocked my head to the side. "Little bit of an understatement."

"Well, it's okay because he's a neighbor. Shoot me if I have to deal with him as a friend."

I grinned. "What make and model for the gun?"

Looking around the home, it was nothing like the outside. Accurately, one of the throw pillows on the couch read, Love, Lives Here. It felt warm and inviting like my mother's favorite blanket that always seemed warmer than the barbie one she bought for me. Knowing a little bit more about him, I knew that his granny had a hand in decorating the inside. Drew didn't exactly scream warmth even when I liked him. He came across as more knowledgeable but fair. Like the tax guy that made sure I got a refund at the end of the year.

A dark grey sectional was set off by a wooden farm table. The walls were bright and inviting. White curtains allowed the windows to let in the sun and the air. Not surprised that there was even a small plant on the table. It was how a home was supposed to look. This place was used to lasagna dinners and game nights with the neighbors. Mine looked staged by the real estate agent as if I never made up my mind about what I wanted. Only to settle on the furniture that came with the house. And it wasn't a far cry from the truth.

"Please, sit," he said, hurrying past me to the kitchen. Grabbing a box of fruit roll-ups out of the cabinet and plopping it down on the table. I grabbed it and smiled. Surprised, when he headed back to the kitchen and pulled out a pan. This hot chocolate recipe called for some stove action. It was good to know that he knew more about the kitchen than just the microwave.

Weirdly, everything in the kitchen was labeled with numbers. There was even a container of straws labeled number 7. I wanted to ask what that was all about, but I knew it would be improper. There were even sticky notes on his fridge with reminders for today's chores. I could vaguely hear him counting to himself as he pulled out items from the cupboard.

I moved the throw pillows over and sat on the couch. Looking back at my shoes that were lined up with several pairs of Drew's in a straight line. Pulling out a small fruit roll up from the package. I'm pretty sure I just kicked those flats off. They were just plain running flats. So he was a stickler for organization, but that wasn't exactly new. My footwear was a little different. After the Manny incident, I decided to avoid The Boxpad for a couple of days. So I was temporarily out of my sneakers. Putting the box back on the coffee table.

He darted back to my side. "You can watch something on TV or something." Shoving the remote in my hand. "I ordered you one of these drinks during our hiking lunch. But I don't think you got a chance to try it. So it's pretty cool that I get to make some for you now."

The last thing I wanted was another reminder of that hiking trip. It reminded me that I shouldn't even be here right now. Drew was just trying so hard that I wanted us to work for the both of us. I turned the TV on even though it was the last thing holding my attention. There was a small table on the other side of the couch loaded with family photos, even some of him and my arch-nemesis Dama. He was all she talked about with her friends. It's crazy I never made the connection before. An everyday layman would have thought him to be royalty with the way she worshiped him.

"Drew, I don't think I ever asked you how you got your license revoked?" Going to the other side of the couch to look at the photos. A fruit roll up hung from my lips as I slowly chewed on it. The TV turned to some random movie channel. More interested in confirming my suspicion that he was adorable in his pumpkin costume for Halloween at 12 years old and cute as a button in a birthday hat at four. Dama was Dama. There was also a dog in some of these photos. A basset hound that looked as old as Drew acted. I almost wanted to laugh out loud.

Looking over at the kitchen, I noticed a dog's food and water bowl on the floor on the side of the kitchen island.

"I had amassed five tickets when I got my last one for driving below the speed limit on the highway. That was a bogus ticket. I was driving the speed limit," he said, taking out two coffee cups from the cabinets. Both were shaped like the bottoms of a rocket ship.

I burst out laughing, imagining cars whizzing past him. Blowing their horns and flipping him the bird. He went over to the screen and opened it, letting in the little old man dog from the backyard. He reminded me of Eeyore from Winnie the Pooh. A melancholic demeanor as he went over to drink some water. Paying my presence no mind as he didn't even bother to bark. Although he clearly saw me sitting on the couch. It only made me want to touch him more.

"Oh, this is Frank. Frank meet Amber."

The dog looked over at me and softly barked as if he knew it was demanded of him. My lips quirked up. I think I liked this dog. Watching him out of the corner of my eye as he struggled to hop into a suede swivel rocker. He fell asleep almost immediately after he placed his face down on his little paws. An old-school style vintage radio was on the table beside it. Somehow I just knew that was where he regularly sat with Drew listening to the radio. A homey contentedness about it that made me want to be a part of it.

"I usually don't ask people if they're okay with dogs because Frank is so mild-mannered. He's usually okay with everyone. But if he makes you uncomfortable, I can keep him outside. He has a rather nice summer house out there."

I smiled at the use of the word summer house. It can get pretty brutal in Chicago in the winters. So it would make sense that he would spend the majority of that time indoors. "No, I'm okay with Frank as long as he's okay with me."

Drew brought over the steaming hot cups of hot chocolate, and it wasn't until that moment that I realized I had no home training. My knees were digging into the soft cushions of their couch. I turned to sit and caught sight of a picture of a retro rocket against a cluster of stars on the wall.

"So what are we watching Daylily?"

I snatched the fruit loop from my mouth. "What the hell is a Daylily? And if you say something wussy I'll punch you."

Reluctantly, taking the cup from his hand. I dropped my half-eaten fruit loop on the table unceremoniously. I took a sip of the drink to find that it tasted like a liquid peanut butter cup. So creamy and rich. Hints of almond milk added to the luscious taste. Like a trip to the ice cream shop with my dad. It filled me with warm thoughts of when I knew magic was real.

"If you don't like it, I'll stop. But I thought it was a fitting name."

My gaze wavered over him, and he smiled bashfully under the weight.

"Do you like the hot chocolate?"

"I do, but I'm not that easily distracted so spill."

I'd never really been hung up on what people called me. My initiation into The Boxpad helped me develop my thick skin. Yet his nickname still hit a sore spot simply because it came from him. So I wasn't sure if I should have even asked.

"I'm surprised that you hadn't picked up on it being a gardener."

"I'm more of a novice, pretender."

"Well, a Daylily is a flower, not a weasel. It can withstand flooding, drought, and even salt. It's strong but beautiful. And the only color it doesn't come in is pure white."

Well, there was no way that I was going to dispute that nickname. Speechless, I threw myself into my drink. The liquid warming my insides confirmed that I wasn't flying. Accidentally, burning my tongue because co-signing the name was also out of the question. After he knew I wouldn't respond, he turned his attention to the movie. The scene appeared to be of one of the main characters talking to her parents about them not butting into her dating life.

"I wouldn't know what that's like. How about you?"

His soft, enticing voice would surely get me into trouble one day.

In my mind, I returned to the moments that I'd had with my parents. The home they'd now made in their little retirement community. Tons of conversations on the phone during our weekly life updates that included my dating status. The TV was merely background noise. I placed my cup down on a coaster on the table.

"Yes, but I doubt that their motives are as innocent. They raised me here in the city, but once they retired they moved to this posh retirement community in the suburbs. They love it there, and it gives them more time to police my life."

"Police your life?"

I folded one leg underneath the other. "I've made some difficult choices without them. My love life was kind of that last thing that I would always go to them with."

"Sounds as if being that open with them would be a blessing."

The word blessing and my parents even being in the same sentence were as foreign as learning French.

"Maybe, when I didn't know any better. Until I told my parents I was done with Manny. They weren't upset about the breakup. Just…the decision I made after it. In their opinion, it was more proof that I'm wasting my life. I just want a change. Yet, their solution was to date people they know, that meet some sort of checklist that they only approve of."

Nearly finished with his hot chocolate, he placed it on the table next to mine. He turned halfway to give me his full attention. "The dating checklist. My granny has one of those for me."

"I hold my parents partly responsible for my twisted sense of love. There was no way that I could figure any of this out with them calling the plays from the sidelines."

He mulled this over like a man at a crossroad. Our gazes reconnected and he looked so lonely that I pinched my inner forearm to keep from hugging him. Watching as he turned back to the TV. "This is why movies like these are so bad. They're not an accurate depiction of real life. The kiss scenes aren't even realistic."

The actors were under the stars on a blanket. Peer Pressure by James Bay and Julia Michaels played in the background from the car radio, and they kissed like Heaven forgot them.

"I think this is where we have to disagree," I said tugging on his arm. "Romance movies suck, but the kiss scenes are real. The right kiss with the right person can send you to the moon, wonder boy."

He looked at me skeptically. "And how often does that happen?"

"Often enough," I said with a determined nod. "Here, I'll show you. Face me, and I'll face you." Like two teenagers playing spin the bottle, we struggled to sit across from each other comfortably. Frank poked his head up like he knew something exciting was afoot. "Now obviously, it matters who you kiss. So we might miss the moon, but I'll still get you somewhere among the stars."

We sat across from each other, and it reminded me that we hadn't been this close since the lock-in. I closed my eyes and listened to the song and somehow, I knew his eyes were still on me. Like a tanning bed, his gaze caressed my body. It flowed over me like the warm surf over sand. My pulse quickened at the thought. "So you have to close your eyes and come towards me. But then take a moment. Pause because it's our last chance to back out."

"Why would we do that?" he asked, his breath tickling my lips.

I nearly fell over in surprise. My heartbeat kicked into overdrive. "Daylily?"

That sweet little word dissolved against our mouths as I closed the gap between us. I claimed his mouth as my own, catching that strong jawline in between my hands. Our lips pressed together tenderly. The kiss was soft and sweet.

"We wouldn't," I mumbled against his lips as I pulled back.

I actually wanted to kiss Andrew Kent.

And I wanted it to be as good for him as he made me feel. Touching my tongue to his bottom lip, I sensed him loosening up, allowing me access to his inner cave. A yummy, sticky slide that only made me hunger for more as I moaned against his lips.

His grip eased from my arms to shift around my waist as he pulled me on top of him. But nothing would stop our momentum now. I gasped for air in between molten-hot kisses that would only be satiated by an eruption. Our kisses devoured every sensation and thought in its path. Including the logical one, we needed to stop. Instead, we were easing each other into something more profound. Hotter. Small mini-explosions set off in my head with every flick of his tongue. A growing ache between my thighs that I found myself rubbing against his thick shaft.

The aim of all this was to prove that magical kisses were real. Forget the moon; I was halfway to Saturn. I think I like it here more. How do I stay? This was what I needed more of, volcanic sparks.

I just don't want him to stop.

Then a hard knock came at the door, and we both froze. I jumped off Drew when my cell began to vibrate in my pocket. Pulling out a text from Layla.

Layla: Be here in 5.

I almost forgot that I asked her to pick me up in three hours. Another brisk knock came at the door. Bowel filled the back of my throat. What if it was Dama? Running into Dama after necking with her grandson was my worse nightmare. "Layla, I asked her to pick me up."

Dama wouldn't knock, would she? She lived here.

He stood up to answer the door. I averted my eyes as if it were illegal to look at our exploits straining in his khaki shorts. A second later, mail was being shoved into the door slot. He picked it up and threw it casually on the table.

"No, Layla," he supplied.

I grabbed my jacket and hurriedly put on my shoes. "Yeah, but Layla texted me that she was on her way. So I should just get going."

He pointed back at the couch with his thumb. "Was that a movie kiss?"

I opened the door and stepped out. At a loss as to what the right answer was because I couldn't tell Drew the truth. It was better. Was our chemistry real? Or real made up? That kiss certainly felt like the former. Suddenly, he pulled me to him and kissed me again. His lips still tasted of peanut butter from the hot chocolate. I think I abandoned that drink in my adolescence. But here I was relishing the flavor and loving it.

Dabbing at the corners of my mouth. "That's a movie kiss."

A car pulled up down the street and honked. I recognized it immediately as Layla's. However, when I turned back to Drew, his face was flushed. Back again was that familiar curtain that made it hard to read his expression.

"I'm gonna go." Leaning down to scratch Frank's ear, who had also gotten up to see me out. Before running back to my ride and throwing myself into the passenger seat.

"Were you just—-"

"Getting CPR. Yeah, I was choking on a cracker."

"See Kim," I said, turning to address her one-year-old daughter in the car seat. "This is why you have to chew your food first."

Layla laughed and pulled off.

Chapter Twelve

Andrew

My nose was buried in a book on using the new rocket fuel when I plowed into Amber the next day. Some of the plants she was carrying toppled over and spilled in front of the open gate of the Garden Love Project. She was positively glowering until she looked up to see it was just me.

"Let me help you with that Daylily." I stuffed the book into my back pocket. Before leaning down to help her. "I'm sorry I wasn't paying attention."

She smacked her lips. "Neither was I, apparently."

I looked at her with a steady gaze. "I was hoping that I'd run into you today."

"Well, I'm here," she said, sucking in a quick breath.

"I have something to apologize for. And I wanted to tell you that I'm truly sorry Amber."

"You don't have to apologize for the kiss."

"I know." This was about a different mistake, but it felt good knowing that she hadn't regretted our kiss. "I made a mistake that I didn't know I was making."

I helped her put the small garden pots back into the black crate that she had been carrying. Just glad that they all seemed to only have had dirt in them. Sweeping as much into the cups of my hand as I could, I dumped them back into the pots. Paying no attention to how dirty my palms were getting. Her gaze on me was so hot it was as if she were trying to predict my next move.

"Okay?"

"The hike we took together. I had gotten some bad advice and ran with it. A true friend of mine set me straight." Admitting that I had made a mistake that was arguable due to my Autism and lack of understanding was hard for me to admit. It showed in my voice and the weird squeak it was taking at the end. She looked at me through narrowed eyes.

"I'm not worried about anything that happened during the hike." She brushed her hand together to get the rest of the dirt off them. After she had gotten up as much as she could from the entrance.

She stood up as if to leave and I knew if I didn't say this now then I'd lose her.

"Buying the roses. Not accepting your thoughtful gift. Lying about the intentions of that girl. All stupid things I did because I thought I had to win you over." Our relationship had entered a new universe. I didn't think I wanted to be her associate or even her friend. I wanted her to really like me.

"Why were you trying to win me over?"

I should have said that I was captivated by her. Attracted to her strength. And positively excited to know more about her. Her expression was apprehensive as if I were a used shoe salesman stopping her on the street. My gaze drifted to the crate in her hand that must hold at least ten potted plants with just dirt in them. Our little commotion already drawing some eyes. I took her off to the side so that we couldn't be interrupted by anyone else from the center or the Garden Love Project.

"Because I was hoping that we could go out sometime. Like on a real date. I like you." It was like a barrier wall made of solid steel was slowly easing up between us. Now I could truly see who was on the other side. And it was Amber, the epitome of strength, love, and beauty. I know I have to give her a chance to answer, but my mind just wanted me to keep talking. The wall lifted and that meant I wouldn't have to be alone anymore. "I think I have since the moment I met you."

"You shouldn't."

So she does like me? "I'll pay for dinner. It will be something nice. I won't buy you flowers. And I'll appreciate the things you do. It wont be the disaster it was during the hiking trip."

She looked back towards the gate entrance before walking towards the parking lot. It looked like she drove her Camaro here. But I didn't care.

"I wont even spill the beans to anyone if you drive your Camaro. I can't exactly pick you up. But I can meet you at your door and we can take public transit together. Or not."

She opened the trunk of her car and placed the plants inside. Twirling the key fob around on her index finger as she leaned against the car. Looking like she was waiting for me to finish my rant. "I don't think you've fully thought out what a date between us would mean."

"Unless it's endless happiness, then probably not. Should you really start a date thinking it will suck?"

"You have a point."

"Then you will go out with me? I could choose the place, or you could. I'm okay with that too."

"I'm not going out with you."

I opened my mouth to protest and maybe demand an answer why but closed it when I saw the look in her eyes. She had made up her mind and no amount of pleading on my part would change that. Especially if she only wanted to ignore the chemistry that kiss sparked. Of course, the only reason she would want to do that was because of my Autism. Not everyone is cut out to be with someone like me. That doesn't make the rejection any easier. It just made me feel worse like I truly was handicapped. "I'm just going to go."

"Drew wait—"

I didn't bother to turn around when my granny appeared.

"There you are. Someone said that you were out here. Why haven't you brought over the palette yet?"

"Sorry I was talking to someone."

"Was that someone Amber Spence?"

I looked back to see that Amber had gotten into her car and was already pulling off. "Yeah, actually it was."

"How do you—"

"I'm going to go get those pallets now." Cutting her off and disappearing into the community center. Because I knew that if she finished the question I'd be forced to answer.

Grandma joined the center shortly after grandpa died. It's where she found her second life. However, she's also a loud talker, who always has a lot of ideas. So when she enlisted my help at the center its one of the few chances I get to see her in action. She certainly laughed more when she was here. Her loud boisterous laughter pinpointed her location even before you saw her. I was happy to show up and see her wearing the tie-dye t-shirt that I made with mom when we were kids. For a second I even missed them.

My mom looks nothing like my granny. She took after her father. In the worse possible ways. While my mother's dresser used to be filled with every aging serum known to the beauty industry. My granny counted her wrinkles like the lines on a tree trunk. They were merit badges for a life lived well.

Her dark eyes carried sadness like a welcoming mat. But it wasn't easily seen thanks to her joyous countenance. Her arms were always available for a hug. Or a shoulder to cry on. Even if it was just the mailman. That friendly face in the crowd that everyone can go to for help. A huge mop of greying blond hair that anyone could tell was her crowning glory when she was younger.

At this age, she was still batting away the attention of dirty old men too. Men who could never keep up with her spry step. Not that her heart could ever be reclaimed. When she packed it away with grandpa. Her olive skin was permanently kissed by the Bermuda sun. With a touch just as delicate as the flowers she tended.

"You're not getting away from me that easily young man. How well do you know Amber Spence?

I had run out of options. The truth was going to come out now. "She's the same girl that I went to court with."

"You're kidding. Amber from the garden. Is kidnapping Spence?"

"She didn't kidnap me, but yes."

"Stay away from her. I can't believe I didn't make the connection before."

I rolled my eyes and got out a small portable pallet driver. "We've talked more than once since then and we've buried the hatchet. I'd even say we were friends."

"But you can't—-"

"Dama, Will is looking for your out in the courtyard. It's about important details concerning the dinner party menu. He's with the caterer."

She looked poised to protest but allowed her friend to lead her away. "We're going to finish this later."

Luckily for me, the garden provided plenty of distraction. I found myself sweating as I lugged pallets of dirt and fertilizer from inside the stock room to the corners of the garden. The seniors gladly directed my movements like they were in air traffic control. Likewise my granny, who notably wanted to be kept abreast of all plans regarding the 2019 Garden Party, was busy picking out items to make this the best party of the year. It was the most important one for her as it might be her last.

I didn't even pay any attention to Amber when she returned. This time with little potted plants with seedlings sprouting. Which it looked like she was planting inside an old wagon wheel. It was so interesting to see her outside the ring, not fighting, or in court looking fierce. But peaceful amongst nature. However, I couldn't let on to granny that I cared.

"I think it's time to go," I said to grandmother. Bringing over the last of the flowers on the palette to be planted. I've got dirt under my fingernails and an itch begging me to grab Amber in my arms like a barbarian and carry her back to my cave. It was more of a statement of how much she affects me now than a need to flee the community center.

"You're probably right," my grandmother chimed in like the boss of her empire. Instead of a woman granted 24 square feet of a raised bed garden. I'd hate to see how she acts if she were ever made President of the Garden Love Project.

"It's already starting to look very pretty."

"Don't worry about the others either. They're just jealous that they don't have a grandson to help them with this stuff. Every year the judges do an audit of my garden. And I'm never found guilty of anything. No matter what you do. My hands still tend the soil." Grandma's little speech wasn't for me, but for the listening ears nearby. The words of a ruler presiding over her garden kingdom.

"You'll be fine." I managed to get out before my laughter threatened to bubble to the surface. "I'm sure that whatever flower you've chosen for this year's competition will win over the judges. Your green thumb cannot be replicated."

I almost forgot that we were playing a mind game called, talk up your granny's skills and planting, when Amber passed by. She looked beautiful carrying in more herbs she had picked up from the store. I knew about grannies clique that excluded certain members of the project. Wrongly, I had classified it as minor contrived drama among old people. However, now I know better, seeing that the ire of their existence was Amber. The fact that my granny would exclude her because of some preconceived prejudice just seemed out of the realm of possibilities. They both were wonderful people who should, in theory, get along.

"The main ingredient is always love Andrew. It may be crazy, but you can even talk to them. And they can never know which is your favorite. It stunts their growth. You have to be part scientist and part parent."

"Completely. You ready to go now?" My question was short and clipped.

"Is something the matter sweetie? Are we running behind schedule? I still need to confirm some details concerning the competition. But then we can go." Grandma's gaze followed my own. I was always a poor liar. "You're looking at her as if you've fallen in love. I know that feeling. The butterflies your grandpa gave me when I first saw him out on that soccer field. Loudly boasting that women can't play. Are the stuff of dreams."

"I don't love her, but I know I'm getting there." Granny's feelings about Amber were obvious. But I'm not going to ignore what I'm feeling. I wouldn't.

"Good. Then it's not too late. You can still turn this around." She grabbed my forearm and led me out of earshot, but still within the limits of the garden.

"Turn what around?" Genuinely mystified as to why Amber's so horrible.

"Love is more than a mixture of neurons," Granny stated, pulling off her dirt-riddled floral twill garden gloves. "It can also be a choice. A deliberate decision that you deserve better in life."

I looked over to see Amber making a decisive effort not to look in our direction. Isolated, alone from everyone.

"Take a good look at her. Her bread and butter is violence. She has no respect for her elders. The cursing is an abomination. There is no way that she knows what she's doing with her life. Hitting women in the face is not a retirement plan." Ticking off all her reasons on her fingers. If allowed to go on I had no doubt she'd be on the fingers of her gloves.

"All of the above. Yet, she's the only star in my universe. Granny, she doesn't even look at me the same way that I look at her."

"Sweetie you know I've always told you the truth. Women like her don't go for guys like you. They want muscles, tattoos, and the smell of alcohol in the morning. She doesn't want the good guy." Granny offered pityingly, her hand on my shoulder.

Her words left a sour taste in my mouth like spoiled milk. Unable to even hold her gaze. All I wanted was to run from this place and seek the solace of my home. I stared down at my feet, uprooting a rock with my shoe. "What happens if she never wants me and all I can do is pine after her? She's carving out this place in my heart just for her. I know every woman I meet is going to be compared to her because I'm already doing it."

"Just try to remember that you deserve better."

It was exactly what I needed to hear for what was said next. "Speaking of what I deserve. I've got to figure that out on my own. Whether you are right or wrong about Amber. The person that's meant to be a warm cozy around my heart, will not be perfect, because I'm not perfect."

"That person is not Amber. I don't want you to be heartbroken." I opened my mouth to refute her statement when I'm interrupted by two of her oldest friends. They wanted details on the food at this year's garden party. When they were really fishing for information on what flower she planned to submit for the competition.

"I'm going to call for a car," I said sharply.

"Thanks, sweetie, you're a doll," she sings, shooting her gaze to Amber and back at me.

I could imagine that the rest of that sentence was you're a doll and she's a dog. Walking away before my mouth got me into trouble.

"Excuse me? Andrew? I'm Agatha. Can we talk?" This request came from a short little old lady who had to be at least 80. Hiding behind a 5 feet tall rack of empty potted plants in various sizes.

I looked back at my grandmother expectantly.

"Your granny will be a minute with her friends," she told me. "No sense in waiting in the car alone. I'll walk you."

I could see that my granny was now immersed in entertaining her subjects.

"I just remembered that I still need to put the flyers in the boss's car. I need to get the keys from the receptionist first."

"That's no problem."

This lady was using a walker though. She couldn't possibly walk all the way to the parking lot. Besides my granny had been going there long enough for us to know everyone. And she wasn't a regular member of granny's ladies-in-waiting. So I couldn't connect the dots on what she could want with me.

Granny hadn't stayed quiet on her wish for a nice church girl for her grandson. This lady just wanted to pass along her granddaughter's information. The thought of sitting across the table from a perfect stranger only caused my stomach to churn. Maybe the next conversation I had with my granny would be new boundaries for setting me up on dates.

"I appreciate the sentiment, but you don't need to walk me."

She shushed me and followed me through the lobby. I stopped at the reception desk where I had placed the fliers. The car keys waiting expectantly on top. The receptionist gave me a knowing wink. Like we know we can trust you. Sometimes I wished I was a bad boy just to see how they would respond.

Agatha's walk may be hobbled, but it was clear that her mind wasn't. She sported a curly salt and pepper pixie cut that made her seem younger than her years. A permanent hitch in her eyebrow indicated an inquisitiveness only seen in children. This was a 5'2" bound lady of fury. That I wouldn't be surprised if she said she had a tramp stamp of the peace sound.

"This conversation is to stay between us," Agatha began, alarming me.

"Have I done something to offend you? Or is this about my grandmother?"

"We don't even know each other. Of course, it's about your grandmother," she scolded. We walked slowly around the building to the back parking lot.

I was just relieved that this wasn't about some granddaughter waiting to pop out of the bushes. "Despite the heavy lifting I do here, I don't have much knowledge on the competition if you expected to pick my brain. In my honest estimation, I don't see her doing anything special to win every year. If she were she wouldn't share it with me. I have Autism which makes it extremely difficult to lie."

"That competition is for people with too much time on their hands," Agatha snapped.

I nodded. But weren't all pastimes that way? Finding our walk painfully slow even for me. "At least this hobby makes a difference. It's something tangible to leave behind. Giving children great joy and adults beauty to marvel upon."

"Until the garden love project gives the plot to someone else," she intoned skeptically, "I only go for the camaraderie."

"Then this does circle back to granny?"

"Moreso about what Dama told you about that lovely lady back there."

"Amber? You know her?"

"Only what everyone else knows. Which is why you should ignore your granny's advice. If you like the girl, go after her."

"But you don't know me," I said growing frustrated. Stopping to lean on the front hood of the owner's car. "How can you give that kind of advice?"

Her breathing turned haggard and I began to wonder if the walk was indeed too much for her. Watching as she flipped the seat down on her silver walker and took a seat. "Are you saying that because of your Autism? Trust me, son, I heard you the first time you said it. When you reach a certain age everyone has something wrong with their thinker."

"Except mine makes it impossible to date without coming off as a weirdo. Or someone who needed to be coddled." I think of Amber during our lock-in, the smile she gave me with her eyes. Before flashing to the kiss I received in front of the TV.

Agatha reached into the pocket of her floral gown and pulled out a pack of Newports and a lighter. "Our life is defined by our missed opportunities. Go after the girl. Maybe you get her, maybe you don't, but at least you'll know. Regret is like cancer. You don't want to take that flesh-eating germ to the grave."

"But what was so wrong about grandma's advice?" I asked, frowning at her. Conflicting information and concepts were usually my worst enemy.

"It's coming from a place of hurt, for starters. I suspect that she has more in common with that girl than she wants to admit."

"What do you mean?" I asked Agatha. "I've spent time with them both. They are nothing alike."

"Maybe not now," she said lighting her cigarette. Inhaling like she was just sent to the clouds. "But something in that girl is familiar to Dama's soul. But they are not one and the same. So she judges her harshly."

Honestly, as lovely as this confidence boost was, I couldn't gamble with the rejection. Amber was the type of girl that you only got one shot with. Agatha's advice felt better, but the solution didn't fit the algorithm. It would take me two or three tries to say the right thing and do the right thing, to get us on an even footing. My flirtation game was located firmly south of the border.

As I hit the key fob, unlocking the door, I put the stack of flyers I made at work in the lady's trunk. "You should stop smoking though."

"I'm 80, if this helps me reach God sooner, I welcome it," she laughed before it turned into a smoker's wheezing.

I rushed to her side. "Do you want me to walk you back?"

"I'm not dead yet son." She nodded to the car. "You just worry about boss ladies wheels."

She put out the cigarette on the side of her walker. Stuffing the half a butt back in the pack. Before looking around her conspiratorially and stuffing the pack back in her pocket. Standing up, I lifted the seat part of her walker. All within two minutes like a transformer. It was all pretty comical. She was a smoking granny superhero.

I called for a car, unable to ignore my guilt at the sight of grandma waiting at the door for me. Lucking out when there was already a car in our area. Her mint canvas gardening bag was in her hand. The bag was filled to the brim with monogrammed tools that I had bought her for her birthday. Rushing out to get the door of the cab for her.

"Where were you?" she asked, as soon as I hopped in beside her, the car pulling off.

"I took a walk with Agatha. At first, I thought she wanted to hook me up with her granddaughter or something. But no she just wanted to talk."

She rubbed my arm lovingly. "I am happy to loan my grandson out every once in a while. Not everyone is as lucky as me."

Chapter Thirteen

Amber

I poured some water over my head feeling a bit overheated. The locker room was dark and loud. I made a mental note to brighten things up in here. Maybe that could be my small contribution to The Boxpad. Coughing into the towel around my neck as sweat pooled down my neck. Taking slow breaths to get my heart rate back in control. Layla was all hips, walking around the corner in my direction.

"This is the last place I expected to see you."

"Were you looking for me or a launchpad for all your anger?"

"I was looking for Shatterproof."

A sensation of anxiousness flooded me. It was as if Shatterproof was an entirely different person and she was the one who inherited The Boxpad. But she had somehow been swapped out by her twin, Amber. I hadn't connected with that woman since college. So I no longer felt comfortable in my own skin. I needed to develop a third personality just to survive life. "What do you want with her?"

"Amber, you know you not acting like yourself," Layla charged, sitting on the bench next to me. "I think you're in a crisis like Manny is."

"Don't compare me to that train wreck. I'm keeping things together because of Don. Everything else is just me trying to figure out life," I said, wiping the sweat out of my eyes.

"Well, you're doing a piss poor job of it."

"Thanks a lot."

I'm starting to feel worse the more we talk. Did Don's death also restructure our relationship? We were constantly at odds now. Most of the responsibility for that was my fault, but she had to meet me halfway. I don't think I could take on the whole gym if she was against me as well.

"You should know, that I saw you kiss that guy outside of his place. The day I came to pick you up."

"It was a thing." Unable to put into words exactly how I felt about it. Or even what it meant to me and Drew.

"Well, this thing would have never happened with Shatterproof. That's just not the type of guy that keeps your motor running. I'm worried about you."

I threw my towel into my open locker. "God Layla, he's not a serial killer."

"No, but he is a symptom of everything else going in your life. You're not in the gym like you used to be. You dumped Manny, even if it was for good reason. Only to end up with a man who looks like he could be a used car salesman. Talk to your bestie. Tell me what you need and I'll do everything I can to help you?"

"Nothing." I hoped.

"Okay well let me help you keep it nothing. Let me set you up with someone tonight? You don't have to get married, but a date isn't going to hurt either."

I looked at her wearily. "If he's such a great guy you take him. Last I checked you were single too."

"This ain't about me. Besides the guy is too much like a brother. I couldn't cross that line, but you could. Even if it's just for some summertime fun."

Maybe, she was right. This date could be my chance to get back into the ring. And away from my weird feelings for Drew. Be more of my old self. "Okay, I agree."

"He'll pick you up at seven. I'll send him your contact info," she said, already on her phone. "But since your fairy godmother is on a roll. Allow me to fix your back-end problems too. You need to get back into the ring."

The only thing I needed now was to hop into the shower. My skin was beginning to feel icky. "Layla, we're literally talking in the gym. I haven't abandoned it."

"Girl, I've been watching you. Suddenly, the punching bag is your new friend. You need to get back into the ring. I'll train you."

A grin spread across my face at the idea.

"You weren't the only one who got a message from Don." Layla reached into her sports bra and pulled out a folded-up letter. "It looks like I was getting a training of sorts myself. He wants me to be your trainer. I have enough knowledge now to be one. I've worked with everyone in the business."

I opened my arms to my friend and she flew into them. Squeezing her until she couldn't breathe. My insides were lit up like a Christmas tree. This was one of the biggest decisions I had to make and I wasn't making it. No one could replace Don. Yet here she was, standing in front of me, with Don's blessing.

"Fine, I'll get back into the ring with you."

She pulled back. "Now that I've fixed your sports life. Allow me to fix your dating life. Let me set you up with someone?"

I noticed another woman passing us to access the lockers. Stepping back out of Layla's reach, I reluctantly nodded my head. "I'm trusting you with everything else. Go ahead."

"You're not going to regret it, Shatterproof." Layla's voice positively sang, and I kind of believed her.

Looking her up and down, she was wearing some black short shorts with red trim. "Are you wearing bootie shorts?"

"I know, did you see Erin walking around this bitch like she was the only one God gifted with assets. I had to show her the truth. She ain't working out in those uncomfortable things either."

I know, but neither was she. "Do I have to institute a dress code?"

"No," she said, clicking her tongue. "Just be honest. My ass better than hers?"

"Oh you already know," I said clapping her hand.

She turned to leave revealing a healthy portion of her lower buttocks as she left. Her chestnut skin was rubbed down with baby oil.

"One man dies and the ladies of The Boxpad decide to pick up fashion tips from the strippers next door." I looked around to see as if no one overheard my comment before closing my locker and hitting the showers.

Since I had a little while before my date. I decided to head home and use my downtime to work on my bullet journal. It had been sorely ignored since I started classes. So I went back to fill in the happenings of my days during Driver's ED. I even got to use some of the stickers I had picked up from there. Laughing at myself as I attempted to draw and color in the various pranks I had pulled on Drew. I was no Picasso, but at least I could tell what things were.

Drawing back on my feelings of being depressed and disappointed when I found out I was being kicked out of the program. Summing my feelings up with a simple boot and the door on that day. Of course, my boots had to be pink. Drawing a cape when I found out that Drew had convinced Joseph to let us stay. A car and a dog symbolized our first stint at trying to get driving hours. Which brought me up to date.

I wasn't even paying attention to the time. And before I knew it I had dedicated an entire page to Drew. Complete with stickers and pink ribbon. I was horrible at drawing people. So there was a simple outline of the side of a man's face in the center. It was so generic that it didn't even look like him. But I knew who it was. And if Layla ever saw it she'd pick up on it too and pitch a fit. I was contemplating adding glitter when a loud knock came at the door.

I put my pencil in my journal and stuffed it under my bed before hopping down to answer the door.

"You are late. What are you doing?" Layla barked in a panic. Taking my hand and leading me back into my bedroom. She picked out my clothes while I showered. Sending this, Kagiso Maddison, an apology text from my phone. This date was happening by hook or crook. She even called me a cab. And an hour later I was in front of Vivere, an upscale Italian restaurant.

"Fucking A." I swallowed the lump in my throat. Approaching the intimidating host. "I'm expected. Maddison is waiting for me."

"Yes, right this way." He led me through the main floor of a place that was both luxurious and whimsical. Deep mahogany booths and brown tiled flooring reminiscent of unknown villages reminded me that I was definitely out of my element. Who was this guy? Expecting him to be just another meathead I hadn't asked many questions. I was regretting that now.

"Hi, I'm Amber," I said when I got to his table. Waving my hand awkwardly as I hiked up my blush pink high low wrap dress and scooted into the booth across from him.

"I half expected to be having dinner with Layla. She seemed determined for this not to go wrong. I think she would have eaten with me if you ended up being a no show."

"We're both lucky to have a friend that will go all out for us."

"Well, I hope today is a cheat day because the food here is exquisite and it would be a shame if it were missed."

I smiled at him and looked down at the menu. It wasn't. "It is a cheat day."

It wasn't but I made it one. Allowing Kagiso to order for me when the waiter appeared. Apparently, he spoke some basic Italian. Everything was so posh. Crisp white tablecloths and clear crystal wine glasses. A low murmur over the crowd played nicely against the piano music. Even my date was decked out in a navy blue suit. He was definitely nightcap worthy, but I was dreading everything.

"So I see that Layla has been talking me up, but I don't know much about you."

"Yes, but not really. I shamelessly follow your career. I'm the owner of a franchise of gyms."

I'm proud of my reputation in the field so I find myself grinning madly. Kagiso's expression is appreciative. Like maybe I was exactly as he had expected.

Some panic took up residence in my heart. Just what was he expecting of me. Should I be crushing beer cans against my head? Or maybe he just wanted to talk boxing all evening. We didn't need a fancy place like this to do that. I cringed at the thought of us only talking about boxing. I already wanted to fall asleep. "So how did you meet Layla? Don't tell me that she's cheating on The Boxpad."

"Nothing like that. A while back one of her trainers was teaching her at my place. I have over 20 locations," Kagiso grinned. He was a boaster, I bet that wasn't the last time I'd heard about his place. He raised his eyebrows at me as if he half expected me to chime in that I had over 5 belts and fought over a hundred fights.

"The Boxpad has been the only place to whip me into shape. But your place must be pretty awesome?"

"It is, and I'm always looking to further expand."

"You can't beat community though. I think that's why the customers of The Boxpad are so loyal."

"Yes, places like mine do wish that we could bottle the loyalty that some of the athletes at The Boxpad display."

Our conversation stalls as our food was brought over. My Chitarra Alla Bolognese actually looks good and doesn't make me want to throw up. Some of these fancy foods can be overhyped. So I was worried about what he ordered me. But I had been prepared to fake interest in it. However, it was simple pasta with three kinds of meat in the sauce.

"So, Layla was telling me that you were getting tired of dating Bro Fit." Spooning some Tortellini in his mouth. "I hope a guy that owns a gym is okay?"

"It is. My statement about bro fit was mainly out of anger. An ex of mine was the reason I got arrested for that DUI and driving recklessly. I just don't want to be in a situation like that again. Bro Fit guys just tend to have fewer brain cells than I need my boyfriend to have."

He was built like a linebacker. So I wasn't entirely sure that he wasn't a bro-fitter. His dark brown skin was radiant as if he came out of the wound as smooth as butter. Ready to model for GQ. An air of exoticism about him because of his Italian African Accent. His tone was pleasing and sing-songy.

"So no daredevils?" He swirled the pasta on his fork and looked up at me. Rolling his r's as he spoke.

"No Evil Knievel."

He probably knew there was more of a story there, I was just glad that he didn't press it. "That story about your arrest was everywhere. I was wondering if you would be honest about it."

"I don't have anything to hide."

"So you're not the huge wild child that they paint you as?"

"My shortlist of exploits include vomiting in alleyways after too much to drink, but bar fights and high pursuit speed chases aren't my thing."

"You're probably the exact opposite of how they paint you then, huh," Kagiso surmised. But if he was disappointed I couldn't tell.

"I think people are often surprised when I tell them how I got into this business. So there equally surprised that I've managed to stay out of the fray." I sound so proud. Practically cleaning my plate.

Kagiso considers my statement. "That has to be due to the community you experienced at The Boxpad. I've been there a few times myself. It's a different connotation when half the people there only want to see you succeed. No one is trying to trip you with steroid use or other addicting pitfalls."

"No, I'd be lying if I said everyone there wants me to succeed. But you don't always need a tribe. Just one person to see your efforts and push you on."

"Now the gym is up for sale." He signaled for the check and handed over his credit card to the waiter.

"The Boxpad has come to mean so much to me. I've shared my joys and tears there. I met Layla there and she's like the best person ever. And it wouldn't be an overstatement to say that I found myself there. So I want the best for that place."

"Sounds like you would want to find an owner that would keep the same spirit of the place."

"Yeah, if it was in my control," I squeaked out awkwardly. Wondering just how much Layla had told him?

He rummaged through his pocket and pulled out his business card. "Maybe you could recommend my name to the new owner then. I know there are a handful of people in the running. A well placed shout-out. Might tip things in my favor."

He grabbed a doggy bag to go and I walked him to his car. Wishing I had my Camaro, instead of having to call a cab. I risked him volunteering to take me home. And I didn't want him anywhere near my apartment.

"Boxing monopolized most of our conversation. I was probably more Bro Fit today than anything. Sorry about that."

"You can always make it up to me later," I replied without really meaning it.

He beeped the key fob and a Ferrari lit up behind him. I was supposed to be impressed but he hadn't seen my Camaro.

"Beautiful car for a beautiful man," I said, knowing only one of those statements was true.

He locked eyes with me and leaned in for a kiss. We could be a couples photo on the tourist site for Chicago under the young, beautiful, and vibrant. The lights from the Ferrari bathed us in white like we were plucked right out of the commercial. My blush pink dress created the illusion that I was an angel. A powerful man with arms like bricks bent me over his arm. It was the perfect setup for a movie moment kiss.

My hand on his shoulder. His massive muscles seemed hard and tough. In a way that I just couldn't appreciate anymore. A familiar feeling that should be a comfort and almost certainly light the furnace. But my flower was drying up.

And I didn't get the movie kiss. Not one spark of fire. No toe-curling, foot popping, eyes rolling back into my head smooch for the ages. My eyes fly open as I implore the heavens above for more. He has to be the one. Or at least the right one for now. And I couldn't get either. His tongue fished around in my mouth like it was a fishbowl. I closed my eyes again and popped them open when we pulled away.

"I'm going to call you."

"I'll be waiting," I smiled pleasantly. Pulling out my phone, slightly irritated that he hadn't bothered to at least ask to drive me home. But instead of calling a cab, I texted Drew.

Amber: I think I want to go out on a date.

There was no competition, that kiss confirmed that Drew was it for me. He occupied my mind and claimed my lips. The crazy thing was if there was no Drew or Manny incident. That date would have exceeded my expectations. As it stood I sat at that table wondering where Drew would have taken me. Reminding me that I'd genuinely prefer to just sit on the couch with him explaining movies.

Fucking A, when did he take over my heart like this?

Chapter Fourteen

Andrew

I'm looking out at the backyard trying to see it from the eyes of a woman that doesn't like me. After she said no to my offer of going out on a date, I was more than a little wounded. Her text last night, however, through things into a tailspin. I had to try harder this time. But I'm so tired of trying and failing with her, and convincing myself that Agatha is right and not my grandmother. But I'll drive myself crazy trying not to think about her at all.

Speaking of grandmother, I managed to enlist one of her long-time friends into getting her out of the house for the entire day. It gave me plenty of time to work things out with Amber. I gave the picnic set up a once over and checked the food that was finishing on the stove. My whole life has been a test to prove that I could. I could do the same things that other people take for granted. Now I can't help feeling like Amber is my test to prove that I could learn to love.

Yes, I'd been in relationships in the past. But are they real, when they already know my diagnosis and treat me with kid gloves? Just because that's what they see my grandmother doing. Or that's what they think I expect them to do so they wont offend. Only to end up being offensive.

I pull out my phone and swipe up to the message I sent her.

Drew: You have such a beautiful soul. Don't taint it by going out on a pity date with me.

Amber: I don't pity you. I don't think I even hate you, anymore. I'm just scared to date you.

For the longest time, I didn't even reply to that statement. Should I be angry? Understanding? Or chalk this up to another awkward life experience because of my Autism. At that moment, I didn't want to be understanding; I wanted normalcy. I wanted a girl to go out with me and not have to wonder if she could or couldn't handle my baggage. But in true Amber fashion, she shocked me once again.

Amber: My dating track record is terrible. I just don't want to fuck this up. I'm not sure I'm right for you.

Drew: That's funny because I'm not sure I'm right for you. Isn't that the point of dating?

Amber: Duh! Yeah, it is.

Drew: I think the idea of dating has us both under a lot of pressure. And we work best when we're surprised. So let me surprise you.

A knock came at the door, and I knew from the rapt forcefulness that it was Amber. I cut off the stove and removed the steak from the heat. I'd been following a recipe meticulously. Never considered myself a great cook, just a good one. I knew enough not to starve. The whole process could also be a source of stress if I didn't know how to compartmentalize it. I hid the cookbook and shoved it into the junk drawer. Scratching Frank on the back of the head as I passed him. Before answering the door.

I opened it to see her in a washed green dress. A triangle bodice showed off her ample cleavage and the slight hint of a pink bra underneath. Some pink suede high-heeled sandals on. That made her almost level with me. Stepping aside, I saw that the dress had a T-back that revealed a healthy portion of her pink lace bra.

"It's okay you can smile," she smirked, raising an eyebrow at me.

"You look beautiful."

"And you look less...old. I think I'm loving the simple white v-neck and navy blue shorts."

I tipped my head back and laughed, stepping aside to let her in. That familiar ease back between us. "I'm glad you approve."

Away from the pressures of the outside world, it was like she looked different. Almost at ease, content. Her hair was down around her shoulders in a curly beach wave. The cotton dress she had on looked soft and comfortable. A slight glittered tan to her toned arms and legs. I was used to seeing her in tight everything, curves for days. But this dress was uniquely her. It was just a pleasure to see the real her finally.

It was also the first time I noticed the bag over her shoulder - a red flower-patterned backpack. A large yellow manila folder stuck out of the side. She followed my gaze. Bringing the bag in front of her. "Sorry I had some business to take care of before I got here."

"No problem. I set things up in the backyard. I hope you don't mind Frank joining us?"

"No, he's a cutie. I think I'd like that."

She walked with me to the back door, pausing as she looked out over the setup. The smell of the steak already spoiled what we were having. I forgot that it was her first time being out here. Huge river rocks covered in moss lined the perimeter of the yard. But not in any linear fashion. Large square stones cut through the grass and led the way to the back garage. A raised and enclosed garden bed, obviously for grandmas projects was tucked in the left-hand corner of the garage. Frank's doggy house was opposite it.

All were positioned safely away from where we would be sitting. On a rocket blanket with a bucket filled with ice and wine. Because I take Lexapro for my anxiety, I'm not allowed to drink. But I figured she was a drinker and wanted to be accommodating. A tray of appetizers and fruit platter was already on the blanket waiting for us. My vintage Bluetooth radio was on the side for our entertainment. I had Frank inside with me to ensure none of it went missing. Her silence, however, was unnerving. "Is it too simple? Do you want something more?"

She touched my chest with the back of her hand. "It's perfect."

Her gaze turned to mine as time stood still. I lowered my head to hers and our foreheads simply connected. As if we could transfer our thoughts to each other without saying a single word. I lifted my lips slightly to kiss her forehead.

"I don't think I need anything more than this."

I wrapped my arms around her waist and pulled her to me until not even air could breathe between us. There was no reason to pretend we needed anything outside of each other. Our lips latched on to one other as if we were the last people on Earth. And maybe we were the last two people for each other. Our noses brushed each other. Her arms circled my neck, pulling me towards her. My body alights with a contained fire that burst to get out. I pushed her against the door jamb. Our bodies pressed together.

Kisses that were probing and deep like we were two halves of the same coin. Her tongue caressed mine in a way that sent shivers down my spine. Not giving a care if our kisses were hot and sloppy. They quenched our ever-present demand for more of each other. The kitchen timer broke into my descent into debauchery as my grandmother would call it. "Isn't our first date kiss supposed to happen at the end of the night?"

She shrugged playfully. "Now there wont be any awkwardness."

I reluctantly pulled her hands away from me so that I could check on the oven.

Her head cocked to the side. "You made peach cobbler?"

My cheeks heated up as I replied, "I just warmed up peach cobbler from the Boston Market around the corner." I pointed to the steak. "I did make the steak though."

She tugged on her bottom lip with her teeth. "Good, I brought my appetite."

Her hot gaze held me in a tight grip. The impact of her beauty was almost impossible for me to successfully compute. Until she broke the spell by heading out to the picnic area. I followed her with my gaze as Frank nipped at her heels. He certainly had the right idea by snuggling on her lap. Although, I suspected his motives were of the food variety. I was starting to need another hunger fed. A pang of jealousy hit me out of nowhere at the thought of that Manny guy touching her.

I finished fixing our plates of steak, fries, and a slice of peach cobbler on glass plates. And brought them out to the blanket.

"I never imagined anything like this," she told me.

"I'm glad it meets your expectations."

"I don't mean the date. Just everything. I thought you lived in a one-bedroom house on a shaggy street. The grass was overgrown from neglect. With blinds permanently open for spying on the neighbors with binoculars and the police on speed dial," she said, as she put Frank aside to dig into her steak. Her knife sliced into the medium-rare steak. Should I have asked beforehand how she liked them?

A small amount of wind carried over her sweet perfume to tickle my nose. "I'm more likely to have my shades closed and the curtains drawn with a barbed-wire fence around the property like a faux G.I. Joe."

We ate and talked amicably about the students in the class who were probably missing us. Jokingly, quizzing each other on impromptu Driver's Ed rules. I even threw in a few fantasy questions about landslides and the zombie apocalypse just for laughs. We only turned on the radio after we finished eating. Hours flew by in a blink. The plates were stacked off to the side on the grass. She nibbled on some grapes absentmindedly. The song, There's No Way by Lauv and Julia Michaels, became the inadvertent soundtrack to the whole day as it played on the radio.

Unable to keep the smile off my face as she lay across my blanket and looked up at the sky. A small pouch poked out from her flat tummy, indicating she was well fed. She discarded the empty vine that she held in her hand. And Frank found his home once more across her lap. Not even realizing that I'd been staring for a long time until she looked over at me.

"Sorry I was staring. Sometimes...it's just with Autism... I."

"Drew it's okay. I kind of like it. It's this weird serial killer-like intensity with edges of infatuation. I just want to crawl inside your head sometimes and roll around. Make a mess."

I laughed. "It's already a mess up there. You'd probably knock some things back into place."

She turned on her side and held her head up with her hand. Successfully, uprooting Frank from his comfortable spot. Angry, he sauntered to his dog house to watch us from afar. Probably, sure that we would call him back. My gaze was back on her as she reached across the blanket to hold my hand.

"Your weirdness fits me almost too well."

"No one's ever said that one to me before."

She shook her head. "Admittedly, it was an affront to my freedom. A noose even. But as I've come to know you better. It's become a comfort. Something solid in my life that I can predict like the rules of gravity. Except these rules keep me tethered to you in a way that makes it impossible to be anywhere else."

I laced my fingers through hers. Hers were arguably more powerful, but mine was bigger and enveloped her in a safety cocoon. "Is that a good or a bad thing?"

"It's a great thing," she said, pulling out of my grasp and turning away. She tried to hide the tears that were just about to invite themselves to our little picnic.

"What's the matter?" I eyed her bag that had the manila folder sticking out of it. Did anything good ever come in those folders? "Is there something you're not telling me? Maybe about your court date? Or The Boxpad? You know you can talk to me."

"How did you know that you wanted to be a computer programmer?" she asked after regaining a bit of her composure.

"It's the only thing that I'd ever been good at?" Everything I do is such a task that finding something I'm good at is fresh air in a polluted tunnel.

"I don't know what I'm good at?" She looked back at me, and there was so much pain there that I wanted to pluck it out like a weed and burn it in an incinerator.

Yet, I was still left with questions. Could she only be saying this to make me feel better about my weirdness? If I fell for her, would I only be disappointed later?

I put those thoughts out of my mind and tried to lean on what I knew. "You are great at boxing. Many have said so. Your championship proved that."

"I was put on that path. What if I was meant to do something else?"

"Then you have time to figure that out? Often in life, you have to try and fail just to learn that something is not right for you."

She scowled. "I don't have time. I'm supposed to know."

"Like you're supposed to know that we're right for each other before we even have our first date. Like the rules of the road are supposed to prepare you for every actuality when they don't." I reached out and laid my arm across her waist. Shaking her waist a bit to get her attention. Nothing but soft femininity at my every grasp.

"You can only say that because you don't know the full story."

"Listen to your heart." Squinting against the sun that was slowly making its way across the sky to disappear for the night.

"My heart is the one throwing me into a tizzy."

"Is it though?"

"Are you suggesting that I'm denying the writing on the wall?" Her voice went up an octave. It felt like I was laying next to a lioness provoking her ire. But I was prepared to face it down.

"I'm saying that sometimes we're just not ready for what we want. So we put other obstacles in our way to make it harder for us to get where we need to be. For instance, you're great at boxing, and you clearly love flowers. But only one of those speaks to your heart deeply."

"*Flowers* are one of the things holding my heart hostage," she said, staring into my eyes.

"Is it?"

"Yes."

"My life is a series of obstacles, in the most mundane ways, and I'm simply trying to get where I need to be. So I sympathize." I had an idea remembering the potted plants that she was carrying out of the garden project the other day. "Is it hard for you to grow plants?"

She pursed her lips. "Yes. That's why I swapped out my flowers for herbs. I fair better in that department, and I didn't want to be the only one at the garden project staring at the dirt."

"So you gave up on the flowers."

A smile tugged at the corner of her lips. "No, they're all over my apartment. They are not fairing any better either. But I call them my little pots of joy, hope, and beauty because they could literally be anything. And the possibility is almost better than the real thing."

"You really are a Disney Princess."

"Only if that Princess is Mulan."

I laughed. "Dually noted." Hours later, my head in her lap, we stared up at the receding Sun and the crescent of colors lighting up the sky. I tapped her lightly on the hip. "It's getting late we should probably go inside."

She helped me bring everything in. Setting the blanket down on the couch. I busied myself washing the dishes as she waited for me on the couch.

"Are you loading those dishes into the dishwasher? There spotless."

"A second round never hurt. Germs can sometimes be left behind from hand washing. Another reason why I can't touch anything until my hands are completely dry."

She got up and opened the freezer. "Then you probably can't hand me some ice cream."

Pulling out a carton of vanilla and getting out a spoon. She ate straight from the carton. My anxiety levels went up a notch. "Let me get you a bowl."

"Oh, that's not necessary. You just did the dishes," Amber said, carrying the carton through the house. My gaze followed her into the living room as she bent to turn the radio back on. What if she spilled something? How was I supposed to clean it? What if it was a tough stain? Were there certain products I was supposed to be using?

She swiveled her hips as the radio DJ announced the song, Slow Dancing In The Dark by Joji. The instrumental was playing in the background. I don't think I'd ever heard this song. The spoon twirled in her hand like a baton. Even in her rawest form, she was a Goddess. Calling for me to come closer, and tangle my hands in her hair, and trace the flow of her hips. But it was competing with the other side of me that was worried about her making a mess and my ability to be able to clean it effectively.

"This is my song. Dance with me," she said, placing the carton of ice cream and spoon down on the kitchen island. Grabbing my hips as I turned away from her.

"I don't dance," I said, placing the top on the ice cream and putting it back in the freezer. One problem was safely tucked away. Another arose as Amber moved my hips in an unnatural motion. I laughed at my stiffness.

Only to pull away and pout. "Come on, it's a slow dance. Just dance with me."

I turned and faced her. Upset that I would have to disappoint her. "I don't think I'm good at it, fast or slow."

"A dance can save a soul," she whispered, placing my hand around her hips.

"How?" I whispered, staring at my feet as she placed her hand on my shoulder.

"It's just a warm hug. A warm hug accompanied by warm music and a sway of the hips," Daylily answered, taking my hand and holding it up. Her chin brushed across my shoulder lightly. Pulling me into a hug, we began to dance across my living room.

I inhaled the sweet smell of her vanilla perfume. Her head came to rest on my shoulder. And I don't know exactly when it happened, but she wasn't leading me. I was leading her. And I wanted to take her to Paris and Rome. Or maybe just the moon on a rocket ship. I'd point out her home and mine, but it would be the same.

I released her hand, and she rested it comfortably against my chest. My finger brushed the side of her cheek. Twirling strands of her blond hair around my finger like I had been dying to do all day. The lyrics, *I want my life in two*, made perfect sense. I think slow dancing just became my favorite pastime.

When my cell phone began to ring, I didn't know who to hate more. The caller or the cell phone company? I reluctantly released her to answer my phone that I had left on the counter. It was a text from granny's friend.

Granny's Friend: Dama is on her way home.

I looked up at Amber sullenly.

She bit her bottom lip and rubbed her hands together. "Our first date is over."

"We can plan another?" I asked, approaching her once more.

She trailed her finger along my jawline. "We can."

I opened my mouth to suggest something, and she silenced me with a kiss. Her lips were soft and inviting. Almost as a promise of things to come. Pushing away from me as if it pained her to leave. Before grabbing her bag from the couch and turning to go.

Chapter Fifteen

Amber

I stopped and wiped the sweat from my eyes. Leaning on the posts of the ring as I tried to catch my breath. Picking up the sweet and simple apple and banana protein shake that I had made at home. The taste was cold and welcoming. A relief. I felt like Layla was killing me in the ring. We were halfway through October and Layla had been training me for at least two weeks now.

I suppose I should be relieved because I didn't have any time to think about Drew. Or maybe that was all I could think about which was why I was doing so poorly? I just wanted to hate Drew again because anything else just might be a mountain too hard to climb. We were already halfway done with our driving hours. It was hard for us not to have grown closer. If he was on the floor right now, he'd probably look up at me with adoration. And then I'd look down like a cat who just wanted to curl up in his lap and be petted.

I placed the shakedown and plopped the towel down next to it. Eyeing the clock that read it was closer to seven pm. We'd be closing in another hour. I didn't want to be the last person to leave this place. It felt like a betrayal considering that I was looking at the profiles of prospective buyers. I wasn't reading them though. More like ignoring them because I wasn't sure I wanted to say goodbye. Just like I'm not sure what to do with my feelings for Drew.

A dance can save a soul.

I felt physically whole with him in a way that I'd never felt before. Looking around the gym at the few stragglers that remained I analyzed how I would look through their eyes. Powerful. In control. A wild animal on the prowl. That used to juice me up, but it wasn't enough anymore. I just wanted to be appreciated the way Drew made me feel.

I turned back to Layla who was grinning madly like a woman who knew she had won. But I couldn't disappoint my fans. After all, they were right about one thing, I was a very powerful girl. I smirked and put my hands up.

"I know it wasn't Kagiso that caused that smile. Because you've been ghosting him."

I circled her and tried to predict her next move.

"So who is it?"

"I thought we were fighting," I said throwing a straight. It missed, but it served as a warning. The tides were changing. "You were right. My body missed the ring. I'm positively an old lady now. But I can still whoop your butt."

"Is that what this is? There is enough sweat pooling on your forehead that you could drown in it. Not very becoming of a reigning champion."

"I didn't win that championship fair and square."

"Then win this one."

That fight was my chance to prove something to myself and Don's memory. Instead, it was stolen from me. How could a technicality be a real win? Now I wasn't sure what to do with my life when that one moment would have defined it. It only left me resentful. So I led with my anger pushing her back with a couple of jabs and then a right hook. Until she was against the ropes. But I knew better. Anger only loses. I had to refocus.

She fought her way back. Boxing me in until I was forced to hug her to get a reprieve. She pushed me off and I worked once more to get the upper hand. Ducking as she tried to take a swipe at my head. Only for me to come back working her midsection. That was enough to send her running. And my jabs were landing with better frequency. But a combo to the head was what sent her backing up. I hoped she saw it in my eyes, she wasn't getting another hit off of me.

And I led with a hit to the chin that sent her careening to the mat. Sending the onlookers, oohing and awwing as they slowly approached the ring. Layla's eyes were open, but she wasn't moving. As if I had short-circuited something in her mind. I fell to my knees beside her, concern racking my brain. El came rushing over and jumped into the ring to check her pulse.

"The back of her head just smacked off the canvas," El said, flashing a light into Layla's eyes.

"I didn't mean for any of that," I replied to El my eyes wide. I turned back to Layla. "I love you. Please be okay."

Someone else came over with a ziplocked bag of ice and applied it to the back of her neck. Slowly, helping her to her feet. She seemed slightly more lucid.

"I'm alright."

El practically snatched the bag from the man's hand and rolled the ice across Layla's neck and cheek.

"Layla..?" I begged.

She broke away from them both and hugged me. "Imagine how awesome it would have been if you did that in the ring to that Second to Nunn woman."

I smiled and positively squeezed her ribs. Just glad that she didn't hate me and I hadn't done any permanent damage.

"Alright, with the mushy stuff," she said, pushing away from me. Her smile was just as big as mine. Leaning down as El helped her through the ropes. "Our first session is officially over, Champion."

Maybe I was a great champion. I hopped down from the ring, soaking in the pats on the back. Like a dog who had just been rewarded a treat for learning his first trick. Or in my case, the seventeenth. But it was the sight of the lawyer Fuschi that stilled my blood. I broke away from the others and showed him into my office as quickly as I could. "What are you doing here?"

"You're ignoring my calls, and I need an answer regarding the prospects I sent you. They were personally, vetted by me I might add. The real person who should be making this decision."

"I've narrowed it down to two. Kagiso Maddison and Piers Ford."

"You want to narrow it down to one?"

"Don't come back here! You don't call me. I'll call you. And since you've made it known on more than one occasion that Don left me The Boxpad. They can damn well wait on *me* to make the decision."

"Amber."

I opened the door and showed him out. "We're done."

His expression darkened, and I knew that I couldn't trust him. Slamming the door shut as I breathed a sigh of relief. I had to do something soon to untether myself from him. Maybe there was some way to turn Manny and Fuschi on each other? Get rid of two pests at once. I lifted my head from the door. Wait, did I actually call this office mine? Thinking back on my arrival. I looked around and everything about it was still very much Don. The way it should always be. I've got to get out of here.

I opened the door and ran smack dab into Manny. The door slammed behind me and forced us together.

"Was that who I think it was leaving here?"

"I don't have time for you. I need to go. Too much on my mind."

"Like how to stiff me of my cut of this place? And ruin it for every-one else who might enjoy the family we've built here at The Boxpad."

I shifted from one foot to the other. Adjusting the strap of my sports bra as if it were chafing me. Trying miserably to come up with a way to avoid another confrontation. Manny had turned into a loose cannon. And it was starting to look like he wasn't showering or eating properly for that matter. His face was a little gaunter than I expected. What was happening to him?

"You know I love this place as much as everyone else. I'm going to do what's best for it. I promise. But this money thing is not helping."

He laughed at me, the sound ugly and harsh. "What I know is that you could never understand it."

"That's not wholly true." It was true in the beginning. However, my relationship with Don changed all that.

"We've poured our heart and souls into this place. And now we don't even get a brick off the wall."

"Who is we?"

As if to answer, Erin and her posse walked through the door carry-ing a gym bag. How much time did they have? Forty-five minutes at the most. What was going on here? They never work out this late. I was tempted to go to El and asked if she knew anything.

"Amber," Erin barked as a hello. Catching sight of me talking to Manny, but if she meant to smile she was positively snarling.

"What's going on with the money?" he asked again.

"I haven't sold it yet."

His eyes roamed over me in a skeevy pervert-ish way. Until I crossed my arms over my chest breaking him from his trance. The faintest hint of amusement in his eyes as if he were no longer attract-ed, but disgusted. But if that were true. Then it was a thin line and he was playing hopscotch.

"You wouldn't be lying to me would you?"

"Why would I lie? I'll give you something."

"Amber, you're going to give me all of it because it's what I demand. And it's time you know I'm serious about that."

He's clearly determined to threaten me again. But powerful women can't be stamped out. "For right now, I do own this place. And I've allowed you to come and go as you please. But push me and you'll be looking at this bitch through google maps because you wont be allowed within feet of it."

"You wouldn't risk exposing yourself that way," he murmured. The implications playing in his head like a hamster wheel.

"Then you're underestimating how much you're starting to piss me off," I said, trying to keep my cool. I brushed past him to the girl's locker room.

"Hey, I saw you talking to Manny by the entrance. You okay?" Layla asked, touching my shoulder. Already dressed to leave. Her bag was thrown over her shoulder.

"I'm okay, go home." I needed to shower and wash the day from my bones.

"You sure. I'm down for a man-bashing session if you need one," she laughed.

I thought about Drew. "I don't need one."

She winked and left me alone to finish getting ready. The showers here were complete crap and needed an upgrade. But I needed to wash off today's mess. And hot water careening down my face would do the trick. Something, I could also do as an upgrade before leaving this place in someone else's hand. They might not exactly know what it needs as I do. It doesn't need an overhaul, just a little TLC.

Energized, after my shower, I dressed quickly. Prepared to go home and make a list of things that I would like to change about this place. Before the sale anyway. Maybe I could do it myself? Don would be happy with that, right?

I walked out of the locker room to find the place shut down. Every-one had gone except El.

"You did a job on Layla tonight," she said.

"It was an accident," I said shaking my head.

"Great champions only make those sorts of accidents. It just comes naturally. Like today, Boss."

I bit my bottom lip, hesitantly. "Thank you."

The Boxpad was in good hands with El locking up. She was a pro at it by now. I, on the other hand, had a long walk to the train. Luckily, the underground tunnel wasn't that long. And brightly lit compared to the street lights that were all out. The Sun long since disappeared as we got further into fall. My music player, my only company as it blared E.T. by Katy Perry.

Looking on puzzled as I saw Erin's girlfriend sitting atop Lolita's shoulders hitting the subway lights with a baseball bat. I frowned, pulling one of my headphones out of my ear. "What are you guys doing?"

Erin's girlfriend dropped to the floor like a gymnast. All three of them turned to face me in a way that made me think that I was probably better off not knowing.

"We just been waiting for you," Erin said quietly. "We needed mood lighting though."

I looked over my shoulder and knew I was already too far in to be able to successfully outrun them. That meant I could only go through them.

"Day after day after day. You prove that you ain't never been wor-thy of The Boxpad. Now Don gave it to you and you sellin' it. So you hot garbage like I always knew you were. But now it's too late for us to run from your bad mistakes."

"Just let me explain," I said, but it was Lolita who shook her head no.

"I'm gone spill blood for that brick," Erin replied.

I slowly pulled the headphones out of my ears. Dropping them on top of my bag. That I cast on the floor. The subway was eerily quiet of any help except for us. "I just have to know, though. Did Manny put you up to this? He promised kickbacks and the possibility of setting things straight. I just want to confirm how dumb you are? Since we having epiphanies and shit."

Erin threw her head back in laughter before lunging towards me. Lolita who had the bat in her hand used it to hold back girly. At least this would be a fair fight this time. It was a long time coming. And I'd finish it tonight.

She was coming at me fast. So I didn't have time to take it slow and calculate my moves. Instead, she hit me straight with a beautiful right hook, her signature. I kept moving, but she still managed to land three solid right hooks. I'm losing this. Fighting on her terms, when I'm not a right, left hook phenom. Falling into the fight that Erin wanted all along.

Suddenly, I heard Don's advice in my ear. You have the tactics all ready to turn it around.

My movements had to be purposeful and less wasteful. Yet, she still managed to avoid my shots. Countering with a combo that sent me back into the wall. Unable to fight back as her right hook smacked against my jaw. My forehead hit the edge of one of the frames of the CTA map. I could feel it rip into my flesh. Blood trickled down my face. Spitting out the taste of blood as I wiped my lips with the back of my hand.

The collision left me dizzy. As Don appeared by my side laughing, *you always waited to the last minute to come out swinging. Get'em Shatterproof.* Disappearing into a fog as Erin grabbed my hand and tried to swing me into the opposite wall wrestling style. I countered by pulling her into me and tripping her. Her head hit the floor hard.

But she wasn't taking it as well as Layla had earlier that evening. The smell of piss was suddenly strong in the air.

A train rumbled across the tunnel and some unsuspecting people began to form behind Lolita and girly. Who suddenly turned into crowd control. I almost wanted to laugh at them, but I was a little busy. Some screamed for the fight to stop. While others pulled out their phones to record. Grumbles of wanting to go home and it being late were felt by all including me. Her punches had me weak, but I wasn't out. Consistently upping the pressure. Doing a much better job of cutting off her hits.

Erin fights outside the ring just as stupid as she does on the inside. Relying on that one punch, she becomes easy to predict. That's what happens when you're one-dimensional. I almost felt bad knowing that she would always be in my shadow. She wanted me to be some rookie that she could easily best. Instead, I was the champ who now knew what she did well enough to counter it. I also knew what wasn't working. Ms. Fast and furious was losing steam. She pulled me into a grappling hold that indicated she was growing weary.

This was no ring fight though. We didn't have to go 12 rounds. I'd proven my point. If her trainer wasn't going to make her go back to basics. Then the video of this fight all over someone's social media would. I could even read it now, *Shatterproof was in a deep rhythm. Proving that she was shatterproof, no matter where you caught her.*

I caught her with the quick hands that were now giving her a bit of a problem. Her punches were coming in wild. I caught her with the quick hands that were now giving her a bit of a problem. Her punches were unfocused, they exposed her to the power behind my jab. I went for the knockout and hit her dead in the face. She was down for the count as her face instantly swelled up. They exposed her to the power behind my jab. I went for the knockout and hit her dead in the face. She was down for the count as her face instantly swelled up.

"Ding. Ding. I win."

The crowd parted allowing me through and I almost wanted to bless them. But it was Lolita who stood in my way. Hitting me in the stomach with the hilt of the baseball bat. "That's for what you're doing to The Boxpad?"

It snatched the breath from my body as I toppled over. The crowd booed in response. But they were finally allowed to leave. So most of them took off. The distant sound of police cars sent Lolita and girly running without Erin. I don't know how I did it but I made it to the train. Unsure of where I should even go.

I thought about yesterday, and how I had never felt more comforted than in Drew's embrace, and I needed that now.

Chapter Sixteen

Andrew

Another loud, forceful knock came at the door. Like they were the police, and we were a meth lab. My granny was peeking out of a crack in her doorway. The whole house was a swirl of confusion and noise as she yelled for me to call the police. Panic set in as I started to get overwhelmed by it all. The knocks were so fast and robust; they seemed to make the walls of the house scream. And all I wanted was to go back to bed and put my head under the covers.

"I'm coming, hold on," I told the door. Opening it to see Amber, a heaving bleeding sack of pulp. I'd never seen so much blood outside a hospital, and inside, for that matter. Before I could even open my mouth to ask her what happened, she collapsed into my arms. Her cheek fell against my chest. I pitifully gripped her waist. Did someone at The Boxpad do this to her?

"Dama close your bedroom door!" I screamed at her.

"Andrew?"

"Now!" I yelled.

"I'm going to throw up," she said, trying feebly to push herself out of my grasp.

"Stop fighting me. I'm trying to help."

She stopped pushing me, and I assumed that meant, help me. Instead, she bent over and clutched at her stomach. Like I was about to see what she had eaten today. I lifted her off the ground and carried her to the bathroom. Making it just in time for her to lean over the toilet. She emitted a horrible, retching sound that made my stomach queasy. Her blond hair barely clung to the rubber band in her hair. As if someone had tried to tug it free. I pulled it off the ends and smoothed her hair back into a perfect pony.

"I got into a fight," she confided in me. Standing up and flushing the toilet. Putting the lid down so that she could sit on the tank. "The throwing up was just a delayed reaction now that my adrenaline is coming down. I took a baseball bat to the stomach."

She was clearly stating the obvious. Her eyes were glassy and slightly dazed. She took off her jacket and threw it on the floor at my feet. Revealing arms with bruises so deep, they were every color of the rainbow: blue, grey, and purple. Blood vessels were clogged and broken just below the skin. She looked terrible. Still, out in the hallway, it occurred to me that granny might be able to listen in. I kicked Amber's jacket to the side and shut the door.

"Are you even still alive?" I approached her tentatively, my brows knitted together. "Can I examine you?"

She lowered her head into her right hand. Showing no signs that she even heard me. She might have a concussion. There was a big gash over her left eyebrow. "You should see the other girl. Pretty sure I almost killed her."

"No, I'm looking at you now. Like maybe we should get you to a hospital."

"No hospital. No police. Promise me." She's rocking side to side on the tank, but this is the most lucid she's been since she arrived.

I made no such promise though, but I did grab a clean rag from underneath the sink. Running some hot water over it so I could clean

Amber's face. Coagulated dried blood covered half her cheek. She looked like the woman from Carrie. It made it hard to determine the extent of her injuries.

"Do I need stitches?"

I focused my efforts on cleaning the wound over her eyebrows. There wasn't much First Aid in the house. But whatever I had was centrally located in the bathroom cabinet. Luckily I had both antiseptic and some antibiotic cream. Most of which I only had for accidents cutting myself shaving. Or the occasional boo-boo when granny bumped into an object that she doesn't see. "You don't need stitches, but you're going to have a gnarly scar."

"Is that your expert opinion doctor?" she asked, wincing against the sting of the antiseptic. "I hate the smell of alcohol."

"If you wanted the opinion of a doctor, you should have gone there first," I said annoyed, especially since she didn't want me to call one.

"But they wouldn't be able to quiet the noise." She wobbled a bit and grabbed onto my shoulders.

"What noise?" I asked her curiously. "You're the one making the most noise here."

"It's loud. In here," Amber replied, tapping the side of her head and wincing. "So many thoughts. I just want you to read to me." She sat back on the tank and rested her head against the wall. Blood and sweat drenched the front of her white tank top. She couldn't stay like that all night.

I pressed the biggest band-aid I had to the cut over her eyebrow. "I'll take care of you."

"I knew you were the right one."

"What do you mean?" I turned to throw the tissue and mess away. Only to turn back and find Daylilies eyes closed. She had fallen asleep. I didn't know if that was a bad thing or not. But I used the time to run her a bubble bath. Heavy on the bubbles for privacy's sake. I stripped her down to her bra and panties. "Daylily, wake up. You're getting in the tub."

She groaned but didn't make a move on her own. It was like she was the last petal on a flower trying not to wilt.

"Okay, I can do this too," I said, lifting her and placing her in the tub.

She gasped awake as if I were drowning her. I almost laughed. She was splashing the water so bad that some even got on me. "Alright, calm down. It's just bathwater."

She sat up and noticed that she still had on her bra. Pushing the bubbles closer to her chest, she unclipped her bra and threw it on the floor. My breath nearly caught in my throat when she took off her panties. I tried to focus on getting her a bar of soap and keeping my breathing under control. Just trying to think of anything else that she might need. "Here, it puts the soap on its skin."

She pursed her lips, but a small smile was playing at the corners of her mouth. She caught my movie reference. "I know how soap works."

"Sounds like the water did more good than I did," I responded, noticing that her tone sounded better. Less tired. I riffled through the bottom cabinet for anything else she might need. There was blood in her hair too.

"I do feel better," she replied.

"Do you want me to wash your hair?"

"Okay," she said quietly.

I used a cup to wet her hair. Pouring some shampoo that smelled like coconuts on the top of her head. I massaged it into her scalp as gently as I could manage. My soapy fingers slipped through the strands of her hair, building up a good lather. Before cleaning the blood from her split ends. I counted the steps in my head so that I wouldn't forget to do it the right way. There was a routine for every-thing, even making hot chocolate. I just had to count it out.

But this moment felt intimate. Like a slow caress. I don't think I'd done anything like this for anyone. An unofficial confirmation that Daylily trusted me, and wanted me close. So I tried to be gentle, but thorough. It was like I was tending to an untouched garden.

"Thank you," she replied when I finished. Her hand lingered on top of mine, just before I rinsed the last of the soap from her hair. Following step five.

"I'm going to wash your clothes and bring you new ones." As I picked up her soiled garments, I slowly crept out of the room to allow her to finish the rest on her own. There were also rules for washing laundry. A little panic was setting in because the main one was that it wasn't laundry day. And there were no rules for how I was supposed to supply her with something to wear. Granny's door was closed, and I couldn't ask for her help now.

I took several deep breaths. First, I needed to focus on what I could control. Do the laundry. Once that was going, I paced a hole in the living room floor, trying to find a solution to the clothes problem. But my mind went blank. It was like I saw everything in color and then everything faded to black and white. I flew to my room, hoping that something there would trigger me.

Only to find out that my granny had placed one of her old pajamas, top and bottoms, on the bed. It was even laid out carefully the way I liked. I grabbed the clothes gratefully and took them back to Amber. Knocking first instead of just barging in.

"Come in."

I placed the clothes on top of the toilet. This time I didn't bother to look in her direction. I just kept my gaze low. "These are for you."

Once my job was done, I waited in my room for her to finish. The place was spotless, and nothing was out of order. That was when it occurred to me that she might actually see my room. Designed much like the outside, it was the only room that Granny had allowed me to touch. I inherited the house from grandpa. She just agreed to allow me to change its clothes and add a second story. But the bones had to remain the same. It was our compromise.

The bed was made as if I had never slept in it. My alarm was already set on an old clock that was so loud it set off my anxiety. A perfect answer to getting up on time. Because if I didn't shut it off, I'd be paralyzed. A white cart next to my bed with all my essentials.

My Nasa Shuttle Xpress rocket model sat on the top shelf. The current books I'm reading for work were on the second shelf. An extra blanket was folded neatly on the third shelf. The whole cart was portable depending on where in the house I might need it. But it rarely moved from this spot.

My social norms notebook was tucked in between two thick encyclopedia-sized software books. However, 21st -century computer code couldn't answer my questions about what happens next. Neither would my social norms book because Amber was a woman of many firsts. Still, my head spun like a rocket from unanswered questions. What would I do if she wanted to sleep? Where would she sleep? How would I explain any of this to granny in the morning? I shouldn't have to explain any of it.

I leaned back in bed and remembered what it was like to have Amber laying on top of me. The last thing a gentleman should be thinking about at a time like this. But as we moved together. She wouldn't need one.

"Drew?" she called, rubbing her hands down the front of her pant leg.

I stood up when she appeared in the doorway of my room. She looked much better now that she was cleaned up. But her bruises still looked like paint blotches. If some kid just knocked over some paint onto a black and white canvas. Then dipped their hands in it and spread it around.

"Do you have any aspirin? Body aches and all."

I looked around as if it might appear on the floor in my room. "Coming right up. There might be some in the junk drawer in the kitchen."

"Okay."

I practically flew into the kitchen. Searching the junk drawer that was mostly filled with granny's stuff. Pulling out a small bottle that upon a shake was almost empty. Except for the 2-4 rattling inside. If it were me, I'd need a glass of water too. Thinking in steps, I poured her a glass and brought both back to her. She was leaning back in the bed when I came in. Her back rested against my black headboard.

"That's my bed." Aware that I sounded like a five-year-old.

"It's okay; I don't think I could sleep if I tried. The water's kind of woken me up."

"Here."

She took the water and pills. Dropping the bottle into her lap before tapping the space next to her. "You going to join me or just stare."

I sat next to her. The clock on her side read that it was now closer to 2:14 a.m. A strangeness to the extra weight in the bed. No woman had ever been in my bed with me. It felt awkward for me just watching her take the pills and drink the water.

"Tell me everything about model rockets? I'm curious." Her voice was weary from everything she went through, but curious nonetheless.

It was rare that I talked to anyone about my rockets. Unless I was out at a con. Probably why I had to picture myself back there to explain the process behind them.

"I only work with flying model rockets. There are only two types of rocket engines to get those off the ground. Black powder and composite. A third has emerged that uses a combination of Liquid Nitro and cellulose as rocket fuel, but I'm still learning how that works."

"Black powder? I'm picturing a cartoon with a trail of black powder blowing up in someone's face."

I pursed my lips. "It's not a hobby for children. If you don't know what to do, then you could hurt yourself or others."

"It's one of those amazing things about you."

I was taken aback. *That's amazing; you're a computer programmer. That's awesome; you have a girlfriend.* All phrases I'd heard in the past with an asterisk attached. Compliments that seemed to imply that it was only amazing because I had Autism. But there was no asterisk in what Amber said. She genuinely thought it was cool.

"Well, it's not a line of black powder from the rocket to my position behind a tire, and all I have is a lighter. It's complex. Yet simple. As it's the same design that everyone has been using since the 50s."

She closed her eyes for a minute and sighed. "How does it work?"

"It's a paper tube with a clay nozzle. And inside is a solid pellet of black powder, a smoke delay charge, and an ejection charge. I simply insert an igniter in the clay nozzle that puts it in contact with the black powder propellant. An electrical current is driven through the igniter and blasts off."

She listened in silence, but when her eyes reopened, it wasn't the wild girl I was used to. Her eyes were lonely, scared, and weary, and it caused me to reach out and grab her hand.

"The blast-off portion is much more complex."

"Did your dad ever get into rockets?"

"Yes, but these times were mostly hidden tests. He would ask me questions about school. Or my personal life. He didn't care about rockets as I did."

I couldn't continue. The ball forming in my throat made it impossible to go on.

"In his defense, how else are parents supposed to find out about their kid's interests?"

"Ask."

"Touche."

Pointing out that I wasn't most kids seemed like a moot point right now. Instead, I sidestepped the whole conversation. "They live on a cruise ship now. They've asked me to come out and visit. I don't mind, but it's getting harder and harder to get away. Granny needs me."

"I don't visit much either, and my parents just live in the suburbs. But what was so upsetting about your dad's questions?"

Running down the list of every inappropriate conversation wasn't possible. I'd get angry. My body would betray me, and I might even cry in front of Amber. Tons of conversations with my dad in our old garage would end in tears of frustration. So I needed to tell an abbreviated version of the truth.

"It wasn't the questions that were upsetting. Moreso, his reactions to the answers. They frequently wanted me to experience normal childhood activities. Like summer camp for instance. These weren't specialized programs, but chances for me to interact with the outside world. Frequently, it didn't go well. He was making it obvious without saying so that he only wanted to hear about the good things that were happening. The bad was too stressful for them both. Not that it was obvious to me, it took me years to pick up on what was causing all the tension."

"They were eternal optimists who gave birth to a pessimist."

"I don't consider people with Autism as pessimists. Just realists."

"The only thing I don't understand is why you're taking care of your granny and there not?"

"They gave up a lot to raise me. Mom was a lawyer and she quit to stay home with me. Eventually finding her way into a nonprofit organization dedicated to making life easier for Aspies. In opposition,

Dad never missed a doctor's appointment of mine. They put in their dues with their freedom, time, and emotional health. It's not fair to ask them to do it twice."

"Sounds like you think cruise ship living was the right decision."

"A good decision doesn't have to be a comfortable one. I'm all she has left. And I don't think that's a bad way to spend your life. Proving you love someone every day by taking care of them without them having to ask. I love them, but that kind of selflessness was not given to everyone."

"Have you discussed with her what she wants? I assume that her condition is only going to get worse. Being a burden to her kids or grandkid had to be a heavyweight on one's heart."

"It's funny to hear that you care considering how much she hates you."

"You actually told her about me?" She looked surprised. "I can imagine how that went over."

"I know that your run-ins at the nursery weren't of the friendly kind. The first time you guys met you were cussing someone out on the phone. She came up to you and asked you to keep it down. Only for you to turn on her like a Rottweiler."

Amber seemed genuinely disturbed at the description of her. So I decided to change the subject.

"When I get paralyzed by any decision. Which is more often than I'd like to admit. I sometimes tape a message to the rocket and send it to the sky. When it comes down over the water and I like to think of it as my answer." I watch her try to piece together the fact that we're talking about rockets again.

"Do you fly all your rockets by the ocean?"

"No, it's not allowed. I'm usually in an open field at the park. My ocean excursions are usually emergencies." I looked down at the book quickly. Sure, that I looked pitiful. Creating an image of a man in an egg yellow button-down and khaki's, crying or yelling at the ocean. The weirdo at the beach that the overprotective mom tells her kids to stay away from.

"Don't be embarrassed." She pulled her hand out of mine and gestured for me to look at her. "I can't get peace anywhere these days. It used to be boxing. Now boxing is the problem. I do more gardening. And sometimes it helps and everything is better, brighter. I can breathe."

"You've never seen one of my freakouts," I said.

"I don't think you've seen one of mine. Tonight was just the result of me not having a proper freak out when I should have."

"I think I want to see one of those."

Her eyes appeared to be very amused. Before she looked straight ahead and closed them. "For the record, I never thought you were weird. Just old."

"Sureeee, Daylily."

"I kind of wish that I knew the things you know. Neither of us will ever see the moon up close and personal. Yet you understand it in a way that will get you a lot closer than I will just by looking at a picture. And it gives you peace. A beautiful state of being."

"So you like rockets too?" Not used to these sorts of compliments.

"Not the same way you do. But I think it would be cool to be inside one, looking out at the universe." She sounded so kind without a hint of pity in her voice that I was happy that she hadn't opened her eyes, because then she would have caught me getting teary-eyed.

She ended up picking up an instructional book on how to put together various model rockets from my bedside cart. It was a thin book that had fallen behind the others. I almost forgot it was there. Knowing the pages inside and out as I did. It was an old book that I picked up when I was younger.

"Daylily?"

Her eyes flickered up to mine from the book. "Yes wonder boy?"

I looked away to smile and she caught my chin with her finger. Pulling my face back to hers.

"Don't try it. I already know you're not a robot."

"Okay," I said, a bit confused. "I just wanted to know if you wanted to talk about anything?"

She handed me the book she was holding. "Read this to me. In that controlled calming voice that you do."

"What's the difference between my voice and anyone else?"

"You command people to listen and it's natural."

"I didn't think I had any natural social skills," I said casually, but from her gaze, she picked up on the hurt.

"Well, I don't know how you'd use it to save the world," she blurted. "But you could save me right now."

I flipped through the pages of the book and looked at her carefully. "Is this about tonight?"

"Yes, specifically The Boxpad." She adjusted her oversized pajama top. "It's all I think about now. I've even started to grind my teeth in my sleep."

I leaned over and she took the bait. Resting her head on my shoulder. "Is there someone there that you are scared of?"

"I'm not scared of anything or anyone." She sounded irritated. "Life just gets hard to navigate. It can become a minefield. And when all you have is a walking stick it can be pretty fucking stressful."

"So what are you leaving out?"

"What do you want me to say, Drew? You want me to admit that I'm scared. That I can't make a decision to save my life. And I literally need to save my life. I have no idea if selling The Boxpad is the right thing to do. But once I do there wont be a soul in the world who will talk to me. I'll lose my best friend. And the only guy who'll give me the time of day. Doesn't even really care for me at all."

"Daylily, that's not true. This decision paralysis you find yourself in is just avoidance. When you find something you're good at it you should attack it with fervor and purpose. You've found that in boxing. You may like flowers, but even you admitted you're not good at it. Life has already shown you what direction you need to go in. You just need to be ready for it a little faster. And I do care for you. You're throwing off the equilibrium in the bed and I haven't asked you to move."

She laughed out loud.

I didn't know I was making a funny, but it was good to see her laugh.

I turned to the first page of the book and began reading. She needed peace.

Chapter Seventeen

Amber

I stirred awake from a particularly nasty dream of being stuck in a fully stocked grocery store. Yet still unable to locate the one item I needed. Sitting up slowly in bed just to realize that I was still in Drew's bedroom. The bedside clock read 5:04 am. Sunlight made an appearance through the blinds. The grayish light blue hue indicated that it would be morning soon.

I peeked at Drew who was still knocked out. The book we had been reading rested on his chest. He was a man of many talents. Most of which gave me a feeling that was better than ice cream. It was better than finding out my opponent had a fighting handicap that I could exploit in the ring. We shared everything last night. Even mundane things like rockets. He now knows about my struggles with The Boxpad and my impending loneliness. The first man to see me outside the ring in all my ugly glory. All of which he seemed to accept with ease.

Like the perfect gentleman, he hadn't touched me all night. And I was still in the ugly pj's, no doubt from his granny's closet. I finally saw that woman through his eyes and I think I liked her more for it. But I still couldn't forget some of the hateful things she'd said to me. So I wasn't planning on leaning on her hospitality too much. I looked around the room for something to change into. At least until he returned my clothes. Surprised that they were sitting on a white chair in his room. I looked back at him surprised, when did he bring this back in.

I ran my hands through my hair. Most mornings it was closer to a lion's mane than actual hair. A slight headache reminded me of my fight with Erin yesterday evening. Easing out of the bed, I shed my clothes quickly. Running my hands lightly over the bruises on my hands and stomach. Some of which had taken on a sickly yellow color. At any moment I expected him to wake up and ask me what I was doing.

I noticed that Drew had morning wood to greet him when awoke. When I grabbed my jeans a condom wrapper fell out. It should have been my clue to run like this was a one-night stand gone wrong. Instead, I approached the bed naked. Pushing the book off his chest without rousing him. Fitting between his legs. As I peeled back the band of his flannel pajama bottoms. Licking my lips at the sight of his navy blue boxer briefs.

I pulled him out of them. His shaft was thick and stout in my hand. But he was a heavy sleeper and still hadn't awoken. I began to wonder just what I had to do to get him to join the party.

His moans were enticing to my ears as I began to lick the tip of his shaft.

He moaned my name, but his eyes weren't open. "Amber."

Did he think this was a dream? Time to make this dream a reality. I took him fully into my warm hot mouth. Closing my eyes as I savored the feel of him. Bobbing up and down as my groans mixed with his. Wanting nothing more than to please him.

His hands crashed down on my shoulders squeezing me tightly. My eyes popped open and I froze. Well, my body froze, because I was still licking him. Staring him down with my hot gaze as I dared him to ask me to stop.

"Amber."

His tight grip on me slowly relaxed. But because of my bruises, I was in a little pain. I thought he was permitting me to continue when he grabbed me again. This time pulling me on top of him. Our lips crashed together like the waves on sand. Hard and unforgiving. Demanding more of the pleasure that had been built up between us.

"More," I breathed. Taking a breath in between the flurry of kisses.

Not at all concerned that I was re-damaging areas that were otherwise healing. Feeling nothing but sheer desire as he gripped my breasts and hips hard. His arms gripped my waist tightly as he rubbed himself against my clit. My back was in a slow roll as little pings of pleasure shot off in my nerve endings. Gasping as he reined kisses down my cheek and neck. Chasing any thoughts of Manny and Erin from my mind.

I pushed against his grip enough, to get a hand down between us. Grabbing his member, I sat down on top of it as he sank into my creamy nectar. He elicited a growl that only made me soaking wet for him. Smacking my ass as he lifted me into the air. His shaft plunged into the nectar between my thighs. Taking control in a way that I'm sure I would never see in any other aspect of his life.

We stared deeply into each other eyes. A painful truth there as if we were mad that it took us this long. We even lost sight of where we were as I moaned out loud and rode him faster. His lips crushed mine once more as he sat up to kiss me. Bruising in its hunger. I tugged on his bottom lip when he pulled away.

"Drew!" I yelled. My fingernails dug into his shoulder. I leaned back as my muscles tightened around his shaft. His thrusts were fast and furious. Until we reached our zenith at the same time. My heart raced as our heads kind of fell against each other and the impulse slowly washed away. His eyes were closed and I couldn't resist planting a kiss across his lips. This one was much softer than the demanding ones we tortured ourselves with.

I just wanted more.

That orgasm was toe-curling. Instead, he leaned back and I eased off of him falling onto the bed beside him. The covers wrapped precariously around our waists. Evidence of our lovemaking was all over the front of his drawers. And I'm staring up at a ceiling mural of the moon landing. Sure I'd have an imprint of his hand on my ass all day.

"Amber."

"I love how you say my name during sex. But you really need to stop unless you want to go again."

I turned to look at him to see a huge crimson blush on his cheek. I gave him a breathy laugh. Staring back up at the ceiling which was a mural of the moon landing in black and white. I turned on my back and felt him trail his fingernails down my spine. Giving me chills. "That was amazing though."

He got up to change his boxers and opened the curtains to allow some light in. And with it some of my sanity. I had to get out of here. This was Dama's house and I just made it with her grandson. "I've got a lot to do today. I should probably go."

"Are you feeling okay to travel? Are you sure you don't want to go to the hospital?" He fussily leaned over and checked the bruises on my stomach and arm.

However, I think that the triathlon I just endured was proof enough that I was fine. As do the goosebumps he was creating on my skin. I pulled away and got some clothes on. "Yeah. I still got to go home, shower, and rest. We are meeting with Joseph tonight for class."

He looked over at me with concerned blue eyes. The memory of him being inside me scorched my thoughts. A look of a man that was concerned about his girlfriend. But we weren't each other's type. Our walk down the aisle would look completely different from each other. Mine would be a shotgun wedding in Vegas and he would be in a small chapel in North Carolina in the fall.

"You could stay. We could have breakfast. Unless you just want to get away from me?" He said with a bitter smile.

Were Autistic men always this direct? No matter. I had to remember that he let me in too. He let me inside his head and risked my ridicule. Also, he opened his home to me when he could have shut the door. Showing immense patience and hospitality. All hidden beneath this hard exterior of the calculated businessman. That soft touch and kind smile wont be easily forgotten.

His lean frame didn't have a speck of hair on it as he took my lead and got dressed as well. Imagining myself planting kisses across his chest. Just for him to grab me impatiently and plant me on his shaft to ride.

"You're looking at me like you want to devour me," he told me. My eyes quickly shot away. "It's okay I want to do the same."

"No, I'm leaving," I said primly and he inhaled a sharp hiss as if he'd been stung by a bee.

"Yeah, that's probably a good idea. Granny is still here after all. Do you need to take these with you?" He asked, shaking a bottle of pills at me.

"No, I have some at home. I've certainly felt worse the day after a boxing match." I throw on my gym shoes. Taking my sweet time tying them because it feels like I'm missing something.

"Are you sure you don't want anything? Like maybe some sparkling water."

"That sounds good."

He nodded and walked towards the door. Staring back at me when I didn't make a move. "Come on."

The thought of running into Dama was not how I wanted to spend my Monday morning. If I had to mumble, bitch please, even once. I'm sure it would ruin whatever goodwill I'd built with him.

"I'm not going to tell my grandmother if that's what you're worried about," he told me stiffly.

He reached out his hand for me to take with a warm smile. That one statement in itself should be a warning sign. I shouldn't be concerned with a guy who lives with his grandmother. Yet I took his hand just the same. "I do think we should talk about what happens now. Which should be secrecy?"

The look on his face melted my heart.

"No one's going to believe that we slept together, Amber. So I don't get anything from spreading it."

He slammed the refrigerator door closed after grabbing my water. My eyes darted around as if at any moment Dama would pop out and yell gotcha. Too busy panicking with worry to acknowledge his statement. Dama would be on the right and Joseph would be on the left. Layla would knock on the door and they would all point their accusatory fingers at me.

How could I even attempt to explain what was going on between me and Drew? I tried to list out all the things I did well in my head. But all I kept coming back to was that Drew was a freaking computer programmer. In comparison, I'm childish and dangerous. So being interested in someone who probably uses pocket protectors was only laughable.

I sat down at the kitchen island. My body aching like I was an 80-year-old-woman. Clearly, I had overexerted myself. Especially after the beating I gave and took. I'm flashing the world a small knot on my forehead. It looked like I'd been in a cockfight all night.

But I don't want to hurt his feelings by just rushing out. So I switched to the one conversation that I knew was always safe. Our past.

"Did your parents think you were going to be an astronaut growing up?" With his smarts the possibilities were endless.

"No," he told me, reaching into the fridge for the water. "Raising me was difficult at times. There were more hospital visits than career fairs. My potential wasn't realized until much later in life."

I was saddened at the thought. How did they perceive his apparent need for organization at such a young age? His addiction to rules and sequences added its own troubles when life called for coloring outside the lines. Developing a mindset early on of cleanliness and order. Opposite of the bird's nest I built in my room. A hodgepodge of things that had caught my fancy that might not even necessarily match.

All of Drew's friends were probably similar to him. Making it impossible to connect with people in the outside world. I wouldn't be surprised if his parents had to leave their old friends behind and gravitate to other parents in the struggle. People who would understand without explaining. Why their child was throwing a tantrum at the sound of a train going by. "Are they proud of you now?"

"More like relieved. Like they pushed me to greatness. Now they can breathe."

"That's a tough one to swallow." I laced my fingers with his. Running my tongue along my bottom lip. It wasn't my intention to bring up anything heavy. I was just intrigued by the large ceiling mural of the moon landing in his room.

"It's not a good or bad thing it's just the truth."

"My brother, older brother, died before I got to college. In my parent's eyes, every moment that my life doesn't live up to its fullest potential is a wasted breath. That's not good or bad either. It's just the truth."

"What did he die of?" He smoothed a flyaway strand of hair from my face.

"He had cancer. He was sick for a long time."

"Do you think he would be proud of what you've done with your life?"

"Yes." I assessed after some time.

"Then your parent's opinion doesn't matter."

"It's never that simple though because it does." This whole conversation became a major downer.

I'd inadvertently turned this man into my therapist, and I should apologize for that but I don't. Because no one is ever this decent and kind to me. We were teetering on the edge of just being a one-night stand to something more. But that only made me feel guilty because we could never be anything more. I wasn't meant for him and he wasn't meant for me.

And I still hadn't properly thanked him for taking me in and nursing me back to health. Although, Layla's guide to dating and life would have said I accomplished that with my bedroom romp. Andrew wasn't some hot, but overzealous fan either. He deserved a thank you note and a box of cookies. Or maybe a gift card?

Of course, I couldn't give someone a gift card as a thank you for sex. This would be a thank you for letting me vomit in your toilet and bleed all over your bathroom. Which required a personal touch. Relieved when I thought of a sneaky way to get him something.

"Tell me something no one else knows?"

"You go first." His tone was warm and innocent.

"I've never been in a bar fight. Manny made sure I watched a few though."

"Until last night, I was a virgin. I've had girlfriends before, but they all wore chastity belts, sort of speak."

"Excuse me?" My voice was thin as I realized the implications of what he said. What the hell was he talking about?

I was hoping for a golden nugget that would end in me getting him a pair of bra crawl tickets or something. Just a unique gift. Now he's telling me that the guy who held my hair back as I vomited and gingerly attended to my wounds like a seasoned cutman. Never folded back the sheets.

"Oh. Sorry, I guess you might've wanted to know that before. But, this morning was a surprise to us both."

"Yes, it's been a day of surprises," I said meekly.

"And it's only nine am."

"So? Your first time, was it okay?"

"It was wonderful. I wasn't waiting for candles or anything. Just dating church girls produces a certain type of woman. I'd certainly take that ride with you any day."

"A certain type of girl." I proved Dama right. I'm a complete hoe bag.

"I think I should go. We don't want to tempt fate."

I handed Drew back the half-empty bottle of sparkling water. He nodded, his gaze drifting in the direction of Dama's room. As if by mere thought we would conjure her up. He walked around the island and escorted me to the door. His hand was on the small of my back as I grabbed my jacket.

He opened the door, but I didn't step through. I watched him fumble with his words. "I wish we had more time to talk about us."

"It was just a morning quickie. For some people that's like a cup of OJ." As soon as it was out of my mouth, I regretted it.

"Yeah, but I hope that we have more going on?" Drew was leaning towards something and I wasn't there yet.

Instead, I was noncommittal. "We dooo."

"And I mean more than just Driver's Ed." He flashed me a quiet smile and a warm feeling consumed me. My inner person kept wanting to mop it away. A sparky flirtatious need to nibble on his bottom lip until he turned tomato red, digging deep into my chest.

"Driver's Ed was what brought us together and we're in a tenuous situation as it is."

"I never thought we'd be here. So how much further we go is a surprise for me too. But like a kid with a gift under the Christmas tree. I'll do my best to wait patiently, but don't be surprised if I can't."

I could appreciate his perseverance in the face of my being so intimidating to most men I meet. But just because I'd come to care about him doesn't mean we're ready for Vegas. Just look at us. We're like oil and water. His dream girl was a librarian. Could he handle my dominance regularly?

"So I'll see you later?" He reached out to hold my hand.

He's the same robot I'd worked with every day for weeks except now he's happy. It was like he had gotten recharged. Inner beauty and strength radiated from him like the stained glass windows of a church. It should be a crime every time he refused to smile. His mouth was completely kissable with a hint of a dimple on his right cheek. And that smile was just as addictive as the sound of his voice or the smell of his skin. All I needed was that smile.

Sure, I had noticed that rare kind of handsomeness that he had, but I didn't know how deep those waters ran. When Drew smiled he was the Mona Lisa. I just wanted to take a picture. Trying to remember the exact moment and place I was when I saw it. It's the only smile I get because it's the only one I deserve.

If only I had never experienced this moment. Then I wouldn't miss it when it was gone. I want to tell him that this meant everything to me. And then he opened the front door and reached for my hand and all the good in the world evaporated. I pulled away from him putting the knife through my own heart. My poor decision-making at this moment will haunt me until I could look at my teeth in a cup.

"Daylily, are we okay?" he asked, clearly picking up on my rebuff.

"Yeah," I told him, even though we were far from it. A tightening in my throat made it hard to lie this blatantly. "I'm just tired."

"Are one-night stands supposed to take this long?" Our audience member reminded me.

I shook off Drew's touch and stepped back. "Bye."

The door closed quietly and I still needed to walk to the corner to wait for my cab.

"So when do I get next?" The neighbor catcalled.

"I will slash your fucking tires if you keep this shit up."

His mouth dropped open and he rushed back inside.

Chapter Eighteen

Andrew

Later that day, I found a note left by granny on the kitchen counter. It said that she had gone on a walk with the neighborhood exercise group. And she would be back shortly. It ended up being enough time for me to shower and change. And I still had to get to work later. This was the first time, I would call in late.

"Oh, you're here," I said, coming back into the living room. Noticing that she had taken to wearing her sunglasses more and more. The discoloration in her left eye was practically visible now.

"And I take it your friend is gone, Andrew?"

"She is," I said, sitting down at my computer to check my work email.

"She looked less than her best last night. I was worried about her blood staining the floor like a crime scene. It looked like she had committed a murder and needed a place to hideout. So I was prepared for you to tell me that she'd be staying a few days."

"It wasn't like that." I started answering my work email in order of emergency. However, it began to occur to me that I may need to call off today completely. Ignoring my granny's statements of exaggeration. "I patched her up a bit. She took a much-needed shower. I washed her clothes while she was in there. She got some much-needed rest then she went home."

I squeezed my eyes shut as she came behind me and rubbed my shoulders. She meant it to be soothing. But she also forgot that it was the complete opposite for me. I had boundary issues.

"Granny," I hissed, shrugging off her touch.

"I just hate to think that she's dragging you into something illegal," Granny said, stroking the side of my cheek. "You've already been through the system once with her. Can she be trusted?"

"I've been through the system twice with her."

She moved to sit on the couch. "Andrew, I want you to turn around and talk to me."

I groaned. Sending my boss an updated email that I wasn't coming in at all, but would be available through email. Before turning back reluctantly to face my granny. Her frown was now a familiar one whenever the subject of Amber came up.

"What do you mean you've been through the system twice with her?"

"Your statement just wasn't accurate," I argued. "We have been through the court system, but—"

"You've also met her at the nursery because of The Garden Love Project."

I was confused as to why she was finding my words so difficult to understand. In my mind, we were talking about simple math, and she was asking questions like it was the complex formula to harnessing energy. I watch her through slitted eyes. Why was this such a problem? There was something I was missing. And she had yet to take off her sunglasses. Which made predicting her mood even harder. It was like I was dancing blind.

"Yes, but that's not a government system," I answered directly. My ability to spill things with no filter was also a detriment.

"How much do you really like this girl?" she asked acridly. Finally taking off her glasses and tossing them on the table. Her look of exhaustion had me worried about her health.

"I like her a lot, but that doesn't make anything I'm saying a lie." I turned and put my computer into sleep mode since this was going to be a while. "I just meant that we'd been through the court system. But we also got scheduled for the same Driver's Ed course for felons."

She looked at me and laughed. "You're not a felon."

"She's..." I stopped when I saw her shake her head in disappointment. It was probably not the best time to bring up that she was.

"How many rules were broken during that little mix-up?"

"It's okay because we've come a long way since then."

"No sort of understanding at all could cover this shit show. I'm getting on the phone to figure out who we need to sue." She made it to her feet. But not past the coffee table before she hit her knee. Moving slower than I had expected even for her. Had that walk taken everything out of her.

"Okay, granny sit down before you hurt yourself." I grabbed her elbow and helped her back to her chair. Leaving to pour a glass of water. Bringing it back to her. I managed to relax enough to take a seat on the couch next to her. Allowing her to lean on me even as her words rocked me to my core.

"Sorry, I just got a little winded." There was a bit of a pause before she placed the cup down.

"We've discussed all this before. I need you to stay out of it," I stated after some time. "She's done nothing to hurt me," I sighed heavily.

"Every time I mention this girl you just get defensive. Why can't you just listen to me?"

"Because you're not listening to me."

"What's there to listen to? You're just like any other man thinking with his penis. I know for a fact that you could do better. But men always want to chase after the bad girl with Chlamydia and not the good girl with the Bible in her hand." She made wild gestures with her hands as if she were acting out a puppet show.

But nothing she said surprised me. "There is no such good girl for me granny. And I don't know who's chasing who in this scenario. I'm just asking you not to hurt someone who hasn't hurt me."

"Would you even feel the prick if she had?" Granny tried to plead with me clutching my face.

"I can only imagine what the pain would feel like on her face."

"I know it's going to be hard, but I demand that you stay away from her." Granny persisted as if I had said nothing at all.

"You can't do that. This is my place and I'll invite whoever I want to it."

Granny wagged her finger at me. "How many times have you had that criminal at the house?"

I gave her the address when I knew we were doing driving hours together. She had already been to the house a few times since then.

"I gave it to her for a good reason. We were studying together. And don't call her that," I said, with growing agitation.

"From last night, it would appear that you guys were much closer than stated, but I know better because you're not her type."

Her statement shouldn't have been such a punch in the throat, but I was gagging. Despite everything that happened last night. She could always have her eyes on the newer model. Maybe it wasn't that I was too much of a loser to get her. I could just be too stupid to keep her.

There was absolute silence between us before she spoke again. "What more do you need to avoid heartbreak?"

"Trust. From you." This one word was meant to shut down any further conversation. Although, I was sure I could hear more of her nonsense in my head.

Granny sighed, heavy and defeated. "I'll always trust you."

"Even threw a broken heart?" I smiled.

"You laugh, but you don't know how serious that is. Which is why I can't give you my blessing."

She just didn't know that I understood perfectly what heartbreak was because it had come to define my dating life. I put my hand over my heart in mock horror, "Will it stop beating, granny?"

She tapped my hand lightly as if to say it just might. Before getting up much more carefully this time to retire to her room to rest. Suddenly, I needed to as well. It had been a long night.

Chapter Nineteen

Amber

I went home and rested before tonight's class with Joseph.

Matters of the heart were the worst kind of limbo to be in. There were so many ways that I could boil down my decision for The Boxpad to numbers and charts. But the possibilities of failure and a lifetime of loneliness were positively debilitating.

The same was true for Drew. If I walked away from Drew, was I walking away from ever being happy.

I picked up the resumes of the two owners vying for ownership of The Boxpad. As much as Drew's talk boosted my confidence in what I do, I still needed to figure out what to do about Manny and his henchwomen. My parents were certainly going to be mad that I decided to keep the place. They wouldn't even be angry if I told them I was being blackmailed over it. They would probably recommend that I give him whatever he wants including The Boxpad. I do have some money stored up that I'd never spent. Maybe some of that could go to Manny just to get him off my back. But would that be satisfactory or would I just be turning myself into a permanent wishing well? He would come and knock on my door whenever he needed me to fill his wallet up.

If I accept The Boxpad and pay off Manny, would I only become resentful at Drew for pushing me into it? Would our growing feelings for each other survive outside the safe walls of his house? Could people accept us being together?

Or would we just face ridicule for being each other's favorite flavor? On the other hand, would he even be happy with a woman like me? I'm just the complete opposite of anyone he's ever dated.

I feel like my relationship with him had reached an impasse. An unscaleable wall that was just beginning to give way. However, my feelings towards The Boxpad had only just begun. I had to figure out how to get away from Manny. Maybe it was time that I asked for a little help in that regard. After all, I'm a champion, I know people that he doesn't.

Needless to say, any thoughts of Drew sweeping me off my feet would have to be put on the back burner.

All of this would certainly be easier if I just hated the man. I headed into the kitchen to fix myself something to eat. Trying to keep the images of him smacking my ass from my thoughts.

Today I was going to be in a class with Drew without any other distractions. Something I was barely managing during driving hours. The music was blasting in the car like we were gangstas. All to keep my mind occupied and my hands to myself. Batting down his attempts for us to talk about the moment we slept together.

So I had to get my head together. My outfit today was a little revealing for his benefit. Even though my feelings were like a bundle of rubber bands. Clarity was always imminent when we were together. He made me nervous. And I craved his attention.

Suddenly, the strap on my heel came apart. I groaned inwardly as I lifted my heel to fix it. Leaning on the wall of the community center.

"Here, let me help."

My skin crawled at the sight of Manny bending down in front of me to fix my strap.

"What are you doing here?" I asked, frowning as he caressed my ankle.

"Just wanted to talk to you."

He clipped the little belt of my shoe back into place. I smirked as I muffed his forehead with my shoe. Plopping him back on his butt. "Surprised that I'm not laid up somewhere."

He wipes the dust and dirt from his jeans.

Adults and children came and went from the community center. None of which I recognized. My thoughts going to my driver's ed class and if any of those people were passing. I'd trust a venomous snake before him.

"Yeah, I heard about what happened to you? Looks like you healed nicely."

His tone was so victorious and indifferent to my pain that I was almost dismayed that I ever thought I loved him. What killed me was the thought that if someone saw us talking they would merely think we were friends.

Instead, I leaned in to make sure that he could hear me. "You can't keep a good fighter down."

"No, but you can send them a message," he said grabbing my chin.

"Let me go."

He shifted his body until it looked like we might kiss.

"You going to kill me," I said through gritted teeth. My hand around his wrist. Ready to bash his head into the nearest wall if I needed to. He looked at my lips with such lust that I almost do it. My hands flinch against his wrist. His pulse betrayed that at least on some level he was scared of me. "Squeeze the money from the blood you spilled in the streets."

"I want an update on the sale. How much longer?"

"You can't intimidate me."

"But I can hurt you bad, Amber."

"You really couldn't." I huffed.

"I kind of did already."

"And you failed." Relinquishing my chin, he laced his fingers through mine and kept it close to his heart. I tried to pull away, not at all interested in playing a faux couple. But he kept a tight grip on the palm of my hand. My gaze darted from his face to my hand in a panic. As I started to lose feeling in my hand. My knuckles turned white.

"What happens to your career if you break every bone in this hand?" He sounded like he cared, but I knew he was playing to an audience of no one. When his eyes cut sideways at me, I thought about my ambush weeks ago with Erin.

"Let me go, you shouldn't even be here."

"Actually someone just invited me to the garden party shindig. Sounds like something I should go to. It's such a welcoming place."

"Well, they recognized that even stray dogs need a home."

He simply looked at me and slowly squeezed my hand until it hurt. I'd never been so scared of anyone. Least of all someone that I once shared a bed with. I winced and the words Fuck repeated over and over in my head.

"If you don't have my money by the end of the week. You're going to find out."

"Let her go," Drew yelled, pushing him against the wall.

I flexed my fingers and inhaled sharply.

"Be easy man. I'm just saying goodbye to my girlfriend before class."

"Is that why she looked like she was in pain? Because lovin' you hurt."

"It's okay." I put my hand on the side of Drew's arm. Drawing him away from the douche-bag. "I'm fine now and we're not together."

He looked at me as if he suddenly realized that Manny had indeed said we were boyfriend and girlfriend.

I'm smiling at him the same way I did that day we picnicked together. Don't worry, I could still be that good girl you want. Manny doesn't mean that I'm too much trouble. Even though I was.

"So you're not together?"

I shook my head. "Some exes, just take longer to get the message."

My skin tingled when he touched my hand. Running his thumb over my knuckles absentmindedly. The complete opposite of what Manny was doing only moments ago. "Are you okay?"

"She's fine."

"Get the fuck out of here now."

I locked eyes with Drew in surprise. The intensity in his gaze was almost unbearable under the heat. It almost feels like whatever powers I have as Shatterproof are being transferred to him through touch. He's angry and strong and couldn't be moved by a bulldozer.

"I was leaving anyway," Manny said trotting off.

"I could have handled that."

Drew just shrugged and kissed my knuckles. And I briefly wondered just how much of the conversation he had seen. "But you didn't want to have to."

"You think you know me so well?"

"I'm slowly picking up on the cues."

I looked at him impressed. Lacing my hands through his arms as he walked me inside. Not at all concerned with what Joshua might think. We even sat at two desks, side by side. Of course, we kept it professional over the next hour. I even asked Layla to take me home when we were done. Ignoring the need to follow behind Drew like some lovesick puppy.

She honked her horn to announce her arrival. And I ran over and got into her car. "I think I miss your Camaro more than you do."

"I know, but it wont be for too much longer."

She looked back out the window at Drew who was already walking home. Slowly, pulling out of the parking lot. "Did I see what I thought I saw? Looked like you two were holding hands."

I watched Drew out of her side-view mirror until he disappeared. Not bothering to answer her question. My leg shaking furiously. It looked like I had to go to the bathroom and was holding it in. Practically bolting for my apartment when she pulled up in front of my house. When I was running away from the pressure in my head to be with Drew.

As predictable as my morning run, I was getting anxious. I don't know why I allowed myself to get so worked up over things. But all I know is that I can't lose Drew. I need to climb this wall. I threw my bag down on the couch, and it bounced like a spring roll. My heart raced.

Layla raised her eyebrows at me and smirked. "What is going on girllll? You been breathing fire since you got in the car."

I turned to look at her. My hands were on my hips as I tapped my foot impatiently. "Tell me I can do it."

"Do what?" She huffed in amusement.

My hands dropped to my side as my stomach churned. I turned away from her, staring up at the ceiling. Why can't anyone see us together? Tension was in my shoulders so tight it could snap like the coils on a bridge. My house was somehow colder without his warm presence. It was disorganized compared to his. Empty beer bottles in every corner of the room. I actually started to go around and throw them away as if he might walk in and catch the mess.

"Okay, stop, talk to me," she said, taking the bottles from my hand and putting them on the table. Before guiding me to the couch.

I sat on the couch staring at the place on the floor where my purse had fallen. "Tell me that I'm okay with him?"

"Your nerd?" She shook her head and sat on the couch across from me. "Did something happen in class today?"

"Just confirmation of everything I knew about him."

"And that makes a difference, how?"

"I know he cares about me Layla and that should matter more than everything because it does."

"How is he not a product of your grief? You don't need some puppy tapping you on the head. You need a man that can tap that ass sort of speak."

"Done. He's perfect for me then."

Her eyes bugged out. "You slept with the nerd? Well, I know you made his day."

"He made mine, but that's neither here nor there," I stammered. "Come on Layla, I just need you to tell me that I'm good enough for him."

"Good enough for him? He's not good enough for you!"

The outcome of this conversation just took a turn that I wasn't expecting. Layla crossed her legs, one on top of the other, as if she were an expert on all things Shatterproof. And maybe she was, but that didn't mean she knew what Amber needed.

When it all comes down to it, I'm going to regret not being with Drew. "And just why not?"

"You're most assuredly going to get tired of his little choir boy act."

"You don't know that," I said stubbornly.

"Maybe Don's death triggered some fears about your immortality, but you ain't ready to be Joan Cleaver."

I appreciated the fact that she hadn't yet said I wasn't his type. But I was starting to feel terrible.

"I keep thinking about you, in and out of the ring. You like to party, not bake cookies. You beat up women for a living. You're not some school teacher."

Outside the window, I heard the faint calling of someone yelling for their friend. Feeling like I was getting further away from mine.

"You're the sort of person that grabs life. You don't need a pros and cons list on what to have for breakfast. We both know his type."

"Maybe you don't know me. Maybe you just know, Manny," I said, punching the pillow out of frustration. "We were always together partying."

"Don't downplay our friendship like that. Yes, we're used to being a quartet, but nothing about what I'm saying is wrong."

"I need you to tell me I'm not crazy. And maybe I wont feel stupid for wanting to run into his arms right now and stay there." I dragged my teeth along my bottom lip until I could taste the beginnings of blood. Wringing my hands as my elbows rested on my knees. "I don't want what happened between us to be a one-off. The thought of going to clubs and picking up some random stranger makes me cringe. I pulled away from him, but I really need to pull back. I miss him."

"Where has he gone? Haven't you seen him in class and stuff?" she asked puzzled. Even as I spoke my truth, her face looked like she had swallowed a sour jawbreaker.

Maybe she just couldn't imagine me being with anyone outside my type. "This could be a lack of vision. Maybe you can't see how great we would be together."

She took the strap of her purse off her shoulders. Placing it in her lap like a mother about to explain to her kid why she couldn't stick her finger in the electrical socket. I stood up needing to flee from her words. Pressing my hands into the couch in the hopes it would give me the strength I needed.

"I know you're going to go through with this no matter what I say. I just don't want you to have regrets."

"I don't know how I could with him."

"That's cute that you suddenly have rose-colored glasses on. They look adorable." She pursed her lips into a cute little duck face. Before going completely blank. "But take them off."

"This goes far beyond who sits in the family section at ringside. We may not work in theory, but this is real life. He makes me feel better about myself and what I do. And the thoughts in my head aren't quite as loud. He is my peace."

"What about the practicality of you guys actually being together?"

I laughed as my nose wrinkled up in distaste. "I can't stand his grandmother and he takes care of her. He knows I'm a boxer, but I don't know how he would react to seeing me getting beat up daily. It does take a certain mental strength to be a partner of someone who does what we do."

"Okay then! I don't have to be the bad guy. Life's circumstances keeping you apart is what is bad."

I hesitated, considering everything that she said. "I love him."

She doesn't try to push me out of this declaration and instead we just stare at each other in silence. And I couldn't be prouder for admitting it.

Yet, I found myself blinking back the tears that threatened to overwhelm me. So I sat back on the couch and caught my breath.

"Don't you freaking dare!" She came and sat beside me. Taking me into her arms.

I pulled back and dabbed at the corners of my eyes with my t-shirt. "I know. It's just...what if you're right?"

"You're happily in love, sweetie. Don't you dare ruin that moment crying! Life will work itself out. Just keep dancing among the poppy fields." The expression in her eyes is softer and I almost don't know how to respond.

"So now your team DrewAn?"

"You've thought of a couple name?" she smiled.

"I like them," I said slyly.

She put her hand in mine. "I'm still not on board, but I'm not the one to stand in the way of love. So I'll support you no matter what you decide."

Inside I was doing the jitterbug. Our heads fell together in support. The truth was Drew fit me everywhere and nowhere at the same time. "Thank you."

"But you should know that you don't have to explain your choices to me or anyone."

I nodded slowly.

"So you gonna go get your man?" She nodded towards the door.

"I think he holds the same doubts as I do without even knowing it."

"Okay."

"But I can't convince him to give us a shot. If I can't convince his grandmother."

"Do you think she would step aside and kind of trust his judgment on this one?"

I looked at her evenly. "Drew has Autism. So probably not."

She pulled her hands away from mine and looked puzzled. "What does that mean? I've heard of that disease, but is he like retarded? Is she worried that you're taking advantage of him? Could you be?"

"Of course not Layla. And he's a high-functioning adult, so I'm not coercing him into anything. He can make his own decisions. He's a computer programmer and he has his own place. I'm not dating a child or anything."

She looked at me wryly. "But you are in love?"

"I am."

She remained silent. This time it was a bit awkward. The fact that I could be with a man with a disability has broken her brain. Unfortunately, what I said next wasn't going to make it better.

"I didn't know when I met him. I just thought he was a douche. But now that I know about his diagnosis, I do look at him differently. Not as someone who can't do something. But as a man who can do everything despite his limitations. And it makes him sexy and awesome."

"You're not going to get a guy like that away from his granny," she pointed out. "There like moms but worse because they smell like cupcakes."

"So what are you suggesting?"

"Frankly, I don't know. You'll have to go through a whole dating boot camp to prove that you're good enough."

"That's it."

"What's it?" she said, wide-eyed.

I got up and pulled her towards my bedroom. We had worked to do. Layla was a genius. I simply needed to start acting more demurely. Tone down the excitement. Act more like the girls he typically dates. Shy, patient dolls, who gesture at stuff delicately with their wrists and drink out of teacups with their pinky out. I remember being one of those carefree girls before my brother died and I found boxing.

Girls who have so many opportunities that life actually was exciting and free. Only for the choices, we made to be boiled down to the choice of husband. I planned to spend the rest of the night figuring out how to get in touch with that girl once more. Going through my wardrobe with fervor. What better way to unveil the old me than at the upcoming garden party.

Chapter Twenty

Andrew

There once was a time when I would walk home from Driver's Ed and only think about the newest rocket model I was going to buy. I would go home, feed the dog, fix myself dinner. Maybe talk to granny about her day. But now all I could think about was Amber. The effort not to think about her, hurt more. Staring down at my phone as I texted and deleted a thousand messages all addressed to her. I picked up Frank and sat him on my lap. Sipping on some hot chocolate as I listened to the radio.

I told myself that I was going to put my phone on the charger to avoid any further temptation. Just as a call came through from my parents. I picked it up and switched to video call. My mother appeared to be in a cafe somewhere overseas.

"Can you see me?" mom asked, squinting at her phone. Her smile brightened when I nodded. "Good, your father's in the bathroom. But he'll be along shortly."

"Where are you guys now?"

She shifted in an uncomfortable-looking wooden chair. Her grip on the phone shook. Making watching her a bit disorientating. A sign behind her in an unknown foreign language. Her shrill voice was only slightly softened by the Caribbean music playing in the background. She only stopped fussing after a waiter brought her over another chair.

"Sorry about that dear," she told me as if she just remembered she was supposed to be talking to her son. "Creature comforts leave a lot to be desired in these places."

These calls seemed to get fewer and fewer every year. I wasn't even surprised that dad wasn't on this video chat with mom. She was always the main force behind everything I did. Dad usually acted like anything having to do with me was just too much for him to handle. She adjusted her eyeglasses as if she were studying what little she could see of my appearance. I realized that no matter how I felt about them they were always there to support my every milestone. Perhaps, mom could help me with the last one. It was the one thing that I usually went to granny with for advice.

"Before I came along, how did you know that Dad was the one? I mean how did you know it was love?"

The question settled among the trees beside her. The palm trees played like the backdrop of a postcard. She doesn't speak as her short hair blows in the wind. Her grey tips created an ombre-like effect that was very becoming. And for a moment, I began to wonder if this was one of those moments where I was supposed to do the adulting on my own. However, when she locked eyes with me again, I knew her answer was about to be a doozy.

"You never really know. But with each passing day, I'm proud of the journey I've taken with him." She nodded to someone off-screen and began to nurse her tea. And for a moment it felt like she was sitting in a chair across from me. No phones glued to our hands. Or the glow of the light bothering our eyes. It kind of felt like she could even reach others and brush my hair out of my eyes like she used to do when I was a child. I wouldn't be exaggerating to say that it was probably the closest we've been since they left. Not even our goodbye was this friendly as it was filled with her barks for me to grab their bags and open the door etc. I didn't bother to ask anything else as a shadow fell across her and my father came into the frame.

"Our second chance at life and romance has allowed us to reconnect in a way that's almost better than it was when we met." It's the answer I was expecting. Yet it still surprised me.

"But you didn't know any of this when you met. So how could you take that chance?"

This time she didn't answer and my father did instead. "What's all this about? Are you seeing someone?"

"Not exactly. There just may be a girl I like...a lot."

"I didn't think you'd ever find a girl you liked enough to feel something more than mild boredom towards. But you want her, I can tell. I can see it in your eyes. You must've stopped letting Dama hook you up, finally. Now you can breathe a little. You have more room to figure out this dating thing as your own man."

"Honey," my mother warned.

"Who is this girl? Does Dama approve? It's probably better if she doesn't. Have they met? I bet there were fireworks!" His grin was wide. Relishing in his son's virility.

"I talked to my mother just the other day. She didn't even mention a relationship to me."

"Then you know that she's really worried," my father chimed in, without waiting for a response from me.

"You may find that hilarious, but I don't know if that's a good thing. I personally have liked the girls Drew has dated in the past."

I rolled my eyes, watching them have this conversation about me, without me."

Dad shook his head. "Maybe if you like watching paint dry."

Frank hopped off my lap at the calling of my granny who just opened her bedroom door. "Frankie, here boy."

I'm starting to feel anxious. There wasn't much I could tell them about Amber that they might actually like and I couldn't lie about her either. I just don't want them to agree with Dama. For once, I want them to support me. I drew the conversation back to my concerns. "If I met someone who was the complete opposite of me and we both liked each other. How would I know that our feelings were real and not fleeting?"

Her answer convinces me that *what if* is a fact of life. "The whole phrase soul mates trivializes the work that goes into maintaining a relationship. There is no invisible force keeping you together. You do it through sheer will, determination, and a lot of prayers. So you never know if you've made the right choice. You've just got to find the right person...for you. And that doesn't mean she is perfect either."

Dad reached over and squeezed her hand affectionately. "She's just perfect for me."

And then they both turned to me as if this call wasn't entirely social. "How is Dama?"

I paused for a moment, trying to make sure that I wouldn't be overheard.

"It's her last year at the Garden Love Project." It's the one answer I knew they didn't want to hear. Even dad recognized what that place meant to grandmother. It was the end of an era. Mom just held my gaze.

"She's going to have an adjustment on her hands, but you keep doing what you're doing. This is for her benefit."

"She'll find something else to do, I'm sure. It's just important that she knows that this isn't the end of the world. And pass along our love."

And just like that Dad gestured to his watch and they both realized that they had somewhere else they needed to be. Waving goodbye before I even had a chance to ask if they wanted to speak to grandmother. Staring at a blank phone when they hung up.

Maybe it would be easier to just tell Amber how I felt at the garden party. Our last day of Driver's Ed was the day after. We both were running out of time together.

Chapter Twenty-one

Amber

Two weeks later, I sat in Don's office chair which was technically now my office chair and twirled around. Staring at my phone of the picture I had taken of Andrew during our picnic. Catching him unaware had truly been an uphill battle. One that I had won with a photo capturing his dazzling smile. But I still lost because I lost him. I was already in love with a man that I could never be good enough for.

I had met my equal and he wasn't some tall, muscle-bound guy dropping nutrition facts. I respect that guy. That guy had helped me get in shape for my fights. But he hadn't been able to touch my heart. That type of guy almost took my life. The guy that touched my heart, was going to make me cry just by looking at his photo. I released a slow breath trying to get my emotions under control.

My dream guy likes rockets and computer programming, and he's a stickler for the rules. He can be annoying, but he's also fucking adorable. Like A1. He's great in bed, but I loved him most when I was simply resting in his arms.

And I could do that forever. But why would I want to ruin his life? I could never be Manny. Yet and still, a homemade bomb was just as dangerous as a real one. Manny was self-destructive and I would never do that to Andrew on any scale. He was too great of a guy. I bit my bottom lip. And I'd miss him forever. My heart sank at the thought that I actually might have to.

"You ready."

"Yes," I said startled when Fuschi appeared in the doorway. Fumbling my phone in my hand until it crashed on the desk. I swallowed the lump in my throat and leaned over and put the black briefcase on my desk. I'd never owned a briefcase for anything. It kind of made me feel important. The clock on my desk read seven p.m., and it made me nervous.

"You sure you're up to this." He looked around before closing the door behind him.

"It was my idea," I replied annoyed. In boxing, I was always better with a team behind me. It was about time that I figured out that I was only going to defeat Manny the same way.

Fuschi got his camcorder out and went into the rather large over-sized storage locker standing to the right of my desk. Unlike the others in the main locker rooms, this one was dark green and rusted. It was cleaned out by El hours ago. Most of the items inside were junk. I had no clue as to what I would use it for in the future. But now I'd keep it. I'd keep everything.

Fuschi groaned like an old man who knew that he was too old for these sorts of adventures. I almost laughed, but time was dawning soon. After today, Manny would hopefully be out of my life. More than that though, I was hoping that Fuschi would change his mind about me. I wanted to keep him on, but I wouldn't do that knowing that he would undermine me. Manny wasn't the only one getting tested today.

"Comfortable in there?" I chimed in.

"If cocoons are comfortable," he said, banging into the side. "You should be in here and me out there."

"No such luck lawyer boy. This is my problem and I'm the solution."

"I'm just supposed to take the video to the cops," he repeated.

I watched the locker as if the boogieman waited within, and not just my lawyer. The tension in my shoulders was so tight that it could snap at any moment like the cables on the back of a truck holding logs down. "Well, it's not exactly the Hilton. So stop moving around in there."

"You come in here and tell me how it feels."

Fuschi was vastly proving himself to be unable to take direction.

When I first came up with the plan, my first thought was to enlist Layla's help. But the idea of her getting hurt in all this made me physically sick. Layla knew what my plan was, and she suggested using Fuschi for his lawyer background. If things went south then Fuschi's presence would be enough to intimidate the guy. I was a gym owner with scary connections, kind of thing. But I still hadn't told her that I was keeping The Boxpad. So much was dependent on how today goes down. That I had been almost too frightened to celebrate.

"I take it this is what's been keeping you from choosing the new owners of The Boxpad?" Fuschi asked me through the slight crack in the double doors. But from my seat behind the desk, it was just a black void.

"Not exactly. I've decided to keep The Boxpad." I took a sip of the scalding hot coffee that El had brought me earlier. The smell filled the room with a homey feel that would have never been there before. Secretly wishing that it was hot chocolate.

"You can't be serious. The guys you narrowed it down to were extremely qualified."

I sighed heavily. Drumming my fingers across the leather-bound suitcase. Staring at the door as if Don would barge through and set the man straight at any minute. "If he wanted those guys he should have chosen them. He chose me."

"Don't let this Manny character bully you into a false confidence. You can't take care of this place the way it deserves."

"I'm in the ring now and no one's going to drag me out."

"Shouldn't you be planting flowers somewhere?" Fuschi barked from the void.

I almost stormed over and threw open the doors. He was going to be doing more than kissing his knees. This was the first time that I had ever told him anything personal about me. I wrecked my brain, wondering if I had ever let anything slip about the community center. Even if my court-appointed classes there were a matter of public record. It wouldn't mention my garden as I specifically hid it. Too scared that because of my connection to the place they wouldn't station me there. And it's too personal of a thing to me for me to blab it around the gym. Layla was the only one who knew about my extracurricular. "What do you know about it?"

"Enough," Fuschi replied.

I stared at the storage locker, helplessness settling in my bones. If there was ever a worse time to get news like this it would be now. I imagined Fuschi taping me in the dark. A proudful sneer about his face as he memorialized having one up on me. However, I was only able to smile back because I knew not even Fuschi's antics could change my mind. I had decided to take on this fight and instead of a championship belt, I was going to win The Boxpad. Suddenly, a realization dawned on me.

"You researched me after you found out that Don was leaving me The Boxpad," I said, running the vanilla cream coffee over my tongue.

"It's my job to execute the best wishes of my client."

"Did Don know you were executing this favor?" I asked, trying to make my question sound as natural as possible.

"No, but he would have if I had found anything incriminating."

His snooping would explain why he was so dead set against me inheriting this place. Like many others when I first arrived, he had found my lack of experience damning. In his head, he had made up his mind about who I was. It was hard not to feel as inferior as the first day I had walked into this place. But I wasn't that girl anymore. I was Shatterproof. And she wasn't about to let an old man derail her plans.

"Who you talking to in here?"

I stood up as soon as Manny entered. Hoping to draw his attention away from the locker. But I didn't have to try very hard as his gaze was glued to the suitcase almost immediately. Before he closed the door, I could see that El wasn't at the desk. She knew how important this meeting was. That lady better be on a piss break or it was her ass.

Record, I hoped my eyes said as I glanced at the storage locker. Reaching for my mug of coffee to keep my hands busy. Then a sudden taste for it.

"Just making some last-minute calls."

I sit back behind the desk as if I always belonged there. Noticing that my movements were a little stilted and if I didn't snap out of it then he would catch on to something being wrong. Although, I doubt he'd ever expect a man hiding out with a camcorder. Dimly aware of his every movement in the small office.

"Let's just get this over with. Why you would be late to your ex-hortation deal is beyond me?" I leaned over my desk and turned the suitcase around. Unlocking it like a woman about to do a drug deal. Pushing it across to him until it practically lit up his eyes. Money that was supposed to be from the sale of this place. When it just came out of my account. Close to $25,000.

"Some of us like to eat dinner."

It was close to eight pm, but who could eat during a time like this? Satan, that's who. A bowl of rusty nail soup. He tentatively approached the money taking out one stack of 100s and putting it up to his nose. Inhaling the way he used to do with my perfume when we cuddled. This man was really a stranger to me.

"Can you eat money? Because I know that's the only thing that's important to you," I said. "Getting your daily roughage."

"I still love you," he blurted out. I realized that I stood up with my hand on my hip.

"You're blackmailing me into giving you $25,000 for monies owed. A debt that doesn't even exist." Not sure how to get him to admit to his dirty deeds before I positively explode. "Love ain't in the mess that you've created for me. The threats you hurled against me. Getting Erin and her goons to come and beat me up."

I'm hoping that no one in the hallway is listening in. But then again, I wouldn't lose anything having a few extra witnesses to Manny's demise. I was never sure about how thin the walls were here.

"Only $25,000?"

"It's next to a strip club." As if that was the only answer needed.

He flipped through the money with his thumb. "You don't give a shit about this place anymore than I do. So let's take this money and run off together."

I rolled my eyes. "That doesn't sound like you're admitting to anything."

"What you want me to grovel? Is that all it will take for you to accept me again? Of course, I hated that stupid plan I came up with to scare you. Erin took it too far."

"I think I need 25,000 apologies." And another twenty years to ever see the silver lining in anything he'd done to me.

"It's just money," Manny told me. "Forget that I forced you to give it to me and let's start over."

My eyes narrowed to dangerous slits. "You want me to forget?"

"I'm sure you're keeping a running ledger of all the times I threatened your life."

"Something like that," I said to him. Furiously glancing to where I hoped Fuschi was recording. "All I want is for you to get out of here. I could never forgive you for stealing from me."

That was the magic phrase because it was like he snapped like an alligator. "I'm not stealing anything from you. This is what I'm owed for all my hard work. Everyone knows that you never should have inherited this place. Do I regret sending Erin after you? Yes. But I'm going to do anything necessary to get my cash. Including blackmailing your sorry ass."

I looked at the locker and smiled. He better had gotten all of that.

"Now if you'll excuse me. I'm going to take my money and go," he paused at the door. Hugging the suitcase like a crackhead who knew what awaited him at home. "But if you want to get your head out of your ass. You know where I live."

"Fuschi, you must be terribly cramped. Come out and say goodbye to Manny," I said, staring him down.

He looked at me quizzically. "What are you—-"

Fuschi practically fell out of that locker. Lowering some of my confidence considering I was deftly afraid of that camcorder falling. It was just a small grey camera that I had picked up at the electronics store. Much earlier in the day.

"Meet your jail sentence. We caught all your little misdeeds on camera. So put the suitcase down on the floor and get the fuck out of here."

He looked between me and Fuschi. "You wouldn't dare."

"You are constantly underestimating me. Something that Don never did. I will fuck your life up right now."

He slowly placed the suitcase down on the floor as if I had a gun pointed straight at his head. But it was Fuschi who he couldn't take his eyes off of.

"What are you going to do?"

"Win the fight." He turned to me breathing fire like a bull. But this dog had been castrated.

"You bitch."

"You going to take this head start I'm giving you or do you want to exchange numbers first," I sneered. He looked like he was prepared to rush Fuschi. Fuschi was a strong man, but no match. "I must've lulled you into a false sense of security because you think I wont kill you right now for that recorder."

He leveled a hard gaze at me before bolting through the door.

"It looks like you did it kid."

I sat down, running my hands over my thighs. My heart raced as my limb shook. "You know what to do with that."

"My connect at the station is just waiting for my call."

I nodded. "Get to it then."

He picked up the abandoned suitcase and placed it back on the desk.

"Just so you know. You disrespect my place here again and he's not the only one I'm going to be chasing off. You're a foot soldier in my army now or I'll replace you."

"Understood, boss."

"Close the door." I waited until I heard the click before flipping my phone over. Pressing the stop button on my own recording. A good fighter prepares for every outcome. I sat back in my chair and spun it around. "Eat shit Manny."

Another knock came at the door. I thought I conjured him like a voodoo doll. I stormed to the door prepared to fight in a way I hadn't been up to before. Allowing Don's death and my depression-like in-decision to keep me down. But when I opened the door it was just El.

"Sorry hun, just wanted to know if you would be locking up tonight or if you wanted me to?"

"Um, no, I'm going to get out of here. You can do it," I said grabbing my bag and picking up my phone. For safety reasons, I wasted no time in emailing the recording to myself. Before giving hugging El goodbye.

Surprised when she spoke up. "I've been silent for a while. But I want to know what's going on with The Boxpad?"

"You're looking at the new owner," I said with a shimmy. "So tell whoever you like. Oh and Manny is banned."

"I was hoping you would say that."

I laughed. "You were the only one."

"You are The Boxpad. I recognized that early on when I convinced Don to take you on as a trainer."

I cocked my head to the side in surprise. My mouth dropped open. Prepared to pepper her with a thousand questions. But she merely winked and went about closing down all the lights. I turned and practically skipped out of the door.

It was late, but maybe I could still celebrate with Layla. All she knew was that I needed her to stay away from The Boxpad today. Which worked out because she volunteered to go on one of her daughter's field trips as a chaperone. But I'm sure she suspected that tonight was execution day. She had been blowing up my phone every hour, asking if I was okay.

But I waited until I got home before responding to the good news. Practically bursting at the seams. But I needed a drink in my hand. For a virtual toast. Checking old mail from this morning that I had absentmindedly tossed on the coffee table. Popping a bottle of wine that I usually only opened on fight nights. My hand was freezing on something from the state. I quickly ripped it open. Narrowly missing a paper cut for the ages. Only to see that it was my driver's license. I jumped on the couch Tom Cruise style and danced. I was zero for two. Manny down and a glorious license in my hand.

Practically everyone had been rooting against me. I accomplished all my goals despite turning away my biggest supporters like a dummy. And there was only one person I wanted to share this moment with. So I sent Layla a hasty text. About having good news and then I hopped on a bus. I should have been heading to her house. Instead, I knew I was going to him.

Dressed in tight jeans and an old top that I dropped pizza sauce on sometime during the evening. My heels clicked on the bus steps as I got off and waited for another. Frowning as the same bus came twice and neither was the one I needed. Threatened to pull over the next bus driver in the name of love and find out just what the hell was going on. It was close to 10 at night, but that didn't mean service had stopped.

Surprised when the third wrong bus came and it was Andrew stepping off.

"Did you have the same idea I did?" I asked tentatively. As if my heart would fall out of my chest. Barely able to find my voice that came out as nothing more than a squeak. Surprised that he was standing in front of me. Pacing.

"I doubt it because I'd been thinking about this since nine am. And I don't do surprises. So this coming off well is slim. But I had to try because not doing anything would be wrong. And my granny sort of gave me her blessing. But she's not the one that matters. Your response matters more. And I can't predict that. It's very unsettling. It gives me anxiety. But not being with you gives me the most anxiety."

I grabbed his shoulders. Stopping his pacing to force him to look at me. "What are you trying to say?"

"I got my driver's license today and I wanted to show you. My driving teacher even said that my driving had improved immensely. That's saying something because he almost failed me the first time."

I pulled out my purse and produced my license. Squealing like a teenager. "I got mine too."

He merely smiled at me and it burst my heart wide open. I pulled him into me and planted a kiss on his lips. His arms circled my waist with that comforting embrace that I had come to miss alone in my bed at night. The taste of hot chocolate on his tongue. Unable to catch our breaths as we quenched our thirst for each other. So sad when he pulled back that I instantly began to pout. My hands playing with the collar of his work shirt. Not at all concerned that he was wearing those old dad pants again.

"You're not the villain in my story. You're the queen. And I'm sorry if I ever made you feel like I don't believe in you because I do."

"I don't think I'm good for you."

"Daylily, I'm no good without you."

Suddenly, something dawned on me. "Why didn't I just drive my Camaro. I would have been at your house an hour ago?"

"Maybe I'm rubbing off on you."

"Am I rubbing off on you?" I asked shyly.

"I told my very supportive granny that I was going to get my women. I'm practically a rebel."

I laughed and leaned my head against his left shoulder. How I loved this little dweeb?

Chapter Twenty-two

Amber

I wouldn't even leave the house until it was closer to 8:15 in the evening. As if the later it got would somehow dull the appearance of myself in a cardigan and a wholesome blue patterned midi dress that Layla picked up at a garage sale as a gag gift. My reflection in the window confirmed that this was probably the most innocent dress I owned. Hitting me just below the knee. I looked like a 16-year-old going to her first high school dance out in the country.

Today, however, I was on the bus. There was no way I could step out of my blue Camaro with the racer stripes in a dress straight out of Little House On The Prairie. I would feel like a fraud. Even when I stepped off the bus at my stop, a little old lady complimented me on my dress. Only used to looks of consternation and constipation, I knew then I had made a mistake. This was not me.

But I'm doing this for Drew, I reminded myself. It's my last chance to prove to him and his grandmother that I was right for him. The garden doors were open in the back of the community center and of course, there are way more people here than there need to be. Why did the community center insist on opening the garden party to everyone? How was I supposed to find Drew like this? I'm sure Dama was posing by the trophies maybe it would be easier to start there.

I was hoping to get Drew alone, maybe next to the pine and cedar planters that had been brought in temporarily. Just to take the place of the empty spot that used to be the rack of potted plants and loaner tools. We could have an honest talk then. But there he was. Talking to a woman that looked a bit older than us. I turned and hid behind a couple at the refreshment table. Peeping over the husband's shoulders to see that Drew's lady friend had desperate cougar written all over her. They even looked good together.

She had on a tight fitted floral dress that was more my style than hers. Showing off legs that went to the moon. The dress stopped mid-calf, but I could ignore the trembles of jealousy. My focus was only on Drew. I was actually in love with a man who wears bow-ties. Moreover, I wanted to tear it from his neck as we made love. The couple in front of me turned and almost ran directly into me. I side-stepped them with tons of apologies. Narrowly dodging a dress disaster.

He lifted his gaze towards us at the commotion. A cup of tea in his hand. His companion nursing a glass of wine I was almost positive she wasn't drinking. But Drew's eyes were only for me. Staring into me as I approached. His gaze was even more intense than I was used to and it sent a zing to my mound. It was like he couldn't wait to see what color my panties were.

"Would you excuse me?" He said to her.

"Sure, but not for long."

My mouth pursed in a frown at the way she was purring at him. She was a bitch in heat alright. Fortifying myself with a deep breath as he took my hand and led me to our little corner. I felt the heavy weight of his hand on my waist as he led me to the gate. Overgrown vines snaking up the black metal like magical roots.

I watched his gaze drop to my shoes and I tried to remember that he's never seen me in flats. He looked dashing, like a man who would own a private island somewhere. Yet, when our gazes connected once more, it was wholly innocent. Like the boy in love with his next-door neighbor. It left me shaking in my heels.

"You're beautiful," he drawled, lightly touching my blond hair that I had curled just for tonight. "This is a garden party, not the prom, Daylily."

I laughed as if I'd be caught dead at a formal event in something like this. "I did work hard on this. So thank you."

"I'm glad you came."

I looked around and pulled us in between two Eastern Redbud trees. They were at least 15 feet tall. There bright pink-purplish flowers like a halo over our heads. Drawing us closer together like two love birds with a secret conspiracy. I'm putting myself out there in a major way and I don't care.

My left hand gently brushed across his. Both of us were worried about attracting attention. But our animal magnetism wont allow us to simply ignore each other. The faint smell of his cologne enticing me to lean in and inhale him. If I turned my focus on this dress then I can forget how much I just want to grind against him.

"My grandmother is here." His voice sounded normal but I didn't think mine would. "Don't leave."

I picked vaguely at a purple petal that had fallen on my shoulder. My dream could burst at any moment because of that woman. Her name alone triggered my flight or fight. I looked up at him through hooded eyes. His blue polka dot bow tie was a little crooked. My subconscious told me that all it needed was a little tug to come completely undone. Imagining myself tucking it into my bra and having him fetch it with his teeth.

My private thoughts can't be trusted. I should tuck my tail between my legs and run. It would be so easy to leave this whole place behind. Except it wasn't easy. Drew was here.

"Don't leave," he said, more sharply. "I want you here with me."

"I just want...you." That came out as more of a surprise. Like finding out your allergic to something you've eaten your whole life. However, if I had to go without then I just might starve. I leaned against the gate feeling like I needed more support.

He stood in front of me blocking my view of the party. "Your hands are sweaty. What's the matter?"

"It's just really hot in here," I said, aware of my fast heartbeat as I crossed my arms in front of my chest.

"There's air conditioning inside. Want me to take you?" he asked, his thick fingers on my neck.

"I think you need to stop touching me because it's really getting hot."

His voice got lower as if he was catching on. "What do you want me to do?"

"What don't I want you to do? Suck me, fuck me, lick me."

He stared straight into my eyes. Before flagging down a waiter to take his glass. Waiting until the man was a nice distance away before speaking again. "What if I took you right here behind these trees?"

"I think I'd squeal like a little girl in a haunted house and completely give away our position."

"No, you wont. Then you'd miss the opportunity to see your panties decorating this tree overhead."

I crossed my legs involuntarily at the image. Completely speechless at this turn of events.

"Tsk, tsk, tsk. You trying to make it harder for me?" he asked, his eyes falling on my legs.

It was so strange to talk to him and not see his face as this robotic wall. Dressed in a pair of cream pants and a matching button-down shirt. A pink cardigan shirt on. I touched the buttons on his shirt lightly.

"Some scandalized old lady will find them tomorrow and have a heart attack," I said envisioning the dream.

"But right now the moment is just between us."

I merely nodded, hypnotized by his voice and words. Wishing I could bottle this moment and take it out whenever he annoyed me. It's not often that he got the upper hand over me. Suddenly, I don't want to just leave lipstick on his collar. I want my bashful baby pink matte gloss on his boxers. The color was reminiscent of a 70s pin-up model. And I was ready to be the face he stared at on his bedroom wall. Tonight, I'm just mush in his hands.

"They may even find it tonight. Curious as to why I'm bent in front of you like I'm about to propose. Your dress slightly raised, but not in any way that she might find suspicious. Their old eyes playing tricks on them and blurring like a kaleidoscope. Just long enough to be our gain. As you pull your panties to the side and I dip my tongue into the inner lips of your flower. Your juices falling down the corner's of my mouth."

My fingers ached to wrap themselves in his hair and pull him into my embrace. Instead, I held the gate behind me as not to be tempted.

"Your legs tremble as they struggle to hold you up. Covering your mouth because you want to moan out, but that would only ex-pose you. Your secret center throbbing under my exploring tongue. Clipped sounds erupting from your throat as if you were being choked. Signs that you're barely able to swallow the crested pleasure of your release."

Even the air between us seemed to weigh more. As if it were waiting for us to need it. His teasing positively torture. My nips hardening and pushing through the fabric of my dress.

"And I frequently have to remove your hand from my head because that would be a giveaway too."

I gripped the gate tightly, the leaves on the vine brushing against my hand. "Can you show me to the bathroom?"

"Right now."

I nodded, unable to speak as thoughts of him naked ran through my head.

"Haven't you been here more than me?" he said, lifting his arm to escort me. When I walked past a group from the garden love project, I half expected them to stop us. There smiles approvingly sweet and that's got to be a bad omen.

"Haven't you heard a girl can't go to the powder room alone."

"If I haven't said this already, you do look nice, Daylily." He opened the side door and held it open for me.

"You have, but you can say it as often as you like." That man sure knows how to dazzle without even trying.

"Where's he going with her?" I heard one of Dama's friends call out faintly. Drew frowned and slammed the door behind us. A huge floor sign directed party goers to the garden party outback. We both nodded, friendly-like, to the receptionist miserably stuck at the desk. A desk decorated with frilly orbs in pink, blush, and grey. Pretty and elegant. We followed the signs that pointed in the direction of the bathroom and I knew I was running out of time.

Then he licked his lips and I knew.

He soaked me in. Slowly dragging his eyes over my body as if every inch of me was important to remember. *Tell me what you want*, I think to myself. *Tell me you want to ravish me in the bathroom and I'll let you.*

"Are you going to use the bathroom?"

"If you come with me?"

I could see his mind filling with doubts. So I did the one thing I knew that he couldn't turn away. I slipped off my panties and then stuffed them in my bra. Fewer things for us to have to get through. Tell me all you want to do is touch me and I'll let you.

"What if we get caught?"

"We wont."

"Someone could come in and report it."

I lowered my voice to a whisper. "I promise I'll lock it."

"Isn't it kind of unsanitary."

So spontaneity was not his thing, but over-analyzing was.

I held out my hand for him. "I think we're the contamination."

He looked around in one final swoop. Before taking me inside and locking the door behind us himself. I threw my bag on the sink. Laughing as he picked me off the floor and my legs automatically encircled his waist. His lips connected with mine. "You really are something special Daylily."

"I was thinking the same thing about you."

He ran his fingers through my hair and cupped my cheek. Smiling warmly as he traced the outline of my mouth with his gaze.

"Wait, I've got protection in my bag."

Still holding me, he leaned over and unbuckled my purse. Rummaging around for this little gold foil and pulling it out.

It occurred to me that he might not be able to hold me up. So I briefly considered guiding him over to the sink area. But my thoughts were silenced, by yet another succulent kiss. Arousal taking over in this animalistic need to have more of each other. An ache between my thighs begging to be touched. My dress hiked up closer to my hips like the harlot I was, and I reveled in it. Wincing a bit as I was slammed into the wall of the bathroom. Aggravating an old injury, that was soon forgotten as I reached for the buttons of his pants. His member straining against the fabric in the best possible way. Like it was calling to me for release.

He actually took time out to unbutton the small blue buttons of my dress. My breasts popping out as if they couldn't breathe in the confinement of my red lace bra. He dragged my lavender-colored panties out of my bra with his teeth and tossed them over his head. I elicited a giggle at his moxy. Was my virgin a real man now?

He nibbled on the pink heaving flesh of my breast. Creating little star hickies across my chest. Causing me to giggle like a little school girl.

Sucking in a harsh breath as he took one of my nips into his mouth. My head falling back in ecstasy as I arched my chest into his lips. His tongue flicking my nips until they were just hardpoints.

Lacing my fingers into his hair as I pulled him into me. Our moans echoed throughout the bathroom like we were in a musical theater. The walls themselves shaking with emotion. Groaning against the force of our desire. I imagined them melting around us unable to withstand the heat emitting from our bodies. The whole building in flames as we withered in each other's embrace.

The only thing I could choke out was, "more."

In response, his pants and boxers seemed to fall to his ankles like an invisible force. Our lips connecting in a kiss meant to caress. Not demand, but love. Not just want with hunger, but to be satiated. We were talking to each other without words. And every touch said we loved each other.

Basking in each other's energies as if that alone would sustain us. His kisses were enticing and probing. Inviting me to stay with him always. The kisses a never-ending flurry of affection and desire. Causing Dama to be nothing more than the wicked witch of the EastWest, sent to keep us apart.

Pushing against his erection I could feel myself wetting his shaft as he eased the condom on. His hand caressing my back as if to let me know that he would never drop me.

I was doing the opposite of what I came here to do. And that was to prove that I could be the demure girl of Drew's dreams. However, I was living for the look of sheer desire on his face now. And it was all for me.

His hands lifted my ass as he lowered me onto his shaft. Staring into his eyes to let him know that it was always just him. Wrapping my arms around his neck as I forgot that there were hundreds of people just beyond that door, any of who could catch us. His kisses gave me a heady feeling as he moved in and out.

Pleasure building up behind my eyes, that I found myself pushing against him. My muscles trembling as I struggled to hold on. His moans drowning out my own. I reached out for something to hold on to find nothing against the wall to brace myself with. Sure that the orgasm alone would send me flopping to the ground like silly string as he moved faster.

My legs began to tremble as he clutched me tightly and we came holding on to each other. Breathing heavily as he eased out of me and slowly put me back on the floor. My legs felt like jello beneath me. Watching as he pulled off the condom and threw it in the trash. I quickly adjusted my dress. Seeing him pulling up his clothes reminded me that I needed to find my panties. They landed underneath one of the stalls. There was no way I was putting those back on, tossing them into my purse.

He came up behind me and wrapped his hand around my waist. Kissing my shoulder lightly.

"I want you to be my girlfriend."

I stared at him in the mirror. Running my hand up the right side of his face. My hands tangling in his brownish auburn hair. And it was like someone had taken over my body because I couldn't believe I said this but, "I want you to love me."

He turned me to face him. "I do...love you."

"Good because I love you too."

I exhaled slowly, my heart finding it almost fantastical to believe. As my came up to caress his face and we kissed once more. Before someone started banging on the door. It sounded like they were banging on it with a hard object.

"We've got to go."

He took my hand and unlocked the door.

Agatha looked on in shocked, but her expression quickly changed to that of someone who pleasantly agreed. The object in her hand, being a walker. "I'd offer to come back, but my bladder isn't what it used to be."

I laughed. "No, go ahead. We were just finished."

Drew blushed as he flew by Agatha as quickly as he could manage. The receptionist looked on curiously as if there was something she was missing. Having all but forgotten that we had gone to the bathroom. It was a perfect crime. Now we had tons of time together to just be. He only dropped my hand so that he could get the door for me. The perfect gentleman. I'd never dated anyone like that.

But if I was planning on breaking out the champagne then I'd be drinking alone. As soon as we walked through the door. We were both accosted by Dama's friends. Talking a mile a minute until it was impossible to think as fast as they were going. All they wanted was to separate us.

"We've been looking for you everywhere," crooned one of the old ladies, who enjoyed taking her teeth out in front of strangers a little too much.

"You're needed to help with the party," said short stuff. The only one in Dama's group of friends that I liked.

"Its last minute, but something always goes wrong during these things," said an older woman, wearing a church hat the size of Texas.

"An extra set of hands will do the trick," said another as she pushed his back. They had clearly never heard of his no touching rule because it looked like his spirit was about to leave his body. Leaving the corpse on the floor.

"Your granny would appreciate it," church hat pleaded.

Drew looked at me with concern.

"Don't worry about it," I said shaking my head. "Just go."

"Okay," he stammered. "Just stop touching me."

He drew more than a few stares with that last statement, but they took heed. The three old ladies flanking him like a triangle. I half expected them to take off on their broomsticks. Drew strapped between them on a magic carpet. Going nowhere as long as it was far away from me.

I noticed that catering had brought out the cake while we were inside. Guarding the table like they were security guards. Smacking the hands of people who dared come to close with a white cloth napkin. It was a four-tiered cake, the bottom two of which were a beautiful lavender color. The top two were white and the whole thing was topped with a matching lavender color fondant flower. Real purple and pink flowers littered the base around it.

The garden love project was in charge of chipping in for it. A necessary expense with a huge payoff. It was dedicated to Dama and I couldn't wait to see the look on her face when they told her. They had to keep it a secret. When I looked over at her it was clear that she knew something was up. It was the first time that anything having to do with Dama brought a smile to my face.

But it didn't stay as the three old billy goat granny's sudden need for help meant Drew and I spent most of the party apart. If he wasn't helping with decor, catering, or other mishaps. I found them introducing him to pretty much everyone. Even people who didn't belong to the Garden Love Project. I was left alone feeling like the odd man out. It became hard to ignore that this help wasn't actually about them needing help. This was a Dama scheme.

I loved the Garden Love Project, but I never would have come to this by myself. It's just not my thing. If Layla was here she would be standing next to me yelling, I told you so. If only because I recognized that it was not my crowd. It was Drew's and he was doing so well with the convo. The guy who has Autism. So what was wrong with me? And this dress was supposed to be inviting and wholesome. But it wasn't working. Admittedly, I supplemented my discomfort with too much of the wine.

Only building up enough liquid courage to go over and say something to the dynamic trio after a few drinks. Knocking a glass out of a waiter's hand that was passing by. Trying to bend down to help, I slurred, "Sorry."

"No ma'am, I've got this. Don't hurt yourself."

Suddenly, I was pulled up by my elbow. Only to come face to face with the author of my troubles. Dama. Her posture bone straight like a Catholic school teacher that just caught a student trying to sneak out of class. She then released me and threw her head back. A huge smile on her face like she was delighted to see me. Waving to a friend that she saw standing across the party.

I used both hands to smooth down my dress, taking this moment to try to impress the old bat. "Hello, Dama. It's a beautiful party that you've helped put together here. Since we're talking I was hoping we could start over. We've gotten off on the wrong foot. But nothing that can't be worked on. Will surprise each other with how much we have in common." My voice was almost hoarse with embarrassment as the waiter brought out a broom and dustpan for the glass shards.

"Are you drunk?" Her finger circled the top of the teacup in her hand. I was almost positive she spiked it, but who was I to call her out on her bullshit. This was a suppress your true thoughts date day.

I moved away from the incriminating evidence riddling the walkway. "I am enjoying myself here, as you are."

We ended up near my small patch of land. It was only herbs and the beginning sprouts were coming in. But it looked pitiful compared to everyone else's land. Completely out of place. That must be a sign that things weren't going to go well tonight. How did we end up back here in the corner of all places? Apart of me wanted to grab Drew's hand and run away with him to Dunkin Donuts because there was a limit on the sweets table. As quickly as that image formed, I imagined him bending me over the sink in the bathroom and taking me from behind. Only to go back to his place and cuddle in his arms. Then I realized, that Dama would just be there. "You look very lovely tonight, as does your grandson."

She was getting a little terse. "Should I have them hide the booze from you?"

That idea wasn't half bad. I cradled the wine glass in my hand feeling a bit foolish. "No more than anyone else. The booze is always the most expensive package to purchase for a reason after all.

"Why are you at this party? And don't lie and say its to support the Garden Love Project. It's not a mandatory gathering. Yet here you are."

I tapped my handbag against my stocking thigh. Putting runs in them. "I'm here for a friend."

"This friend. The one you have wrapped around your little finger. When he asks you why you left early, tell him that your stomach was a little upset. The food didn't agree with you. So he wont push it."

"I'm not leaving here without speaking too Drew." I'm gripping the wine glass in my hand so hard that I was surprised that it hadn't cracked. If I thought that I could somehow repair my relationship with Dama, it was all disappearing with the trash. I looked around trying to get rid of the drink in my hand only to throw caution to the wind. Completely downing the drink in one go.

"Drew has seen enough of you for one night." The crease in her brow deepened. "And frankly so have I."

"We don't have to be enemies. Drew can be this uniting factor for us."

She ignored me. "I want you to turn and look over your right shoulder."

I stared down at my empty glass for a moment, not sure if I should give in. Only doing so at her gentle prodding. Fucking A, be a big girl.

"That girl Drew's talking to in the white and yellow dress is his ex-girlfriend. And you notice how there is no one else around because there doesn't have to be. She holds his attention astutely. Something you can't do by merely spreading your legs." She took my empty glass from my hand.

"Getting rid of me wont be that easy Dama. Drew is important to me. I hated him and he disliked me and now we're turning into more than friends. Whatever is going on between us can't be stopped," I hastily tack on. I just told Dama, without telling Dama, that I loved Drew. Practically confirming that we were friends. Now she was ready to spit on me.

"No one can stop it, but Drew you mean."

"Drew is why I'm here. Look, I know about your diagnosis. Let's face it, we have all faced some life-changing events. At least one of those can bring us closer together."

She ignored me again. "The good thing about Drew is that once he really knows someone. He can smoke out there lies. So I'm confident that you wont be able to hold on to him if you tried. Cheap women always smell like old perfume. No matter what they're dressed in."

Stubborn as the day is long, I replied, "I'm going to bite my tongue because Drew choosing a woman who could fit on the front of a Wheaties box is a lot for anyone to take. But you should get on board as soon as possible because you're making it harder on him and that's not fair."

That last little nugget of truth must have hit close to home because it sent her scurrying into the embrace of her yes only, girlfriends. I turned and looked back at Drew who was still, in fact, talking to his ex. How much more was there to say between exes? A waiter passed me and I picked up another glass of wine from off his platter. I don't need to be sober for any more of this.

The sun dropped lower as I passed one couple after another, whispering about me. The Garden Love's designated gossips wasted no time in sharing my occupation and my penchant for everything wild and unruly. At one point, a guy even came up to me and asked me for my autograph. I couldn't tell if it was legible or not as my signature had turned into chicken scratch. But I was to sheets to the wind and couldn't care less.

I felt positively stupid. Even when I was putting on this silly dress, I felt sure that it was my stepping stone towards at least getting invited to afternoon tea. This was my only chance to make things right for Drew and I. Only in my exaggerated worse case scenarios would Drew be spending all his time with an ex. While his grandmother looked on in delight. At the very least I'd hoped to be talking about the weather and dying inside in a poor attempt to have something in common with Dama. That wasn't happening either.

I tried to catch Drew's eye more than a few times to no avail. It seemed like everyone in the world except me knew that I couldn't hold his attention. I was a lot of things, but boring wasn't one of them. Who knew a stuffy garden party was all it would take to see the truth about Drew? All I wanted was to escape from the accusatory glances that said I wasn't good enough to even be in there presence.

To break the awkward silence playing in my head as the party spun, I said, "Fucking A, the only losers here are you guys."

The owner of the center, usually only seen in pamphlets of the place, approached me. Placing his hand on my elbow. I couldn't push Dama when she tried that shit, but no one said he was off-limits. But I misjudged how stout he was. Falling back into the sweets table. Sitting on Dama's going away cake. A gasp shook the crowd.

I could only laugh. "Dramatic much, guys."

Slipping and sliding in vanilla icing as two men came over to help me up. "Please get up young lady," the owner demanded.

I licked the icing from my fingers. "Very good." Making it to my feet through no real help from those now crowding me. I jerked away angrily. Almost stumbling on the white table cloth that now decorated the floor. But I righted myself.

"You did this on purpose?" Dama screamed indignantly.

"What if I did?" I said without thinking.

"You never should have come in the first place. At least now everyone sees you as the trouble maker you are."

The owner sighed and cut both of us off. "Miss Spence, why don't you go home and clean up?"

"Roaches will find a better home here than you ever will," Dama fumed.

The owner spouted off instructions to the waiter to bring in a janitor and get this mess cleaned up. Salvaging the rest of the food and directing the music to play again. By this time, Drew had appeared in the thicket.

"You just going to continue to allow her to talk to me like this?"

He looked disappointed in me. "You shouldn't have come if you weren't going to behave. This party was important to granny."

"Behave," I said, approaching him with indignation dripping from my voice. "This is me, and I'm not a pet to be trained. Maybe you thought you were brave hunting on Safari, but this animal wont be trapped in a Zoo."

I bumped his shoulder as I filed past him. Running out of the community center with my tail between my legs and cake in my hair. Only to see Manny getting out of his car out in front.

He looked on in amusement. "What's going on? Was the party a little too sweet for my Sangrita?"

I shook my hair back and allowed the crumbs to fall to the ground. "Get me out of here."

He looked like he wanted to eat me up. And it kind of made my skin crawl. But looking back and seeing Drew with his granny at the reception desk made me feel worse. So I ran to Manny and hopped in his car. Ignoring the fact that I was taking a ride with the devil.

23

Chapter Twenty-three

Andrew

The way she approached the community center the next day was slow and shaky. It was hard sometimes for me to read cues, but she looked positively scared. She was like this crumbling, dark, shaky mess walking towards the building. I rushed to hold the door open for her and it was like a bolt of lightning rushed past me when we accidentally touched.

My first thought was that I needed to apologize. Even though I don't know what for.

My second thought was that I wanted to carry whatever was weighing her down.

This was our last Driver's Ed class together, and we had already completed most of our driving hours. If we weren't careful this could be the last day that we would ever see each again. Each day that I didn't see her felt wrong. Even after everything that happened last night. She looked worse for wear, however. The long blonde hair that I once twirled around my finger looked wet and stringy. Her arms wrapped around her torso. And I still don't hate her for last night's mistake. Not even if it was on purpose. I couldn't hate someone I loved.

I put my hand on her shoulder to stop her from going into the classroom. But removed it quickly, knowing how much I hated to be touched. It looked like she had barely slept. We just needed to talk.

"Daylily." I needed her to know with that one word just what she meant to me. "We need to talk?"

She seemed to be startled by the fact that we were even talking. Her eyes were practically vacant. "What?"

"I want to talk about last night," I said, trying not to touch her when my arms ached for her body.

"I don't even remember how I got here."

"A cab dropped you off just now."

She seemed genuinely shocked. "I went to the club with Manny and then back to his place."

She looked out of sorts as if she had just been dropped from the sky. Dressed plainly in some grey sweats and a tank top. A hoodie thrown over it, but the type that looked like it belonged to a man. Maybe one man, in particular, Manny. "He took care of you?"

"No," she said grabbing onto my arms. My muscles tensed up, but I didn't pull away. How could I when tears were falling down her face? A light sheen of sweat across her face. Her fingernails dug into my skin through my long-sleeved shirt. I pulled one away and kissed her hand lightly.

"I need you to tell me everything that happened." I pulled her away from the classroom door and back to the waiting area. There wasn't much to it. Just a couple of chairs, a table, and a potted plant. It was an afterthought that didn't get much use. But it would get her away from Joshua who may feel compelled to report whatever he heard.

"I think he drugged me."

I pulled her chair out for her. Pulling mine closer to hers as I held her hand between mine. "Did he rape you?"

The question fell to the ground like a broken wine glass. I looked over at the receptionist who was doing her best not to listen in. It was past five o'clock and she was preparing to leave. The place stayed open until 9, but there was no information desk available. Most assumed that if someone was in the building after hours then they should already know where they were going. Anything valuable was already locked down.

"No," she said after a long pause. Her hands visibly shaking in mine. "I don't think so. When I got up this morning. I was in his bed and he was sleeping on the couch."

"So how do you know that he drugged you?"

My hand slid over her neck, and I run my thumb along her jawline. I can barely think straight. I'm so worried about her. Hoping, that I'm doing this comfort thing right.

"He told me so. Sort've."

"Goodnight, you two."

I looked up and nodded to the receptionist who was looking at us both with concern. "What's sort've?"

But Amber didn't acknowledge her. Staring down at our hands as if she were only upright because they were giving her strength.

"He just smirked as I walked out and said good luck on your piss test today?"

"How would he know about those?"

"I don't even get advanced knowledge on when she shows. Unless he called in an anonymous tip."

"But it will be okay because you're clean." I tried to reassure her.

"I wasn't going to drink with him, but he insisted. I just had one and now last night is a complete blur. I don't remember anything after that drink. And I feel icky. Like my head's coming out of a fog. I know he gave me something. I know."

Her head fell against my arm and I could feel her tears wetting my skin.

"It's going to be okay." I kissed the top of her head softly.

Joshua appeared in the lobby, clearly looking for us. He gestured to his watch demandingly. We were on his dime and the other class was still starting at seven. I merely nodded and hoped that would be enough. He stormed back to the class and I rubbed Amber's head gingerly.

"I'm going to go to jail for close to two years because of this." She lifted her head only slightly. Enough for me to see that her mascara was running. Black streaks underneath her eyes made her look like she just left a clown shop.

"Let me help you."

"You can't help. If you could that time has long since passed. I probably shouldn't have even told you. I just need to pull it together."

"You did the right thing telling me."

She sat up straight and dabbed at her eyes. Only serving to make it much worse. "Class is starting and we can't be late either. We're the class."

I'm painfully awkward when we both stood up and I blurted out. "Allow me to give you my pee."

She looked at me puzzled.

"I'll pee in a cup for you. Some people do that, right?" I wanted to stop long enough for her to answer, but I couldn't catch my breath. "I see now that you don't deserve to be in jail and I want to do my part to keep you out of it."

"I can't ask you to do that," she said hiding her hands in the sleeve of the hoodie.

"You didn't. And I get that you don't get any forewarning usually, but let's think about this rationally. When do you think she's most likely to pop up?" I asked reaching for her hand.

"After class."

We walked back to the classroom together. "Then I'll wait in one of the stalls. You go into the one beside me. I'll pee into a cup and pass it to you."

"When did you become a criminal?"

I smiled. "Just think of me as Batman. I do what I need to ensure that justice is carried out."

"Okay, wonder boy," she said with a wistful sigh.

During, the whole class I unreasonably felt like a complete caveman with her. Biting down Joshua's throat when I felt like he was being overly critical. Making excuses for when she would nod off. I'm not a hundred percent sure, but that could have been why he ended the class 15 minutes early. Which was fine by me. It wasn't like we were taking a test or anything. That would have to be done at the DMV. Today, was mostly about picking up our certificate of completion. A document that would have to be shown in court for those who were required to go back. If requested he would email a copy to everyone's lawyer.

"How are we going to do this?" she asked once we were outside the classroom. Nodding friendly like to some of the early birds that we recognized from the beginning of class. Tilting my head so that we wouldn't accidentally be overheard. If we were going to do this I had to act fast. The fewer people that saw us together the better.

"I'm going to go to the women's bathroom. The second stall and lock it. I'll wait on top of the toilet with my feet up. Tap your foot twice on the floor and pass me the cup. I'll piss. Tap your foot twice when it's safe to pass it back."

"I don't think you should be doing this."

"Merely, imagining him taking advantage of you makes me want to turn into The Hulk. You can't trust him and you never could. Just tell me that you trust me?" The thought of her seeking solace in another man hurt me.

"I trust you."

I got situated in the bathroom. While Amber waited for her parole officer outside. Every time the door opened, my heart picked up speed like a racehorse. I could be overly paranoid, but every potential footfall was an officer with a gun ready to blow me away for committing fraud. Only to feel relief at the sound of peeing and eventually the washing of hands.

Only to be caught off guard by the sound of Amber entering with a shadowy figure behind her.

"To what do I owe this little drop-in? Or should I say who?" I watched her break into a knowing smile in between the cracks of the door and the stall. But I wasn't brave enough to continue looking out for fear of being caught.

"Just pee in the cup, Miss Spence."

I could hear the officer checking all the stalls. She stopped in front of mine when she couldn't open it. I imagined her bending down and looking underneath the door. Only to see the bottom of the bowl and the empty tile. I was practically squatting on top of the toilet. Briefly, wondering what this yoga pose would be called?

"Is someone in there?" she asked, rattling the door once more.

"It's probably just out of order," Amber said covering.

Meanwhile, I was close to peeing myself. Too scared that my hiding spot would be found out. Then Amber would be sent to jail, and I'd never see her again.

"These sorts of places, do the most good. And never have the resources they need. I'm familiar with the struggle," the officer replied, mildly.

I heard Amber enter the stall to the left of me. Unsealing the cup. It sounded like she was peeing. But two-foot taps sounded, and as quickly as I could manage I stuck my hand underneath her stall. Frowning as she passed me a half-full cup. I dumped out its contents and peed in the cup. Just as she had stopped. Giving off the illusion that there was only one person in the bathroom. Waiting for two more foot taps to pass it back. It felt like a full minute of me holding warm piss in my hand before I could hand it over.

Louder than Amber had to, she exclaimed, "There I'm finished."

I took a chance and looked through the little slot allotted to me. It looked like the officer was placing a little sticker on the cup filled with my pee. Her hands were covered in those plastic gloves that I seldom see outside of the hospital. This huge case sitting on top of the sink looked like the kind of forensic kit I sometimes see on those cop shows that my granny watches. Would she test it in front of her now?

Was there a way for her to distinguish it from male to female? Should I stay hidden even if Amber was getting arrested? Or would my attempts to save her just be her damnation? This parole officer didn't appear to carry a gun, but there was a taser strapped to her belt. I only knew what it was because the walkie-talkie was next to it. Sucking in a harsh breath at the idea of a thousand volts ripping my body in two. But none of those questions would be answered because she merely closed her bag and turned to leave. The badge around her neck was clear.

"Then we are finished. Don't leave town. You'll be hearing from me soon enough."

"I look forward to it...not."

I could hear the door open and then close again, but I was too scared to peek my head out. Freezing at the sound of the toilet flushing next door. And then Amber appeared to wash her hands in the sink.

"Please tell me that you flushed that piss that was in the cup?"

Slowly, I set my feet back on the floor. Cleaning myself up a bit before flushing the toilet. Coming to stand beside her at the second sink. Cleaning my hands thoroughly, like a doctor at a hospital. "I did."

"And it looks like our little plan worked. She didn't suspect a thing. I may finally be out from under this."

We both dried our hands with hard brown paper towels. But it was Amber who went out first to make sure the coast was clear. Even if the parole officer was gone. There was still Joshua to contend with. It would be an instant disaster if he suspected that something was going on. But she waved me on.

"The coast is clear."

I was just glad that no one saw us. My heart was practically giddy at the thought that she might be able to overcome the mistake I had made so long ago. But that wasn't the only thing on my mind. She stopped her as we waited outside for her ride. "We need to talk about everything that happened yesterday. You ruining grandmother's cake."

"I was just drunk," she said banging her head lightly on the wall of the community center.

"But was it on purpose?"

She hiked one leg up on the wall and didn't bother to look at me. "No."

"That garden party meant a lot to grandmother. It was her last one. And the people of the Garden Love Project chipped in to pay for that cake."

"Yeah they did and I paid for the other 75% of that four-tiered cake with fondant flowers," she said, sounding disgusted.

I grabbed her hand. "I figured because of your relationship that you might not have helped at all."

"I can't believe you," she said, pulling her hand away from mine and twisting a nail into my heart. The caveman in me wanted to grab it back and cart her off to my place. "I didn't mean to offend you."

"Yeah, but you did."

"I wasn't holding it against you or anything. You've got to believe me." I watched her mull over my words.

"What I believe is that nothing today convinced me that we belong together? You giving me your pee just confirmed that we live too vastly different lives. And I shouldn't taint yours with mine." I was hoping for a restart, but her tone is withering.

"I love you, though."

"Do you? Because I'm kinda feeling like I should show you receipts for the cake. A cake I paid for not to get in your good graces, but because I know Dama loves this place despite our differences. It was her last hooray. And I truly wanted to start fresh. To be her friend because I care about you. In a dress that you probably never noticed wasn't my style at all. Just to be the girl that you two would want."

"I don't know women's fashion." She directed a gaze toward me filled with such deep regret in her eyes that I had an awful thought. Maybe being with me was just too complicated for her. She doesn't feel the same way that I do. It would even explain her bias against granny.

"It's what you don't know that I can't handle. I'm a leather jeans, studded heels, shot glass taking boxer. Who occasionally plants flowers. I'm not a church girl, and I wont pretend to be one. Just to get your granny to like me. Or to get you to take up for me. If I'm always the villain in your story that's fine. But you're not going to get me to love you too."

A cab pulled up and she hopped in without another word.

Epilogue

Two Years Later

We walked out of the dealership and I twirled the ring of the key fob on my index finger like a basketball. Andrew was purposely avoiding my gaze and it only made me want to laugh. One of those gut-busting laughs that always made me want to pee. But that would be a bad idea right now.

Stuffing my hands into my overalls. My casual gray shirt rolled up at the sleeves. I put my sunglasses up on my head as our new car pulled up.

The car salesman hopped out and handed Andrew the second set of keys. "It's all yours now. Nice doing business with you two."

A flutter in my stomach alerted me to the baby's movement and I rubbed my stomach hoping to avoid a few kicks. Not at all above rubbing our newest acquisition in his face. Even though I completely agreed with the purchase. The man still deserved to squirm for my dead homie.

"You're still angry with me," he stated flatly.

I approached our new car tentatively as if it were a rabid dog I was trying to domesticate. Squinting against the setting sun as I turned to face him. Unable to get past how far I'd come.

"I'll always remember the moment you neutered me," I scolded. "And it wasn't when you knocked me up."

He came up and opened the passenger side door for me. He even waited until I was safely situated inside before going around to the driver's side seat. I hopped inside and adjusted the seat and mirror in the position he was most comfortable with.

And instead of finding it annoying, that I'll never be able to change it, I just wanted to kiss him. But I was supposed to be freaking out. So I tried not to lose focus.

"This will always be the moment that I had to trade in my Camaro for an SUV."

"You secretly love this car. You picked out the model. And the color. More than the Camaro it's safer for Helen. Every day, when you two leave the house, knowing that you are safe and not in a deaf trap on wheels. Is invaluable to my sanity."

Ever since we agreed to take our relationship seriously, every decision we made was to make each other proud. And when I got pregnant, it felt like we were being rewarded for all that effort. It felt silly not to say goodbye to my past and the car was a big part of that. I'd settled firmly in the boxing gym owner camp, and now I was owning the title of mother.

"I'm not agreeing with you," I pouted, in loving memory.

He looked over at me and kissed the back of my hand. Rubbing my stomach lovingly before pulling off.

"That's a shame. I was hoping that since you got our baby the gift of safety. That I could give you a gift," he said, pulling in front of the house almost thirty minutes later. He quickly piqued my interest. My ears turned towards him like an antenna. A hunting dog out in geese season. Overly excited to see what zaddy had gotten me.

It's like he knows that I can't get out of the car without his help though. Because he quickly unbuckled his seat and rushed around to the passenger side seat to grab my door. I felt as big as a double-wide. Watching him grab both my hands to help me out. In my seventh month, I was eagerly awaiting the end. It was a special kind of torture to be pregnant in the summer. And it wasn't that I was super huge being in perfect shape. It was just huge for me, never having been accustomed to carrying so much extra weight.

But Helen was worth it. Not that I was super in love with that baby name. Andrew was quickly turning me into a convert though. He told me one night that he wanted our daughter to be beautiful, yet fierce like her mother. A true woman of history like Helen of Troy. It was hard to argue with a statement like that coming from your baby daddy.

"Does this gift have something to do with your big project out in the backyard? I feel like you've been working on that thing as long as I've been here. Pulling out a small grocery bag of items that Dama wanted me to pick up for her. At this point, Hubert knew more about the gift than I do. Dama has been dropping horribly unhelpful hints."

He held out his arm for me to hold, not bothering to take the bag from me because he knows I'd bite his arm off. The actions of a woman determined to do things for herself before her husband turns her into an invalid.

With the help of Hubert of course, they drag this huge blue tarp off this small structure. It was a circus funhouse-shaped greenhouse. The structure itself was made out of reclaimed wood from the community center. Two of the front windows had been spray-painted pink, and the others were a greenish turquoise.

I covered my mouth with my hands. Holding back tears, laughter, and just everything. "Fucking A, it's awesome."

I walked around the entire thing, and my cheeks hurt from smiling so hard. Laughing at the baby columns that he used to hold up the large picture windows. "I love it."

"Good because this isn't all of it."

Inside were huge planters, big and small, of every color of the rainbow. Filled with dirt.

"Some have seedlings and some don't. But only because I wanted to fill this place with hope."

I laughed. Unable to believe with my own eyes how much thought he put into this place. Covering my mouth with my hand as I tried to breathe. There were even two small white chairs and a table opposite the planters. A matching green vintage Bluetooth radio similar to the one he uses in the house sat atop the table. I followed that up to where a row of small planters sat in a trough labeled Herbs close to the ceiling. The only greenery in the place and I loved it. I loved it all.

I leaned over and turned on the radio to see that he had already programmed it to all of my favorite stations. I stopped on a station that was playing, All I Need By Brandy. It was hard to feel sexy with a tummy, but at this moment I wanted to be sexy for him. With my back to his stomach, we swayed back and forth to the music. Smiling at the fact that he didn't even complain about having to dance or being touched.

"Marry me?" He whispered into my ear.

I closed my eyes and continued to sway. "Yes."

Kissing him softly as the song went off. I took a seat to rest my swollen ankles. Unable to relinquish his hand because surely this mythical creature would disappear. Or maybe I would be the one to fly away on a cloud of his love. Only to wake up next to Manny because this would all be a dream.

"I'm sorry that being a boxer has sort of put you in a box where people expect a certain kind of thing from you. You can't plant flowers. You cant have other dreams. You can only date…"

"Bro fit guys."

"Yeah, it's an attack on your very person. And I know because people do the same with me. As soon as they see me I'm automatically put in a box filled with their preconceived notions. And it's okay, but sometimes it gets downright hard to deal with."

I was about to ask him if he was thinking of someone specific, but he continued.

"I can't change how they see us. Individually or together. But I want you to know that under this roof I will make it my business to give you everything that your heart desires."

"I know that wonder boy," I managed to get out. "And together we both have a new little one to spoil."

"I know. And I'm overjoyed with how far we've come. I can't tell you how sorry I am for almost getting you sent away for kidnapping." He dropped his mouth to the knuckles on my hand.

"I forgive you. But you forget that if It hadn't been for those series of unfortunate events, I never would have met you."

"I was an idiot. Especially since I loved you from the moment I saw you."

I looked at him wryly like he was selling me a story. "You didn't?"

"Our first meeting in court anyway. I didn't see much outside of the police's twirling lights that first night."

"Okay."

"You challenged me. You stood in front of me and commanded my attention. Like this Amazonian warrior."

"Stop," I blushed.

"Now I've created this place for all your heavy thoughts to be stored. A place just your own that can never be taken away. Maybe you could decide if you're going back to boxing after the baby is born now?"

"Just being in the gym with the others has been oddly comforting." I sit back in the chair and stared up at the glass ceiling. Slightly shaded by a nearby tree. "There is always something exciting going on. Layla is doing a great job of keeping me in the loop about her potential prospects. Everyone, in general, has been super excited and supportive of me and the baby. I do get the occasional whisper. But I ignore it." Looking back at him as I marveled at how he was able to keep this all a secret.

"Are you starting to feel pressure to make a decision?"

"If I am, it's all contrived by myself." I thought that I'd be struggling with this decision for months. All the way up until Helen's birth. Instead, that tugging feeling on my head and heart was just fear of me ignoring what I already knew. "I know I took a year off to focus on The Boxpad and the new renovations. So I wasn't defending my title. But six months after Helen's birth, I'm going back to boxing."

"I was afraid that you might say that. I've been trying to mentally prepare myself for how that might affect our family. When I think of you and boxing my only form of reference outside of old videos is that street fight you had with Erin."

"I'd like to say that things are less bloody, but I can't exactly promise that. I can promise that I'll always come back to you and Helen. I'll play it safe as much as I can, but I still got to keep it rough if I'm going to be a winner. I just really need your support on this."

"You always have my support. This place is meant to be physical proof of that. A place here at home, where you can go, when the worries get a little too loud in your head. And your not limited by time or availability. These listening walls are for your voice only. You can scream whatever you want. Even if one of those screams is really worry that Helen will turn out just like me."

"We didn't get the Amniocentesis because I told you I wasn't worried about that. I will love this baby in every form that it comes in."

"I know that's what you said, but it's okay if you feel something else. This place will absorb all your secrets."

"Okay. Thank you."

"You're very welcome," he replied, more to my stomach than me as he bent over and rubbed my tummy.

"You know what this moment is missing?"

"What?" he said, looking up from his discussion with the baby as he described the greenhouse.

"Hot chocolate."

His eyes begin to twinkle. "Now you're speaking my language. I'll go make us some?"

"Oh no you don't," I said gently, pushing him back down. "I'm going to make it."

He crossed his hands on his lap. "Shouldn't you be the one enjoying this beautiful house?"

"Yes, but you worked your fingers to the bone. I think I should give you a minute."

I entered the house and made his favorite hot chocolate. It wasn't the right weather for it as it was closer to 85 outside. But in our household, there was never a wrong time for hot chocolate. Fifteen minutes later I had poured the concoction into two rocket-shaped mugs and put them on a tray with a small vase and a single rose.

"Did you make enough hot chocolate for me?" Dama asked. Coming into the kitchen from her room.

"Of course."

"Oh, he finally unveiled the greenhouse today. How do you like it? It has been a terrible slog for him to get through."

"And it was worth every moment because I love it."

"I thought the funhouse aspect might appeal to you."

"That was your idea?"

"Why are you so surprised?" She took the offered cup from my hand.

I put Drew's and I cups on the small tray that I intended to carry out to the greenhouse. "We are alone. So you don't have to pretend like you like me."

She turned to look at me, her eyes a filmy gray. Sometimes it was downright scary, that I recoiled if caught off guard. She was almost 75% blind. "I wont even report your messy ass to Drew."

"The baby," she said, using her white cane to make her way over to the couch. The TV was already on the game show network. Her only afternoon programming. It was usually nothing more than white noise as she drifted in and out of sleep. Causing me to tiptoe around her to avoid getting in her way.

"What about the baby? Any child of mine is a demon reborn." Although we have come to tolerate each other. No movement had been made over the last two years that even suggested we would ever be friends.

She smiled and sipped from her mug gingerly. "Of course not, it is half Drew's there is no way that she could completely be a foul-mouthed little shit."

"Well, this conversation has been enlightening because I wasn't expecting you to say that at all. Not."

"How's this for enlightening then. We both need to get our shit together for this kid. In a way that we couldn't for Drew. I only want this little one to see us smile at each other not throw insults. Also, I wish to be a true grandmother. And having a good relationship with you is a part of that."

"That's very adult of you." My stomach trilled.

She shakily placed the mug down on the table in front of her. "We have both been more than a little juvenile. But I'm the reason that it has lasted so long."

"We both agree on that."

"Since you have moved in here Andrew genuinely seems happier. You seem to take heed to my warnings when I tell you that you're pushing him past his capabilities as an Aspie. You love him. And every day I see that a little bit more."

"I never questioned your love and concern for Drew. Just your ability to allow someone else to do the same?"

"You cracked the code," Dama agreed. "Just like I've deciphered yours. I know I'm the reason that you haven't accepted any of Drew's proposals."

"I'm not—-"

She interrupted me. "Ready to pack up and leave with the baby, possibly, if things go south? This is your home now. You and Helen, and there is no need for plan B. We both need you here."

"And the brick wall around your heart is gone?"

"I'm glad you loved the funhouse idea, but let's take this peace offering slowly."

"I knew you couldn't resist me." I temporarily abandoned the tray on the counter. Approaching her and bending over to kiss her cheek. But I didn't wait for the rebuff. Bouncing over to the tray, I went back out to where I knew Drew was waiting.

"Silly granddaughter-in-law," I thought I heard her giggle. She'd never called me that before. Usually, I was just Amber. But I didn't turn back around and risk ruining the moment.

"I almost sent a search party out for you," Drew said, getting up quickly to take the tray from me and place it on the small table between us. The small vintage radio turned on. Playing the song, Paris In Love by Lauv.

"What for? I'm never gonna be without you."

Afterword

Thanks for giving this book a chance. It was my first attempt at writing a character with a disability. I sincerely hope that I did the subject justice. If there were some things that were a little insensitive, please allow a little grace as I'm still learning. Meanwhile, a new couple enters the boxing ring in The Straight Paint, with Tabatha and Bryden.

Sign up for my newsletter and get new release updates and be the first to find out when The Honey Strait Novels come out. To sign up just fill out the form on the following page:

http://newsletter.trsbooks.com/signup

As a thank you for signing up, you'll receive a starter library.

If you enjoyed reading The Parry Garden: A Honey Strait Novel, I would appreciate it if you leave a review on your platform of choice.

Your sneak peek of the next novel awaits —>

Book Playlist

The Straight Paint
You can listen here on Spotify or
search TRSBooks.

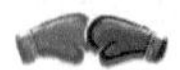

The River by KT Tunstall
Dancing With A Stranger by Sam Smith and Normani
I'm So Tired by Lauv and Troye Sivan
Peer Pressure by James Bay and Julia Michaels
There's No Way by Lauv and Julia Michaels
Slow Dancing in The Dark by Joji
E.T. by Katy Perry
Nothing by The Car
All I Need by Brandy
Paris in The Rain by Lauv

Discussion Questions

1. What kind of concerns would dating someone with a disability raise for you? If you are currently married to someone with a disability please share your highs and lows?

2. Do you think society as a whole frowns on an able-bodied person dating or marrying someone with a disability?

3. Michelle was used to dating *bro-fit* guys. Can a dating preference become a crutch?

4. After reading this novel, would you be open to dating someone with a disability?

5. Why do you think Dama and Michelle didn't get along?

6. Have you ever been at a crossroads in your own career? If so why and how did you get out of it?

7. What do you think was the defining factor in Michelle choosing to stick with boxing?

8. Michelle and Andrew got involved during her hiatus. Do you think Andrew will be able to adjust to Michelle being a boxer? Yes or No.

9. What problems might Michelle's renewed Boxing career cause Andrew?

Excerpt: The Straight Paint

The Honey Strait Series #3
Copyright 2019 Paige Lynn Hoving

CHAPTER ONE

Working at The Boxpad, only called one question to mind; why was it built right next to a strip club? I was fresh out of the Army and had gotten a job here through my best friend's connection with the secretary. His mother was a ten-year staple of the place. Most of the time the place was quiet. But I started on a Friday and we stayed open late on the weekends. My first chance to see how busy the back gets during smoke breaks. Feather Boas, strong perfume, and circus-sized heels were the thing in that crowd. It was also the first time that I'd seen anything like this. Craig swore that I'd passed the place a few times when his mom would pick us up from school and take us to the fast food place down the street. But I never paid attention.

But from my over-excitement, Craig thought I needed some ground rules. It was only day two and now there were rules.

"Number one: Don't go to the strip club as long as you work here."

"But..."

"Listen to me, bro. No buts. I love the place, but I have been on a steady diet of the crazy shit that can go down at both places since I was a kid. So just steer clear."

I pulled my work bag out of my car. "Okay, what else?"

"Number two: See no evil, hear no evil bro."

I frowned at how dramatic he was being. It was like he was talking me through how to survive a haunted house. At any moment, he was going to pull out a cross and some holy water. When did my boy turn into such a chicken shit? "You want to tell me what that's about?"

"Angry girlfriends, lying strippers, and pimps gone crazy. You ain't seen none of that shit."

I shrugged. "Makes sense."

Throwing the bag over my shoulder I followed him inside. Kissing both cheeks of El lovingly. The woman had been like a second mother to me. And I was happy to know that someone had been praying for me when I was gone.

Especially someone as beautiful as El. Growing up she was the *Jessie's mom* of our neighborhood. Even now El was still aging like a fine wine. Past 50, she now had a beautiful head of gray hair, Beyonce style. And working in a gym must be paying out because she still had her beautiful figure as well. I could probably pinpoint my appreciation of the African American female form to my bestie's mom. That tidbit could never leave my head, however.

"How you doing baby?" she asked, grabbing my chin and shaking my head.

"Good," I replied, pulling away from her.

"You already know where you need to go?" she asked, looking between me and her son.

"Yeah, thanks," I said, knocking on her desk as I made my way around her.

"Don't be distracting him, Craig," she yelled, like an annoyed mother.

He kept his head low, rubbing his fade, clearly embarrassed. I wondered sometimes why he even worked out here. "I do need to get to work. Is that all the rules?"

"Number three: After your shift, just go home. Do not hang around here."

I shook my head. "Man, you trying to make it sound more dangerous than all the 'stans combined. If it was this bad why did you get me a job here?"

"Because you wont get this kind of love anywhere else."

I looked back at the locker room. "What happens if I break the rules?"

(End of Sneak Peek)

What does happen, be sure to pick up the next Honey Strait Novel and finish the chapter:

THE STRAIGHT PAINT

About Author

Paige Lynn Hill is an entrepreneur and multifaceted author. As a businesswoman, Paige has spent half her life writing and now she gets to put a little romance into every pen stroke. She first became a lifelong writer and first began creating lovebirds in the seventh grade and published her first poem in high school. Her love of reading started even before then. However, life's interjections sent her into poetry and eventually business. But she managed to find her way back to her first love, writing novels. Propelled like everyone else by a terribly written TV show that used to be one of her favorites. She thought she could do better and then she did. Now it's all she loves to do.

Author Links:

Website: www.trsbooks.com

Facebook: www.facebook.com/authorpaigelynnhill

Instagram: https://www.instagram.com/authorpaigelynnhill

Newsletter: https://trsbooks.com/newsletter/